Jailbird's Daughter

Praise for Irene Carr

'Another turbulent tale in the Cookson mode . . . so well does she bring the gritty world of 1900s Sunderland to life, that you can taste the sea air, the fumes from the dockside pubs, timber yards and the smell of money . . . there's no quenching the appeal of stories like this.'

Sunderland Echo

'A splendid tale of jealousy, revenge and hard-won love.'

Bolton Evening News

'Irene Carr knows the world she recreates in her tales and it shows in the detail . . . Lovers of North East sagas won't be disappointed.'

Newcastle Evening Chronicle

'Sheer descriptive talent shines through here . . . gritty, powerful stuff.'

Dorset Evening Echo

'This novel has the clear ring of authenticity . . . the depth of the setting gives it its richness.'

Northern Echo

'A warm-h⸍   *Daily Express*

'In the best⸍   ⸍kson.'

Middlesbrough Evening Gazette

By Irene Carr in Hodder paperbacks

Mary's Child

Chrissie's Children

Lovers Meeting

Love Child

Katy's Men

Emily

Fancy Woman

Liza

Rachel

About the author

Irene Carr was born and brought up on the river in Monkwearmouth, Sunderland, in the 1930s. Her father and brother worked in shipyards in County Durham and her mother was a Sunderland barmaid.

IRENE CARR

Jailbird's Daughter

HODDER

First published in Great Britain in 2005 by Hodder and Stoughton
A division of Hodder Headline

A Hodder paperback

4

A CIP catalogue record for this title is
available from the British Library

ISBN 978 0 340 83669 9

Typeset in Plantin Light by
Palimpsest Book Production Limited, Polmont, Stirlingshire

Printed and bound by
CPI Mackays, Chatham ME5 8TD

Hodder Headline's policy is to use papers that are natural,
renewable and recyclable products and made from wood grown in
sustainable forests. The logging and manufacturing processes
are expected to conform to the environmental regulations
of the country of origin.

Hodder and Stoughton Ltd
A division of Hodder Headline
338 Euston Road
London NW1 3BH

I

Sunderland's East End, February 1895.

'When's me dad coming home, Mam?' The child, just five years old, stood in the middle of the kitchen, her dark eyes huge in her thin face, raven black hair tied back with a strip of rag. Her white pinny was grubby with wear, the brown dress beneath it threadbare and too short, barely covering her knees. Holes showed white in her black stockings, in legs and heels. Her shoes were cracked and the soles parting from the uppers. She was not conscious of her shabbiness; this was normal. She waited for a reply.

Her mother gave it: 'He isn't.' Doreen Grant was a young woman, voluptuous when dressed up but slovenly now in dirty skirt and blouse, her lank black hair hanging loose and tangled as she had just crawled out of bed. An old woollen shawl was wrapped around her shoulders against the cold; there was no fire in the grate, just cold ash. The floor was without covering and the bare boards needed sweeping. An old couch stuffed with horsehair that sprouted through cracks was set against one wall and four chairs stood round a table, its surface stained. The window, washed by the rain that pattered on its panes, looked out on a yard with privy, coal-house and tap dripping water.

Doreen glared at the child standing bewildered and shouted, 'He's in a prison three hundred miles away and will be for the rest of his life! But he's lucky they didn't hang him because he killed a feller. God knows what'll happen to us now. Not that he'll care. He only married me because he had to, and to give you a name so you wouldn't be a little bastard.'

The child stared, still uncomprehending.

Doreen muttered, 'What's the use? You don't know what I'm talking about.' She took a part loaf of bread from a crock, tore off a hunk and gave it to her daughter. 'There y'are, Alison. Now get away to school.' She kissed the child, pushed her out of the kitchen into the passage and closed the door behind her. Then she passed from the kitchen into the bedroom, the only other room, and crawled back into the crumpled blankets.

Alison walked down the uncarpeted passage and out of the open front door. The street was a long terrace of houses, all let for rent, each occupied by two or three families. Children were emerging from them now, in a trickle that would soon become a flood. The men were already at work, the din of the riveting hammers in the shipyards a familiar background noise. She started along the pavement, eating hungrily, trying to understand. She saw the next door neighbour out early and kneeling on a scrap of old carpet, washing her front door step despite the rain.

'Good morning, Mrs Cavanagh.'

The woman, her red hair streaked with grey, looked up and round at her. 'It's not very good, Alison.' Then she peered at the hunk of bread. 'Wait a minute.' She rose with creaking knees, wiped her hands on her apron and said, 'Come in for a minute.'

Alison followed Mrs Cavanagh along the passage to her kitchen. This had cracked linoleum on the floor and a fire burned in the grate. Mrs Cavanagh poured brown tea from a brown pot keeping warm on the hob, added sugar and a spoonful of condensed milk, then spread a scrape of butter and jam on Alison's bread. 'There y'are.' She watched as Alison ate and drank; it did not take long for her to finish it.

'Thank you.'

'You go on to school and let me get back to my step.' She wiped the child's mouth with a corner of her apron and shepherded her back to the street. She watched Alison run off through the rain, shook her head and sighed, then knelt down to her bucket and whitening stone again.

Alison was grateful for the kindness and not surprised. It was not the first shown her by Mrs Cavanagh and other neighbours. She ran on to school, trying to sort out in her mind what her mother had told her. She knew a prison was a place where bad people went, but the father she loved, and who loved her, was not bad. So how could he be in prison? She had to find out the truth because she missed him so much. Somebody would know and be able to tell her.

Matthew Grant was a seaman. In a London pub a man called Sean Rafferty had called his wife, Doreen, a whore. Matthew knocked him down and Sean tried to attack him with a knife but in the fracas fell on it himself. Matthew still did not know that Sean had spoken the truth. He lay in his cell of a night and wondered why he never had a letter from Doreen.

Alison was right. Somebody did know the truth about her father. Adults talked and children listened. She heard nothing in the schoolyard when she reached it that morning because her breakfast with Mrs Cavanagh had almost made her late. She was just in time to take her place in the line of girls waiting to march in. The attack began in the morning break.

Oliver Crawshaw led the charge. He was a big boy, the son of a shipyard foreman, a worthy man. Oliver was different, a great one for bullying, and for cheating at games at which he was unskilled, then blustering his way out when he was caught at it. He confronted Alison gleefully and bawled, 'Your da's in prison!'

Alison could only stare, could not deny the accusation

because her mother had told her: 'He's in a prison three hundred miles away . . .'

Oliver saw her flinching under the lash and laughed. He licked his thick lips and shouted, 'He's a jailbird!'

Inevitably there were others, boys and girls, who were ready to follow his lead and they gathered around Alison, chanting, 'Jailbird! Jailbird!'

She looked around her, head turning desperately. She sought a way out, the chance to run and hide somewhere, anywhere, but her tormentors fenced her in. Oliver was dancing now, savouring this opportunity to hurt, and he went a step further and yanked at Alison's hair. She cried out at the pain of it but she knew what to do about this, had seen what some of the bigger girls had done when Oliver pulled their hair. She struck out, a wild swing but her open hand slapped across his face and wiped away his jeering grin.

'Ooh!' said the crowd, just as happy to see Oliver hurt.

'Ow!' he yelped. Then, furiously, 'I'll bash you for that!' He lifted his fist.

Alison put her hands up before her face to guard against the blow, but then someone came between them.

Simon Stothard was not as big as Oliver, but sturdy in his patched old jacket and shorts. He stood with small fists clenched and raised, ready, and defied Oliver. 'You leave her alone.'

The bully hesitated. He was not a coward but now he was not facing a little girl. He sneered but did not act. 'Are you king o' the lasses now?'

Simon ignored the jibe and repeated, 'You leave her alone.' Then he added, 'Or else.' He took a pace forward towards Oliver and it was clear what 'else' he intended.

Oliver jeered, 'Aw, you play wi' the lasses, then.' And he turned and swaggered away.

Simon watched him go. The group around them shredded

and slowly drifted off, whispering among themselves and covertly eying Alison. Simon turned to her and said indignantly, 'Take no notice of him. He tells a pack of lies.'

Alison said, 'It's not a lie.' And when he stared, disconcerted, she went on, 'It's true. Me mam said me dad's in prison.' She stopped herself then, her own confusion closing her mouth – and not wanting to talk about it or even think about it because of the pictures that were brought to mind, of her beloved father peering out at her from behind bars. She turned and ran and little Simon Stothard watched her go, unhappy for her.

Alison hid in the girls' lavatory and cried until the break ended and school started again. At noon she ran home and found her mother there. Doreen had lit a fire and was sitting by it, staring into the glowing coals and toasting bread on a fork. She greeted Alison: 'Here y'are. Have some o' this.'

'I'm not hungry, Mam.' She was sick with worry.

'O' course, you are!' Doreen smeared dripping thinly on the toast and shoved it at her daughter. 'Get it down ye.'

Alison chewed obediently, swallowed and said, 'They were mocking me at school over me dad. About him being in prison, I mean.'

Doreen scowled. 'I expected they'd get on at ye. But you don't need to worry because you won't be going back to that school. We'll be getting out of this.'

Alison paused, mouth open to bite, eyes round. 'Where are we going?'

'Never mind. Just you wait and see.' That was said with relief and gratification because Doreen was eager to get away. But then she glowered and warned, 'Mind you don't say a word about this outside!'

'No, Mam.'

But Alison did not go out again that day, reluctant to face

the world. She hid behind the dirty curtains in the bedroom at the front of the house and surreptitiously watched the other children playing in the street when school ended for the day. She saw the lamplighter come round with his stick and reach up to switch on the lights, saw the last child called home. She clutched Sadie, her doll and her only comfort. It was second hand, a Christmas gift from a neighbour. Doreen had said they could not afford treats.

Her mother made up a bed on the couch in the kitchen. 'You can sleep on here tonight, our Alison.' She put her little girl to bed then dressed herself in her best, a costume sporting a jacket with huge puffed-out 'leg of mutton' sleeves, and a skirt that swept the floor and hid her buttoned boots. She paused a moment beside the couch to say, 'You get to sleep now. I'll be back later on.'

Alison wriggled to fit her little body around or into the lumps and dents of the couch, tickled by the horsehair that oozed out of holes in the imitation leather cover. 'When will we be moving?'

'Never you mind. It might be sooner than you think. Now shut up and go to sleep like I told you.' She turned out the gas lamp and left. Alison heard the tap-tap of her boots as she walked down the passage, then the slam of the front door.

She lay in the half-dark. There were still embers glowing in the grate and shedding a little light. The neighbours were walking about in their rooms above her head with a creaking of boards. Mice skittered across the floor and under the couch. She wondered where she and her mother were going. Just *where* they would live, not what it would be like. She assumed their destination would be another two rooms like the ones she was living in now because she had known nothing else. She thought about her father and cried as she had done before.

She woke to the clatter of feet and slurred voices. Her mother's – 'Make less noise. I don't want you waking the bairn. It's bad enough that old cow upstairs shoving her head over the bannisters and seeing the pair of us. She'll tell the street tomorrow.'

A man grumbled, 'I can't bloody see where I'm going.'

'This way.'

They moved from the door around the table. There was no light now from the fire, the embers dead. Alison made out their shadowy forms, close together, and she guessed one was leading the other.

'Mam?'

'Aye, it's me. Now go back to sleep. I'll see you in the morning.'

'Goodnight, Mam.'

'Goodnight.'

The figures moved again, passed through the doorway into the bedroom at the front of the house, and the door closed behind them. Alison wondered who the man was and why her mother had brought him home. But her eyelids drooped. She slept.

She woke to sunlight filtered through narrow cracks in the torn curtains. No one was stirring but the door to the bedroom stood open. She slipped out of bed, dressed only in her cotton shift, crossed the floor on tiptoe and peered cautiously around the door into the bedroom. Her mother lay curled up in the bed but there was no sign of the man now.

Alison was uneasy, knew her responsibilities but was reluctant – afraid – to wake her mother. But then Doreen's eyes opened and she peered blearily at her daughter and winced in the light. 'What d'ye want?'

'If I don't go to school the schoolboard man will come for me.' He patrolled the streets looking for truants.

Doreen said with grim humour, 'He won't find you

because you won't be here. We'll be out of here before tomorrow. Now go and get dressed.' And she added, as Alison obediently pattered back into the kitchen, 'That old cow upstairs can talk all she likes an' all; she'll be wasting her breath.'

The man came again in the evening when the shipyard hooters blew raucously to signal the end of the working day. He clumped along the passage and shoved in through the doorway. He was a coarse featured, thick bodied man in old working clothes, stiff with dirt and grease. He glanced once at Alison, playing with her doll on the couch, then ignored her. He demanded of Doreen, 'Have ye got my dinner ready?'

Doreen answered, 'Aye. It's in the oven, Cecil.'

He handed her his empty tea can with the big red and white handkerchief that had held his sandwiches for the mid-day meal. Doreen had set a bowl of water on the table and he washed his hands and face.

She took away the bowl and called, 'You come and set the table, Alison.' And as she went to empty the bowl down the sink in the yard, 'This is Mr Tobin. He's like your father now.'

Cecil glanced at Alison and nodded curtly. 'Don't forget.' He sat down at the table.

When Doreen returned she served up the meal in rough and ready fashion, Cecil first. Then in an aside to Alison, 'You don't want the name of Grant round your neck like a millstone, people pointing you out because your da is in prison.'

Alison did not, had suffered enough already. 'No, Mam.'

'We'll see about another name for you,' said Doreen, but left it there. She washed up after the meal while Cecil sat scowling into the fire. When she passed close to him he would reach out to fondle her and she would squeeze his hand and tell him, 'You'll have to wait.'

Alison wondered what he had to wait for and why. She shyly took her doll to him. 'She's called Sadie.'

He stared at her blankly and Doreen steered her away. 'Don't bother Mr Tobin.'

Alison went back to the couch and played a game with Sadie.

The hours passed, the house became silent around them, all movement ceased in the rooms above. Alison lay sprawled on the couch, half-asleep, with Sadie in her arms. She watched her clothes being parcelled up in old newspaper by her mother and wondered. She did not ask for an explanation and Doreen did not give one.

At last Doreen said, 'We can get away now.' She brought out from the bedroom the cheap and battered old suitcase she had packed that afternoon.

Cecil said, 'Aye.' He pulled on his jacket and took the suitcase from her. 'My case is at the station.'

Doreen stuffed Alison into her coat and boots then pulled on her own coat. She picked up the newspaper-wrapped parcel and put a finger to her lips as the child gazed sleepily up at her. 'We have to be quiet now.'

The fire was almost dead. She turned off the gaslight, opened the door and the three of them went softly down the passage and into the street. They walked in silence still until they rounded a corner with its street lamp. Then Doreen muttered, 'Good riddance to that place. And the rent man can whistle for his money.'

Alison knew the rent man, portly with cheeks that wobbled pendulously as he warned Doreen, 'You'll have to pay something on account or it's out on the street for you.' But how would whistling get him his money? Like the singers who walked the streets bawling the latest music hall hits, some of them with dented tin megaphones? But she knew better than to ask for an explanation.

The ferry was not running at that time of night so they crossed the River Wear by the bridge. It was empty; the trams were not running either. Alison had never been this far from home before. She was curious but too tired to take an interest in the ships lying in the river, as if set on a sheet of black glass. Nor to stare at the shipyard cranes standing silhouetted against the night sky like storks. Her legs ached and she could scarcely set one foot in front of the other. She only pleaded, 'Are we nearly there? Is it far?'

'Just a minute or two,' Doreen replied. 'We're in Monkwearmouth now.'

Then they left the last of the narrow streets behind them. The road ran between fields, dark in the night and bordered by black hedges. To their right there were sometimes glimpses of the sea and the lights of ships. It was a strange land to the child raised in the labyrinthine alleys of the East End.

They came to the house, set in the fields and standing back from the road, inside its own encircling hedges. Doreen said, 'Here we are: Bellhanger.' It stood, square and substantial, three storeys with steps leading up to the front door. It was in darkness save for one lit candle set in an upstairs window. Somehow that one faint light only added to the gloom of the place. The house seemed to hang over them, threatening. Alison shuddered and clung more tightly to her mother.

Doreen muttered to Cecil, 'He's still mourning her and drinking himself to death. I'll lay he has a woman up there now and he's pretending she's his wife, that Esme, or trying to forget her. I worked here for the first few years after I left school. He never tried to touch me or me mam though, I'll say that for him.' She laughed earthily. 'I might ha' stayed if he had.'

She walked past the door and round to the rear of the house. Here was a cobbled yard and a stable block, dark and silent like the rest of the house, but with the smell of horses.

Doreen turned away from the stable to stop by another door set in the wall of the house. She yanked at the bell pull that hung beside it and they heard a faint and distant jangling within. Minutes seemed to pass, then they heard shuffling footsteps and a key turned in the lock. Bolts were drawn and the door swung open.

An old man stood there, holding a paraffin lamp in a shaky hand. Its trembling glow showed him skinny and toothless, his nightshirt tucked into trousers held up by braces. He peered at them while shadows shifted huge and grotesque on the plastered wall beside him. 'Aye?'

'It's me, Silas,' said Doreen, stepping further into the light. 'I've come to see me mam, Francie Bailey.'

'At this time o' night?' His voice was shrill with age and incredulity. 'She'll be in bed and asleep like everybody else should be.'

'She'll want to see me.' Doreen pressed forward and he had to fall back a pace.

Silas grumbled, 'Aye, all right, then. Come in.' And then, 'Who's this?' Because Doreen had dragged Alison into the passage with her.

She answered, 'My bairn, Alison.'

'She should be in bed an' all.'

Cecil sat down on the suitcase and grumbled at Doreen, 'Don't be all bloody night about it.'

Then he was lost to sight as Silas closed the door on him and led the way along the passage.

They passed through a kitchen, deserted and dark at this hour, with only a faint glow from the banked-up fire by the oven. It reflected faintly on the hanging spoons and ladles. Now they mounted a narrow stair, following the trembling light from the lamp clutched in their guide's clawlike hand. Alison was towed along by her mother, to a landing with three doors, all closed.

Silas knocked on one and after a moment or two a voice, high and querulous, demanded, 'What is it?'

He answered, 'I've got your Doreen here with her bairn. She's wanting to see you.'

'*Doreen*! What does she want? But never mind; I'm coming.'

Now Doreen shoved past Silas, muttering angrily, 'Can't get in to see me own mother. I never heard owt like it.' When she tried the door she found it locked. She swore under her breath, exasperated, but when the key turned in the lock she twitched her features into a smile.

The door opened and Frances Bailey, Francie from childhood, stood on the threshold. She was a tall thin stick of an old woman, wrapped in a frayed and faded dressing-gown, with her grey hair hanging down her back in two plaits and a hooked nose in a bony face. She peered at them, sharp-eyed and resentful. 'All right, Silas, you can leave them to me.' Then as he shuffled away down the stairs she stepped back and held the door wide. 'You'd better come in.'

Doreen simpered, 'Ta. How are you, Mam?' She passed into the room. It was small, lit by an oil lamp standing on a table that was flanked by two straight-backed chairs. The embers of a fire glowed in the grate. A rocking chair stood at the fireside and a bed occupied most of one side of the room. A china bowl and jug stood on a chest of drawers and a chamber pot could just be seen, pushed under the bed.

Francie took her seat in the rocking chair, huddling over the fire and pulling the dressing-gown about her bony knees. She grumbled, 'Sit yourself down, then, and tell me what you want. You couldn't get away from me fast enough but now you want something, I'll lay.'

Doreen dumped the parcel containing Alison's clothes on the bed and sat in one of the chairs by the table, her little daughter standing at her knee. 'It's Alison here, Mam. Have you heard about her father? Where he is?'

'Aye, I've heard,' said Francie heavily. 'I don't know him, never saw him because you never brought him here. If it comes to that, you've not shown your face here for years, never brought the bairn for me to see. But I'm sorry for – Matt, wasn't it? It's an awful place he's gone to.'

'Aye,' Doreen agreed, but pressed on. 'I have to go away for a bit and I can't take Alison with me. It will be better for her if she stays with you.'

'Me? Look after your bairn?' Francie stiffened and her eyes narrowed. 'You've got another feller, haven't you.' That was a statement, not a question.

Doreen did not deny or explain. Mindful of Cecil waiting, she glanced at the clock on the mantelpiece and kept to the point. 'I'll send you money for her keep.'

'I've heard your promises before,' Francie said sourly. She shook her head. 'You want me to take on a little lass at my age? I should be sitting back being looked after by me own bairn but there's damn all chance o' that. I'm still working early and late in this house and only that old fool Silas to help me.'

Doreen sighed. 'Then there's only one place left.'

Francie's head snapped back and she looked down her nose. 'That place? No! But I believe you would do it.'

Alison was afraid, not sure what was going on, not understanding what they were talking about except she was being discussed – and some strange place that appalled the old woman. She quavered, 'Mam, I'm frightened.'

'Ssh!' hushed Doreen. 'Keep quiet when we're talking.'

Francie said with bitter resignation, 'All right, you can leave her with me.'

'Ta, mam.' Doreen glanced at the clock again and rose to her feet. 'I think it would be a good idea if she used your name: Bailey. Not his, you know? She should forget about Grant.'

Francie said, 'And now you're away.'

'Aye. We're getting the first train out in the morning.'

The old woman stood up stiffly, took a tallow taper from the mantelpiece and lit it from the fire then passed it to her daughter. 'That'll light your way out.'

Doreen took it and opened the door. Then, remembering, she turned back and stooped to kiss Alison's brow. 'You be a good girl for your Gannie.' It was a local word for grannie, peculiar to that part of the world but familiar to Alison. Doreen went on to warn, 'And never mention your father. If anybody asks you about him, just say he's dead.'

Alison took this in numbly, another blow. She blinked at this strange grandmother, then looked up at her mother. 'When will you be back, Mam?'

'One of these days.' Then Doreen was out of the door and it closed behind her.

She found her way back to the entrance by the light of the flickering taper. Cecil still sat on the suitcase but stood up when she emerged. He complained, 'You took your bloody time.'

'It wasn't my fault,' Doreen excused herself. 'I couldn't finish quick enough for me.' And she consoled him, 'Never mind, I'm here now. Let's get away from this benighted hole. It gives me the creeps.'

She hurried him away.

In the house, Francie glowered into the fire and muttered to herself. 'She was never any good, never will be. The trial she's been to me.' She ran over in her mind the lies and failings of her daughter, the betrayals. Then she became aware of the child still standing forlorn by the empty chair and wilting, leg-weary. The old woman stared at the full mouth now turned down at the corners and quivering, the huge dark eyes under drooping lids. She said softly, 'Come here, pet.'

Alison went to her, but warily. She was afraid of this old woman with the hooked nose and fierce eyes. But then she felt the bony arms wrap her around, surprisingly warm and comforting, and she snuggled into them.

Francie tucked her inside the folds of the dressing-gown and rocked her, crooning under her breath.

Alison was worn out, on the verge of sleep, needing only security and finding it now. Her own arms crept up to slip around her grandmother's neck. Just one question still worried her. She had not ventured to ask her mother, fearing the answer. But now: 'What's a bastard?'

Francie sighed. 'Poor little lamb. Not you, so don't worry your head about it. You're a bonny little lass and you're mine now.' She knew her daughter would not return.

When she looked again, Alison was asleep.

2

Monkwearmouth in Sunderland, February 1895.

'Mam?' Alison awoke, at first frightened by her strange surroundings and calling for help. Her mother did not answer and now the child recalled Doreen's leaving.

Francie replied to her cry, 'Whisht! I'll see to you in a minute.' She was dressed and performing her toilet, washing in a bowl of water set on the table.

Alison realised the dusty old curtains were still closed against the last of the night and the oil lamp burned. She herself wore only her shift in which her gannie had put her to bed. She lay warm in the bed where she had snuggled close to Francie all night, and she still cuddled the doll, Sadie. She lay still in that warmth that cocooned her but she could see the fire was cold and dead, could feel the cold inside the room. She repeated the question she had asked the night before: 'When will my mam come back for me?'

Francie evaded it and replied, though certain that in doing so she lied, 'One o' these days.' Then she hurried on, to avoid more awkward enquiries, 'Now it's time you were up and we'll see about some breakfast.' She finished drying herself and instead washed Alison then dressed her with clothes from the newspaper-wrapped parcel left by her daughter. There were few of them and she muttered under her breath, in early morning bad temper, 'This will cost a pretty penny.'

'What's a pretty penny, Gannie?' Alison asked, voice muffled by the dress being pulled over her head.

'A lot o' money, that's what it means.'

'What will cost a lot of money?'

'A few clothes for you. We'll have to buy some.'

That silenced Alison. She could not remember having clothes bought for her before; they had always been handed on from someone else. Matthew Grant had given money to Doreen for the purpose but she had spent it on drink. When he came home from sea she lied to him that the hand-me-downs had been new, but, 'That bairn is always getting dirty; I've washed them to rags.'

Now Francie stood back. 'Let's have a look at you.' She inspected the little girl in her brown dress and white pinny, the black stockings with their holes and darns. Alison stood with her hands by her sides and looked up at her gannie trustingly. Francie's temper fled and she smiled. 'You're a bonny little lass.'

Alison's smile matched hers. 'That's what my dad used to call me.' Then she remembered and the smile was swept away. 'Sorry. Mam said I wasn't to mention him.'

'Aye,' said Francie, heavily. 'It could cause you a lot of trouble. Just forget about him. You have a life of your own.' She hugged and kissed Alison then drew the curtains to show the first light lifting above the distant sea, the frost riming the windows. She took Alison's hand with one of hers and picked up the lamp with the other. 'It's time we made a move.'

The old woman lit the way with the lamp as she led her granddaughter through the gloomy passages of the house. When they passed a window they saw the outdoor light growing. They still needed the lamp and its glow showed stone floors under their feet, cobwebs above their heads. Their footfalls echoed.

There was a light in the kitchen already. Silas had lit a lamp and was stoking up the fire in the stove, part of the black-leaded kitchen range that filled most of one wall. He was raking out the dead ash and shovelling more coal onto those embers that still glowed. Cupboards flanked the range and a dresser holding racks of plates and other crockery stood opposite, with a long scrubbed table between. A window, uncurtained, looked out on the stable block and cobbled yard, vague in the dim pre-dawn light.

Silas was dressed in a suit now, black and shiny with age, a stiff white collar and a tie. As they entered he mumbled toothlessly, without looking round, 'G'morning.'

Francie put the kettle on top of the stove. ''Morning to you.'

Alison added shyly, 'Good morning.'

He turned at the sound of her voice and squinted at her but addressed Francie. 'What's she doing here?'

'Staying with me.' And she added, to Alison, 'Sit up to the table and I'll get you some breakfast.'

As she obeyed, to sit straight-backed, Silas said, 'What? All day?'

'Every day and every night. This is my granddaughter, Alison, and she's living with me from now on.'

He looked from her to Alison and she smiled, hoping to please. He said, 'What's he going to say?'

Francie was busy preparing the meal. She shrugged. 'Nothing. He'll take no more notice than he does of anybody else in here.'

'Aye.' Silas nodded agreement, head bobbing on skinny neck, and told Alison, 'I'm Silas, the butler.'

Francie let out a snort of derisive laughter. 'And valet, groom, gardener, footman and odd-job man.'

Silas cackled. 'Aye. All them an' all.'

He washed the fire grime from his hands at the kitchen sink while Francie went on with her work. Alison sat quietly, listening to their talk and not understanding much of it. Once Francie asked, 'Did he have anybody in last night?'

Silas shook his head. 'He sat up there with a bottle o' whisky. Might still be asleep in the chair.'

Francie grimaced. 'That wife of his has a lot to answer for.'

'Aye.'

They breakfasted on porridge and Alison ate hungrily. Francie watched her and thought, correctly, *the poor bairn's probably not had a proper feed for weeks.*

The light grew, pale and wintry, as they ate. The meal over, Francie said, 'I'll clear this place up and leave his breakfast in the oven, then we're off.'

Silas wiped his mouth on the back of his hand. 'I'll see to him.' He took from his waistcoat pocket a stubby clay pipe, its stem bound with thread so he could grip it better between his toothless gums.

Francie said, 'Not at the table. I've told you before.'

'You're too bloody fussy,' he grumbled, but he put the pipe away. 'Where are you two going?'

'Shopping. Here, Alison, help me to put this stuff away.'

Together they cleared the table, Alison returning porridge oats to the cupboard then drying plates as Francie washed them, and placing them in their racks. All the while she cherished that word: 'shopping'. This would be a new experience.

Francie climbed on a chair to reach down an old tea caddy from the top of a cupboard. She opened it on the kitchen table, delved inside and brought out a fistful of coins, most of them silver but one or two gold sovereigns amongst them. She counted out several shillings, her lips moving silently, and put them in a worn leather purse she had in a pocket of her apron. The other coins she returned to the tea caddy, then mounted the chair again to replace it on top of the cupboard.

She saw the child watching her, wide-eyed, and explained,

'I don't trust them banks.' And with a nod at the caddy, 'That's my bank.' She patted the purse bulging out her apron. 'Now we're ready.'

Alison asked, 'Can I bring Sadie, please?'

Her grandmother looked at the old rag doll in Alison's arms and remembered how fiercely the little girl had clung to her in the night. 'Aye, you love it.'

They crossed the bridge over the Wear riding on the lower deck of a tram drawn by two horses. Francie paid the half-penny fare. Alison, excited, peered out of the window at the ships lying in the river or being built on its banks. The drumming of the riveting hammers could be heard above the clanging and grinding of the tram, the clopping hooves and jingling of gleaming harness.

On alighting in Fawcett Street Francie produced crusts of bread she had brought for the purpose and handed two to Alison. 'Go on, feed them.'

Alison fed the horses, feeling their soft muzzles nuzzle against her hand. Francie stroked their necks and grumbled, 'They're talking about bringing in electric trams and getting rid of the horses. It's a lot o' daftness, if you ask me. You can talk to a horse. If you talked to a tram they'd put you away.'

Alison giggled at the thought and the grim old woman chuckled with her. It was the first time she had heard the child laugh.

They shopped in Blackett's and along Fawcett Street and the High Street, not wildly but well, Francie cautiously dispensing from her carefully hoarded savings. There were two new dresses, overlong, their hems coming down below the tops of Alison's new button boots. Francie muttered, 'That'll allow for you growing.' And while she bought new shifts, drawers and stockings she pursed her lips and said, 'Your pinnies will last a bit longer.'

They returned to Bellhanger and, in the light of day, albeit with a grey lowering sky hiding the sun, the house seemed less threatening to Alison. It was still a tall, grim pile. They passed the front door, Francie muttering, 'That's for gentlefolk, though none of them call here now. It's the back door for us.'

They walked round to the rear of the house and found Silas in the kitchen. They shared a lunch of bread and cheese with him and as they ate Francie asked, 'How is he?'

Silas mumbled, mouth full, 'Scoffed his breakfast and went riding. Brought the horse back in a lather. Had a whisky and a sandwich and set out to walk. I expect he'll come home when it's dark.'

Alison's curiosity had built up during the course of the morning. Now emboldened by her growing familiarity with this new-found grandmother of hers, she asked, 'Who are you talking about, Gannie?'

Francie pursed her lips, considering how much she could tell the child. 'I work for the rich man who owns this house: Michael Tarrant. His family left him money; he made a sight more by building ships, and he owns a lot of properties. But his wife, Esme, ran off with another man so he took to the drink. She was twenty years younger than him and no good, but he still hopes she'll come back to him.'

Silas supplied, 'He rides like a lunatic. He's trying to kill hisself, I reckon.'

Francie muttered, 'Burning the candle at both ends the way he does, that will do for him. He looks twice his age.'

Silas put in, 'Folks call him Mad Michael.'

Francie sniffed with disapproval, eyeing Alison. 'They don't call him that to his face without paying for it, and don't let me catch you calling him that. D'ye hear?'

'Aye, Gannie.'

Francie nodded. 'That's right. He's always treated me fair, though it's hard work here.'

'Aye, that it is,' put in Silas. 'I'm the groom as well as the butler and the kitchen hand and everything else around here. There's a stable at the back o' the house wi' two horses and a carriage, though that comes out once in a blue moon.'

'You work just as hard as I make you,' Francie told him tartly. 'If I didn't, you'd ha' been sacked long ago and in the workhouse.' Silas scowled but did not deny it. Francie went on, 'He's given us shelter here.'

'He's given shelter to a few,' sniggered Silas. 'Here tonight and gone tomorrow, they are. Why, I could tell you—'

Francie cut him off. 'You'll tell her nothing, or I'll see you rue it!'

He quailed before her hard eye. 'All right.'

She rubbed it in. 'I have work to do and so have you, so you'd better get on with it.'

'All right.' He shoved up from the table, querulous, and made for the door. 'All right, all right, all *right*!' His whining faded away down the passage.

Francie muttered, 'Old fool!' Then she said briskly, 'Now then, Alison, we have this kitchen to tidy and then a bit of cleaning to do.'

Alison helped with the washing up, then they left the kitchen to thread the passages to Francie's room. There they put away Alison's new clothes in wardrobe and drawers, then moved on to the cleaning. They left the servants' quarters at the back of the house and moved into the front. The rooms now were spacious with tall windows but the furniture was covered with white sheets, like spectres in the dim light of a winter afternoon.

Francie explained, 'He only uses a few rooms and the rest are like this. I give one or two of them a turnout every day. You can give me a hand.' So Alison helped unsheet furniture, dust it and cover it again. Then she sat with Sadie in her arms and watched as Francie, on her knees with dustpan and brush, swept the carpet.

Later that evening she helped her grandmother in the kitchen as she cooked dinner for Michael Tarrant, then followed her – 'Here, Alison, fetch that dish o' taties' – as the old woman carried a loaded tray to the dining-room. She waited outside the door with the potatoes as Francie went in with the tray, to return and take the dish from her. As the door opened and closed, Alison caught a glimpse of Michael Tarrant, sitting tall and broad at the head of the table. He was a man of forty-odd, dark but with greying hair. He was in evening dress, black-suited with a gleam of white shirt front. He sat sombre, mouth a hard line. Then the door closed and Alison saw him no more that night.

Nor did she see him for many days. Francie warned, 'Don't let him see you. He doesn't know you're here and what he doesn't know won't hurt him.' Alison would have hidden from him anyway, feared him as she had been frightened by the house, Bellhanger. And yet she felt a sorrow for him, left alone and so lonely.

For a time she missed the sights and sounds of Sunderland's East End, the blaring sirens of the ships in the river and the hooters of the shipyards calling the men to work, the drumming of their boots as they had passed below her window and the screeching of the scavenging gulls, swooping down for whatever they could find to eat.

Now she attended a different school and none of the other children knew her or her past. She played among them, was absorbed into their games and made new friends. When they talked of their parents she said her father had died and her mother had gone away to work. Francie invented that last explanation for Doreen's absence. It was accepted and Alison was happy there.

Francie asked, anxious, 'Do you like your new school?'

Alison nodded enthusiastically. 'Um!'

But she liked playing in the sheeted rooms, games of hide
and seek when she hid from an imaginary pursuer, or when
she was a princess or a great lady, ordering her servants from
a throne of a sheeted chair. That was her playground and
Francie's room was her nest to which she returned. Bellhanger
House had become a home.

She saw Michael Tarrant sometimes when she played,
sighted him at the end of a passage or descending a stair,
but he never saw her.

When she was not at school, on weekends or holidays,
Francie would take her walking by the Wear so she could
see the ships moored in the river or being towed by fussy
tugboats. Often they would wind up at the Folly End, a quay
where steps ran down into the river. When the tide was in
the steps were nearly all covered, but at low tide they were
exposed, slimy with weed. There were iron rings set in the
wall of the quay so boats could be moored. Standing at the
top of the steps, Alison could see along the reach of the river
where ships were building on the slipways.

Afterwards they would walk along the sea front on their
way back to Bellhanger House, and on one of these excur-
sions they saw Michael Tarrant out riding on a big black
horse. He galloped along the line of the surf, raising and
trailing a plume of spray and hurdling whatever rocks lay in
his path. He soared over one outcrop, only clearing it by
inches, and Francie caught her breath as the horse stumbled
on landing. Then it recovered and she let out the breath in
a sigh. She shook her head. 'That's one of the reasons they
call him Mad Michael.'

Alison would usually help with the cooking and serving
of dinner, as she had that first night. Sometimes, though,
Francie would take her back to their room, saying, 'I don't
need you tonight, bonny lass. You can stay up here with

Sadie.' And then warning, severe, 'Mind you don't stir out
of here.' And Alison was left in her little bed – she had one
of her own now – clutching the doll and with the lamp burning
for company. She was usually asleep when her grandmother
returned and climbed into her own bed.

It was on one of those nights that Francie came back to
her bed and Alison stirred then opened her eyes and said
sleepily, 'Gannie?'

'Aye, it's me. Hush now and go back to sleep.'

Alison obeyed but in the seconds before sleep claimed her
she heard Francie mutter to herself, 'I'll have to go and cast
an eye over the place later on.' Then she slept.

When she woke it was to hear the tail of a distant call, a
voice raised. The room was dark save for the glow from the
embers of the fire. 'Gannie?' She looked for her grandmother
but Francie's bed was empty. Alison got out of bed and set
out to look for her, taking Sadie with her because of the
darkness. She padded barefoot through the passages, following the sound of the voice or voices. They led her not
to the kitchen but to the green baize door that opened on
the front rooms of the house. She opened it a crack and
peeped through. There was a corridor stretching away from
her, windows on the right with sight of a full moon flooding
it with silver light, closed doors on the left, sheeted chairs
standing like ghostly sentinels. One door at the far end was
open and more light, this time yellow from a lamp, streamed
from it. And a man's voice growled from inside, 'Now come
back here.'

It was addressed to a young woman who stood in the light,
looking out of one of the windows. She held a wine glass in
her hand and was tall, long-legged, shapely and stark naked.
Her hair hung down her back to her waist. She answered,
'You just wait a minute.' She drained the glass and set it on
the windowsill then ran her hands over her body. She stood

like that for a second then turned and walked sinuously back
into the room.

At that instant Francie seized Alison's arms from behind
her and drew her back. 'Come away,' she whispered. As she
hurried Alison through the passages, returning to their room,
she hissed, 'I didn't want you to see what goes on in here
sometimes. He has lasses come in to share his bed, to fill his
wife's place. They're low class, all of them, and after his
money. What were you doing there out of bed, anyway?'

'I was looking for you, Gannie. I woke and you weren't
there, but I could hear voices. I thought that might be you.'
She swallowed, then admitted, 'I was frightened you might
be leaving me.'

Francie tucked her back into her little bed. 'I'll never leave
you. Remember that: *never*!' She stopped and kissed her. 'If
you wake up like that again just wait for me. Do you hear?'

'Aye, Gannie.' Alison's eyes closed.

'And forget what you saw tonight; don't talk about it or
think about it.' She went on, muttering to herself now, 'Them
he brings in here, they're all of a kind, the same kind as that
wife of his that ran off.'

But Alison did not forget, could not banish from her
memory the picture of the young woman with her silver
body. She never did.

Her life resumed its placid flow of school and home. She
had been living with her grandmother for six months or more
when she finally, inevitably, was found by Michael Tarrant.
She was playing happily on a summer's evening, winding in
and out of the sheeted furniture, secure in the knowledge
that Michael had gone walking. Francie had told her so. But
he came upon her suddenly, walking long striding, his boots
making little noise on the carpets. He towered over her, his
mouth set grimly, his eyes wild. He glowered at the small
girl with her rag doll and she saw there was blood on his

face and hands and shrank from him. He growled, 'What the hell . . . ?'

Francie came scurrying behind him, anxious. 'She's my granddaughter, Alison. Her father's dead and her mother gone away. She's got nobody else but me. She doesn't do any harm and I'll keep her out of your way. We didn't expect you back so soon. You took us by surprise.'

'You're not the only one to be surprised,' he said grimly.

Now Francie saw the blood. 'You're bleeding; your face and hands . . .'

'A pair of louts thought they would have some fun insulting Mad Michael. They got a beating they didn't expect.'

'I'll wash and bandage the cuts.'

'I'll do that myself. You keep the brat out of my way.' He stalked off.

Francie heaved a sigh of relief. 'I didn't think he would turn you out but I'm never sure of him. Still, now he's said it will be all right for you to stay wi' me, he won't go back on his word.'

Alison whispered, 'He'd been fighting, hadn't he?'

Francie sighed. 'Aye, and it's not the first time he's fought, by a long way. People with no sense or manners bait him and regret it. Still, it's over now and you can forget about it.'

But Alison would remember the fighting.

3

Monkwearmouth in Sunderland, July 1902.

'Good morning, Gannie. I've made your tea.' Alison greeted her grandmother as she had since Francie's sixty-fifth birthday three years ago. She had made the tea – scurrying down to the kitchen and back again, balancing the cup and saucer carefully – as a birthday surprise, but then kept it up.

Francie sat up in bed, yawning, and made her own regular reply: 'That's kind of you, clever lass.' She sipped at the tea, brown and strong. 'Just as I like it.' Then she peered at the clock on the mantelpiece and cried, 'Look at the time!' She sucked the tea down and swung her skinny legs out of bed, nightie clutched around them. 'We have to be moving. He told me last night when I served up his dinner – and me about ready to put my feet up – "Francie, I have a fourteen-year-old nephew coming tomorrow to stay for a few weeks." I wasn't going to start doing a room and making a bed at that time o' night so it's an early start today.' She began to wash in the bowl on the dresser, splashing and blowing.

Alison, already washed and dressed, said, 'I'll go down to the kitchen again and make the porridge.'

They broke their fast with Silas and then prepared a room for the guest. That finished, Francie looked it over and nodded with satisfaction. Then she eyed Alison. 'It's Saturday, so there are no more jobs for you this morning. I'll have to stay here in case I'm needed but you can take yourself down to the beach. Would you like to do that?'

Alison nodded vigorously. She returned to the kitchen with her grandmother, packed in a bag a bottle of home-made lemonade and sandwiches wrapped in a cloth, then left the house by the back door. Francie watched her go, fondly. The young girl was a huge help to her now, about the house and as a companion. Alison had nursed her through a bout of bronchitis in the winter just past and the doctor who came told Francie, 'You're very well looked after.' Alison had even cooked all the meals for Michael Tarrant, but had Silas serve them and claim the credit.

Now Francie called after her, 'Enjoy yourself, bonny lass!'

Alison waved a hand in acknowledgment.

Silas had opened the double doors of the stable and was washing the carriage. A big black horse was saddled and its reins hitched to a ring set in the wall. Silas turned from his task to wring out his cloth and saw her. 'Now then, Alison, where are you off to?'

She crossed the yard to him and stroked the horse's neck. 'I'm going down to the beach.'

'I wish I was.' He leaned against the carriage and took from his pocket a plug of tobacco, black from the molasses in it. He used a clasp knife to saw shavings from the plug, rubbed them between his palms and stuffed them into his clay pipe. 'But I've got to get this carriage ready for the afternoon. He's using it to go to the station to fetch the young feller.' He scraped a match on the iron tyre of the carriage and it flamed. He held it to the bowl of the pipe and said between puffs, 'He'll be – no company – for you, though. Him being – a young – gentleman.'

Alison froze, taking this in. The pipe was going well now but suddenly Silas plugged it with a scrap of paper as he shoved away from the wheel and warned, 'Here he comes! Hide before he sees you.'

That jerked Alison into life. The horse was between her

and Michael Tarrant, concealing her. She slipped into the stable and crawled behind a pile of straw. Peering out she saw him come striding to the horse, heard him call to Silas, 'You'll have that ready.' It was a curt statement, not a question. 'Master Richard is arriving on the five-nineteen.'

Alison saw he was dressed for riding in jacket, breeches and boots. His expression was grim and his eyes haunted. He unhitched the horse, swung up into the saddle and rode out of the yard. Alison waited until the clatter of hooves died away, then crawled out of the straw.

Silas muttered, 'You shifted fast. Good lass. It's best you keep out of his way.' He pulled out his pipe again and re-lit it.

Francie had seen them from the kitchen window and came down through the passage to stand at the back door, wiping her hands on her apron. She called across the yard, 'You should be getting on with that job!'

Silas took the pipe from his mouth to answer shrilly, 'You look after your kitchen, missus, and leave the yard to me.'

Francie glared but accepted the division of responsibilities, withdrew and slammed the back door.

Alison set out for the beach but warned, 'Remember what he said.'

'Damn me, but you're getting to be as bad as her!' Silas cackled with laughter. 'But enjoy yourself, bonny lass.'

Alison tried, but all that day she recalled his remark, that young Richard Tarrant would be no company for her. She remembered her mother warning that she would be treated as a pariah if it was known her father was a jailbird, remembered also the jeering mob at school led by Oliver Crawshaw. These memories were always near the surface of her mind, and comments like that of Silas brought them back. She tried to shrug them off now, and thought she had succeeded, absorbing herself in games that were all products of her fertile imagination. In all of them she was a princess or a lady, looked up to and respected. They summed up her ambition, her aim in life.

She ate lunch on the shore, watching the ships entering and leaving the river, and finally wandered home in the dusk. She was approaching the house when the carriage, drawn by two horses, came racing up the road from Monkwearmouth and the station. She drew back into the shadows and it rolled by with its iron-bound wheels bouncing on the cobbles, the horses' hooves striking sparks. Michael Tarrant sat on the driver's seat, the reins in one hand, whip in the other. Silas stood on a step at the back of the carriage, clinging on for dear life. Alison saw the wild progress of the carriage and thought: 'Mad' Michael. There was a boy on the seat beside him, laughing, his head thrown back. He was bare-headed, with a shock of black hair blowing on the wind.

Michael reined in the horses and the carriage stopped at the foot of the steps, the horses blowing. Silas scuttled round to hold their heads and Michael leapt down to be followed by the boy. They climbed the steps and Francie appeared at the head of them, opening the door wide. Michael called back over his shoulder, 'Put the carriage away and take the baggage to Master Richard's room.'

They vanished inside the house as Silas answered, long-faced, 'Right y'are, sir.' And he led the horses away around the side of the house.

Alison saw the coast was clear, followed and caught up with him before he reached the stable. She fell into step alongside him and said, 'I thought that boy was arriving on the five-nineteen train.'

Silas grumbled, 'He was late. Said he missed his connection. The boss left me to wait with the carriage in the station yard, while he sat in the Palace Hotel, reading the paper and supping. Then I had to load his baggage and he has a trunk that weighs a hundredweight. Now I have to haul it upstairs.'

They were in the stable yard now and Francie called from the kitchen door, 'Come and give me a hand, Alison. He wants his dinner and so will Master Richard.'

Alison helped with the serving, carrying dishes, trays and plates, but only as far as the green baize door. She caught barely a glimpse of Michael and the boy, seated at either end of the long table.

She saw him briefly the next day when she walked down to the shore. He rode one of Michael's horses, galloping recklessly along the water's edge. His uncle was in hot pursuit. They rode at Alison where she paddled in the surf and she could hear Michael shouting furiously, 'Rein in! Damn you – rein in, I tell you!' But the boy paid no heed. Alison realised they were charging down on her and sought to run out of their path, but at the same time Richard tried to evade her and only turned to follow her. Then he reined in and his mount came to a prancing halt only feet away from the girl.

Alison had been frightened and now was angry. 'You have no business riding like that! You could kill someone!'

'No, I won't. Sorry if I scared you.' He grinned down at her, confident, stroking the horse's neck.

Alison had more to say but now Michael stopped beside his nephew. He glanced at her and asked, 'Are you all right?'

She answered, 'Yes, sir.'

He turned to Richard then, raging, 'You deliberately flouted my orders! Galloped off like a lunatic! Ignored me when I called on you to stop!' Richard opened his mouth to reply but Michael went on, 'Don't pretend you didn't hear because lying will earn you a beating! Now get down.' Richard shut his mouth again, flushed now. He slid out of his saddle and Michael snatched the reins from him. 'You can walk home. Follow me. And you will never mount a horse of mine again.'

He urged his mount forward at a walk and young Richard followed, face red. But as he passed Alison he said again, 'Sorry.' And grinned and winked.

She was taken aback by the size of him. Francie had said he was fourteen, two years older than she, and until then she had only seen him seated on the carriage or the horse. Now she saw he stood head and shoulders above her.

She watched him go and thought: *serves you right*. But she still felt sorry for him.

She saw him no more that day, but during the week that followed she saw him several times on the shore when she was on the way to school. She did not wonder at that because school was only compulsory up to the age of thirteen and Richard looked to be that and more.

Alison was in the top class now and that week the head-master, Mr Twentyman, tall, thin and enthusiastic, gave them a history lesson. His subject was the Duke of Wellington and the Napoleonic wars. Alison was interested, but what stuck in her mind most of all were Mr Twentyman's windmilling arms as he described the battles, and the picture of the Duke that he showed to the class. He said, 'This drawing was made just after the battle of Salamanca. He looks like a man who has just woken up from a nightmare.'

Alison stared at the picture and agreed. And she had seen that look on the face of Michael Tarrant.

On Saturday she helped her grandmother to do what cleaning and cooking was necessary. Then Francie dismissed her. 'You can get away down to the beach now, if you want.'

Alison did, spent every hour there that she could. She took with her sandwiches and lemonade as before. Being Saturday, there were many more people, but she took off her black stockings and paddled along in the surf past Roker Cliff Park until the last house was behind her. The beach was empty there and she could wriggle her toes in the cool sea and pretend to be a Venetian princess, digging with her hands a network of canals.

A voice said, 'What are you doing?'

Alison turned and saw Richard Tarrant in shirt and shorts, a haversack slung over his shoulder. He stood by her bag that held her stockings, sandwiches and lemonade. She was surprised again by the size of him, had to look up to meet his grin. Now he said, 'Aren't you the girl who thought I was going to ride over you the other day?'

'Yes,' she replied, nettled. 'And I saw you walk home.'

He pulled a face. 'That was my Uncle Michael. He was a bit annoyed.' He asked again, 'What are you doing?'

'I'm making a model of Venice.' She would say nothing of her dreams of being a princess.

'It won't last long; the tide's coming in.'

'I know that!' The boy was irritating her. 'I'll pretend Venice is flooded over.'

'But the real Venice isn't.'

'I know that as well!'

'You know a lot,' he laughed.

'I know I wouldn't miss my train and be late.'

That wiped away his grin. He stared at her, startled. 'How did you know that?'

'Never mind.' Let him wonder.

But he shrugged. 'Servants talking, I suppose.'

That was true. Alison remembered Silas telling her.

But Richard was going on and the grin was back. 'I didn't miss the train accidentally. I took a couple of hours to go to a music hall.'

Alison was scandalised. 'But—' She stopped, had been about to say that his uncle had been waiting for him, but she did not want the boy to know too much about her. She said indignantly, 'What about the people waiting to meet you? They must have been worried.'

He shrugged. 'I didn't think about that at the time and I needed cheering up. And I wasn't in a hurry to meet Uncle Michael.'

Alison could understand that last. 'Why did you need cheering up?'

But he said, 'Never mind. Look, your Venice is flooding now. Why don't we build a castle and try to stop the sea coming in, like Canute?'

'He didn't stop it.'

'We could try.'

And Alison could pretend she was queen of the castle and he was her man-at-arms. She agreed, 'All right.'

He pulled off his stockings and shoes and they went to work, splashing in and out of the surf, brown and bare-legged. They built a castle just above the line of the surf, laboured frantically to repair the breaches in the wall as the tide came in until they lost their battle and the sand edifice melted away. Then they built another higher up the shore. The tide stopped short of that and they were able to flop down and rest, triumphant.

Alison's stomach told her it was time for lunch and she delved into her bag, unwrapped the cloth and offered her sandwiches. He laughed and took a similar cloth-wrapped bundle from his haversack, and a bottle of home-made lemonade. 'Snap! There's a coincidence. My uncle's cook gave me these when I said I was coming here. She's a funny old stick, bit of a tartar, but I'm glad she gave me this lot because it saves me having to go back to the house for lunch. She's a good cook, better than we have at school. What is yours like?'

Alison thought of Francie. A bit of a tartar? She would not argue. 'She's very good.'

They ate in silence for a while as she thought about what he had said. Then she asked, 'You're still at school, then?'

He swallowed and grinned. 'Not really. I was but I was expelled. That's why I'm here. My guardian, Uncle Geoffrey, is away in Canada so I had to come and stay with Uncle Michael until he returns.'

'Oh.' Alison was intrigued. 'Why were you expelled?'

'I broke out of school at night, climbed down a rainwater pipe and went poaching game in the wood with an old villain called Billy Tighe.' He grimaced. 'Billy is an expert. I caught nothing but he came back with a couple of rabbits. All I had was a few apples. They were stuffed inside my shirt when I got back to school. My housemaster caught me halfway up the drainpipe.'

Alison mouthed silently, *Oh!* And asked, 'What happened then?'

'My guardian had arranged with the school that Uncle Michael would stand in while he was away. They sent him a telegram saying they were sacking me and he sent one back asking them to send me here. Meanwhile I was in a room on my own in the sickbay, like a prisoner.' He was silent a moment, eyes cast down, then said in a low voice, 'That's why I needed cheering up and went to the music hall.' He looked at her now, miserably. 'I'm an orphan, you see. My parents were lost in a shipwreck three years ago. My father was a major in the army and they were coming back from India when their ship sank in a storm. That's why I have a guardian. I suppose you have a mother and father?'

Alison quickly amended her story, reversing the roles to meet this situation because she was determined that one day she would be a lady. 'My mother died when I was five. My father is a sea captain and I don't see him very often. My grandmother looks after me.' Though lately Alison had cared for herself and Francie a lot of the time.

Richard's grin had returned with this recital of troubles shared. 'So we have some things in common; we're a bit alike.'

'Yes.'

Later they started for home, Richard walking along the shore towards Monkwearmouth and Bellhanger, Alison heading inland to hide her destination from him. She would return to the house by a circular route.

She trudged round to the kitchen door in the dusk. Francie was cooking the meal and called as Alison entered, 'There you are! You're late tonight. Come and help me with these. We're serving a bit late because Master Richard only got back about ten minutes ago and he's dressing for dinner.'

Alison took a knife and began to peel potatoes. She knew an explanation was required for her late return and gave it. 'Master Richard came along to the beach where I was.'

Francie paused in her peeling. 'I made some sandwiches for him. He said he was going for a walk. How did you get on?'

'All right, but he's another wild one.' Alison told of the poaching and expulsion, the illicit visit to the music hall.

Francie pursed her lips. 'Little divil. It sounds as though he takes after him upstairs. Did he know you came from here?'

'No, he remembered me from the other day, when I thought he would run me down. I told you about that.'

'Aye, you did. It's just as well he doesn't know you live here. It might be awkward.'

'That's what I thought.'

'Good lass.'

'He thinks I live in a house like this with a cook. He said his parents were drowned and he lives with his guardian, another uncle, so I told him my mam was dead and my father was a ship's captain.' Alison looked round at Francie.

'I know it was a lie but a white one. You told me never to tell about my dad. And Richard was a bit miserable and I thought it would cheer him up to know I was in the same boat.' She paused, then finished, 'I couldn't tell him the truth.'

Francie had watched her at her games of make-believe, when she was a lady and respected. She knew the reason for them, the desire to be looked up to, not derided as the jail-bird's daughter. Now she sighed but then smiled down at her granddaughter. 'You did right.'

Alison met Richard almost every day in the two weeks that followed. They invented games together but frequently argued. Neither would give way but they would finally agree to differ. It was in the last few minutes of his last day that he said, 'I'm going home tomorrow. I expect my guardian will send me to another school and later I'll be an officer in the army like my father, with a sword and a gun. What will you do later? Marry someone and be his wife, I suppose.'

He annoyed her because she knew what she wanted but had no idea how she might achieve it. She flared at him, 'That's none of your business! But whatever I do it will be something useful. I won't be shooting people. You should find something better to do, like being a doctor.' The one who had tended and cured Francie had seemed a godlike figure to Alison.

Richard was taken aback by the storm he had unwittingly raised. 'Here, steady on. I'm not going to shoot anyone.'

She turned her back on him.

He joked, 'I'll think about being a doctor.'

She started to walk away.

He followed. 'It's time I was getting back. Can't we part as friends?' But when she did not answer, he said, 'Very well, then.' And strode away.

She knew he was unhappy, looking forward to the morrow

and the meeting with his guardian with apprehension. And she felt guilty now, because for a while she had thought of training to be a nurse. But she had reverted to her original ambition to make her way in the world and be looked up to.

Impulsively she ran after him and stopped him with a hand on his arm. 'Of course we're friends, now and always. I'll pray for you. Good luck, whatever you do.' Then she stood on her toes, kissed him and ran.

He put a hand to his cheek and watched her run up to the road, on her way home, as he thought. She turned once and waved, then she was gone. He did not see her again.

Alison saw him once more. She was standing outside the dining-room door with a loaded tray, waiting for Francie to bring more dishes. The door was slightly ajar and she could see Michael and Richard, in evening dress, sitting again at either end of the long table gleaming with polish. Michael said, 'You're going home tomorrow morning but it's been good to have you here. I'm a melancholy man but you have cheered me. I've had to rein you in on occasion but I believe you will turn out all right. I will just ask you to bear this in mind: your father did his duty and so does Geoffrey, my younger brother and your guardian. You are here because you failed in yours. Don't do it again.'

Richard, straight-backed in the chair, answered low-voiced, 'I won't, sir.'

Michael raised his glass in a toast. 'I drink to your health and your future.'

Richard responded, 'And to yours, sir.'

Alison wished the boy well but thought he would need to mend his ways.

The following day Geoffrey Tarrant, Richard's guardian, stood before his fireplace and said, 'You are acting irre-sponsibly and it won't do. I will find another school for you but first I need to know that I am not wasting time and money. I'm talking of your time and the money left to you by your parents. You are dear to our hearts and we worry over you.'

Felicity, his wife, looked up from her sewing to nod and smile at Richard. Before Richard was called to this interview she had pleaded, 'Don't be hard on him, Geoffrey. He has been punished and I'm sure he has learned his lesson.'

Now Richard met Geoffrey's eye and replied, 'I realise that I've caused you a lot of trouble and I'm determined to improve.'

'Good.' But Geoffrey added severely, 'Let's say you're on probation. Now there is a matter to be addressed: what do you want to do with your life? Do you still wish to be a soldier?'

Richard saw, with his mind's eye, a small face, indignant and solemn. He answered, 'I want to be a doctor.'

Alison skipped across the yard to the stables in the bright sunlight of a fine morning. She stopped in the doorway to call, 'Silas! You're to come and have your mug of tea!' There was no reply at once so she urged, 'Tea, Silas! Now!'

He came out of a stall then, brushing straw from his creaky knees. He grumbled, 'Hark at you giving orders. Little madam. It won't be long before you go into service and about time an' all.'

'Service?' The word brought a chill to Alison's day.

'Aye. If not here then at some big house.' Silas started towards the kitchen. He saw her crestfallen look and said, 'What's wrong wi' that? There are plenty o' lasses like you, wi' neither mother nor father, starving and in rags. They would be glad of a job in service, a roof over their heads, food in their bellies and ten shilling a month.' He went stiffly on towards his tea.

Alison followed at his heels. Lasses like her with neither mother nor father? That virtually described her. So she was destined for a life of waiting on some wealthy employer. She felt as if a prison was closing around her, remembered her father and was on the verge of tears for him and her.

She entered the kitchen and Francie hailed her cheerfully, 'Come here, bonny lass. I hear Silas has been talking to you. I put a flea in his ear.' He sat at the table, sipping at his mug, sulky. Francie slipped her arm about Alison. 'Take no notice of him. Hold on to your dreams. You'll be a lady one of these days.'

Alison said, 'A lady like you.' She thought that would be no bad thing.

They smiled at each other.

4

Monkwearmouth in Sunderland, June 1903.

～～

'He's looking very ould,' said Francie. She was looking out of
the kitchen window to where Silas stood grooming one of the
horses in the stable yard. Alison stood at her elbow, tall and
slim, all arms and legs. At thirteen, she was soon to finish
school. She had always thought of Silas as old, but . . .

Francie sighed. 'He's still doing all his bits o' jobs but
there's no energy in him. He's only got two speeds these
days, dead slow and stop. It comes to all of us. I can't work
like I did once.'

'Oh, you can, Gannie.' Alison supported her loyally but
knew she lied. A lot of the work about Bellhanger was done
by Alison now. Reflecting, she recalled how she had taken
on more and more duties over the years. She had always
helped from her first days of living with her grandmother,
but now she played a major part in the running of the house.
And Silas? Watching him now she saw the slow sweep of
the brush, and his dragging stride as he crossed the yard.
His movements were deliberate and shaky. She remembered
his brisk shuffle, the way he would scurry around when sad-
dling or harnessing the horses.

She admitted, 'Silas is tardy now.'

Francie said heavily, 'Mad Michael wanted to pension him
off but Silas wouldn't have it.'

'Why not?'

Her grandmother looked up at her. 'What would he do?
Where would he go? This is the only home he has.'

Alison realised she was taller than her grandmother now because Francie was stooped. 'You'll always have a home with me, Gannie.'

'Ah! Bless you,' said Francie and squeezed her hand. Then briskly, 'Now then, let's get on wi' this baking.'

They turned back to their work but Alison remembered her promise.

It was a week or so later that Alison went down to the kitchen first thing in the morning to find the fire not stirred up and no sign of Silas. She was not surprised because this had happened several times lately. She had not mentioned it to Francie to save Silas from a ticking-off. Now she sighed and dealt with the fire herself, made the tea and took it up to Francie. But when they came down to breakfast Silas had still not appeared. That was unusual.

Francie clicked her tongue worriedly. 'Ah, dear. I wonder what ails the man. We'll have to go and see to him.'

They retraced their steps but this time they went not to their room but that of Silas. Francie rapped on the door with her knuckles. 'Silas? Are you up yet?' He did not answer. She tried again. 'Are you all right? Can we come in?' Still there was no reply. Francie sighed. 'We'd better go in.' She turned the handle and opened the door. The curtains inside the room were drawn across the window but enough of the morning light filtered through for them to be able to see.

The room was like their own and familiar to them because they saw to the cleaning of it. Silas lay in his bed, the blankets pulled up over his head so his face was hidden. He was quite still. A worn pair of bedroom slippers and a pair of boots stood on a strip of carpet by the bed. The boots were clean and polished, ready for the day ahead. His clothes, similarly ready, lay neatly folded on a chair. He would not need them. Francie gently pulled down the blankets and they saw his face, toothless mouth open but eyes closed. She said,

'He's gone. Poor ould soul. You'll have to help me lay him out and then fetch the doctor.' So Alison learnt about death and the performance of those last offices.

They buried Silas at the end of that week. There were four pallbearers and they carried the coffin easily. Francie murmured, 'He was just a bag o' bones.' Then, reflecting, 'He never saved a penny. He liked to go down to the pub and have a crack wi' the men there, and he was always an open-handed man, ready to stand his round and a bit besides. But he had no family, nobody but us.'

Alison thought that heart-breaking and wept for him.

Michael Tarrant attended the funeral and grieved. 'He was a good man, faithful, honest and hard-working.' He paid the cost of interment and for a headstone.

Francie climbed onto a chair and lifted down her old tea caddy. She took money from it and told Alison, 'We'll buy a few flowers for him.' They bought a wreath and Alison laid it to save Francie's creaking knees. So they laid Silas to rest.

A man came from a livery stable to care for the horses for a few days but soon his place was taken by a new groom. He appeared at the kitchen door one morning, a gangling youth of eighteen, looking about him with a vacuous grin. His straw-coloured hair, combed with his fingers, stood out from under his dirty cap. He nodded at Francie and Alison. 'Now then.'

'It's usual to knock first,' snapped Francie. Then she demanded, 'Who are you and what do you want?'

'Cuthbert Price. I'm the new groom, just started this morning. I've put my case in the room over the stable and thought I'd have a cup o' tea. The boss said I was to get me meals in here.'

Francie sniffed. 'I make tea at eleven and it's only half-past ten. I'll call you when it's ready. And next time wipe your boots and take off your cap.'

Cuthbert grinned vaguely and took it off. 'I heard the last feller snuffed it a couple o' weeks back. When I told my old boss I was going to try for this job he gave me a good reference. This Mad Michael, he wanted me to work about the house but I said I only knew horses. He still took me on because of the reference.'

Francie flared. 'Don't give him that name! He's Mr Tarrant to you. He told me about you, said if you couldn't do old Silas's jobs I was to do what I could and leave the rest. I told him there was a lot being left already but he took no notice.' She glowered at Cuthbert. 'I don't want you working in the house. There's all kinds o' vases and pictures and suchlike, easily broke and worth a mint o' money. And if you're only to look after the horses you'll find them in the stable, so off you go.'

He wandered out. Watching from the kitchen window, they saw him stroll lethargically across the cobbled yard, still with that vacant grin.

Alison said, 'Oh, dear.'

'Oh, dear, indeed,' echoed her grandmother. 'He's not going to be any help at all.'

Alison silently agreed, knew Francie would not be taking over the duties formerly done by Silas, was already leaning heavily on Alison to perform many of her own. The routine of cleaning the sheeted rooms day by day was done entirely by the thirteen-year-old schoolgirl. The prospect of taking on Silas's work did not frighten her. She had carried on with his stoking of the kitchen fire since he had died. She would do the other jobs for her gannie's sake.

Now Francie said, 'There's no good will come of that lad, you mark my words.'

They would be proved true some years hence.

Alison took on the extra work, before and after school. It was on a fine summer's evening that she went to clean one of the sheeted upstairs rooms. She had to pass the room that had been Esme Tarrant's, that had never been touched since she ran off and nobody had seen but Michael. He would go there with a bottle of whisky and lock himself in. It was – just – open now.

Alison paused. Francie had told her that Michael had been called to attend a business meeting in the town and had gone off in a great hurry. Alison reasoned that he had been in the room and forgotten to lock it in his haste to get away. She was curious. Through the inches-wide crack of the door standing ajar she caught a glimpse of a chair and a pier glass, a tall mirror between two windows. Neither pier glass nor chair were sheeted but both were coated in dust and draped with cobwebs. She could see, reflected in the mirror, a four-poster bed and a dressing table, with another mirror. She pushed the door open wider and entered cautiously.

The red light of sunset flooded through the two windows and showed that nothing was sheeted, all was covered in dust, save one chair and a portrait. She guessed that this was where Michael Tarrant sat when he visited the room, staring at the picture. Alison looked at it now and saw a young woman dressed for a ball, her shoulders bare and showing creamy, opulent bosom. Her hair was dark and glossy, her eyes green and slanted, cat-like, bold and inviting. And mocking; Alison could almost hear this woman laughing at her. She turned away uneasily, avoiding those eyes.

There was a wardrobe and she tip-toed to it and opened it. The dresses hanging in there had avoided both dust and the moth, so far as she could see. She glanced at them one by one, flipping along the rail. Then she found one she thought she knew and took it out. It was the dress in the portrait, a gown for a lady going to a ball. One day Alison would go to a ball as a lady, she was determined on it. She slipped off her own plain brown dress and white pinny, donned the gown and stepped in front of the pier glass. The gown was too big, too old for her. She showed thin and her hair still hung down her back as a young girl's should. She thought she looked awful and would never go to a ball.

Michael Tarrant, striding in at the door and gazing into that red evening light saw only the familiar dress and thought he saw – 'Esme?' He put a hand to his head, staring.

Alison whirled, clutching the dress to her, shocked.

Now he saw this was not his unfaithful wife who had come back to him. He was looking at a frightened adolescent, skinny and gawky, one he knew, the grandchild of his housekeeper. She had no business in this room, in this place of private grief.

He shouted, 'What the *hell* are you doing in this room! My instructions have always been that none of you come in here! Make no excuse! You're a thief!'

'No!' Alison denied the charge. She wanted to explain, apologise. 'I—'

He was in no mood to listen. 'Aye! A thief and a liar to boot. You should be locked up in jail, like, like—' He paused, momentarily lost for words.

Alison misinterpreted the pause, guessed at what he would say next, and burst out, '*No*! Don't dare to say "Like your father"!'

'What?' Now he was bewildered. 'How d'ye mean? What about your father?'

'Nothing.' Alison saw she had let the cat out of the bag and tried to remedy the situation. 'Nothing.'

He would not have that. '"Nothing" be damned! You've spoken too much or too little. What's this about your father?'

Alison, trembling, saw there was no help for it and confessed, 'My father is in jail. He killed a man in a fight.'

Michael whispered, 'Oh, my God.' And then, angry again, 'Why wasn't I told of this? Surely Mrs Bailey knew about it.'

'My mother – before she went away – said we had to pretend he was dead. And my gannie said it would save a lot of trouble. They mocked me at my old school.'

He could understand that. He said heavily, 'Aye, bairns would. And so would some folks a lot older. They call me Mad Michael.' He was silent a moment, looking down at her. Then softly, 'You poor child.'

Alison set him straight. 'That was a long time ago, before I came here, and I'm not going to be poor always. One day I'll be a lady, and respected.'

Now he stared because it was said with such confidence and determination. 'I hope you will.' He looked around at the dust-covered furniture, the dresses in the wardrobe and the portrait. He shook his head and turned back to Alison. 'I thought you were someone else. I'm sorry if I frightened you. She'll never come back, I know that now, so I'll just go to hell my own way.' He spun on his heel and strode to the door but checked there to say, 'Tell Mrs Bailey to burn all these dresses then shut up this room. The key's in the door. She's to bring it to me.' Then he was gone.

Alison called after him, 'Aye, sir!'

She put on her plain brown dress and hung the ballgown in the wardrobe. Then she locked the door, took the key down to Francie who was knitting in the kitchen, and told her all about it.

Her grandmother let the knitting fall into her lap and put hands to her mouth. 'Glory be to God! What possessed you to go in there? I saw him come back early and he said he'd met a chap on the way – Arkenstall, the solicitor – that said he wasn't needed at the meeting after all. But I never thought you would be in there. He must ha' been demented and you're lucky to be in one piece. I've known him nearly kill fellers for less than that. And haven't I told you often enough to keep out of that room?'

'I'm sorry. The door was open and I thought I could just peep in, doing no harm.' Then Alison admitted, 'I let it slip out that my dad was in prison.'

Francie threw up her hands in despair. 'Will he sack me and turn us out now?'

Alison hurried on, reassuring. 'No! He seemed to understand why we had kept it to ourselves. And at the finish he said his wife would never come back. You're to burn all the dresses in there and give him the key.' She handed it to Francie.

The old woman scratched absently at her thin grey hair with one of the knitting needles. 'Aye? It's time he forgot her, but it's one thing saying it, another to put her out of his mind. I doubt he can do it, but we'll see. And it seems he felt sorry for you.'

'He said, "You poor child".'

Francie nodded. 'There you are.'

'I told him I wouldn't always be poor,' Alison admitted. 'I said I'd be a lady one day.'

Francie stared at her, aghast. 'What did he say to that?'

'He said he hoped I would.'

Her grandmother shook her head. 'I can hardly believe it. You've had the luck of the divil. He'd ha' murdered anybody else he caught in there. But keep out of his way in case the sight of you changes his mind.'

On the surface very little changed. Michael stopped keeping his vigil in his wife's room but his drinking went on. He still brought nubile and willing young women to the house to spend the night. He might have forgotten Esme. He never mentioned her, but as Francie said darkly, 'That proves nothing.'

Alison took her advice and avoided him as she had always done.

Her school days ended and her headmaster, Mr Twentyman, told her, 'I wish you could go on to higher education. You could do well, become a book-keeper or a teacher, perhaps.'

'I can't, sir,' Alison explained. 'My gannie needs me to help about the place.' She knew Francie, like Silas, would never retire, fearful of confinement in the workhouse. She would fight for her independence so long as she drew breath.

Twentyman sighed, had heard the story before with variations of plot and not only relating to a promising child being denied further education. He heard it weekly, sometimes daily, when girls were kept off school, needed to help with the washing their mothers took in to make ends meet, turning the handle of the big old mangle that wrung the water out of the clothes, or to care for younger brothers and sisters while their mother scrubbed floors.

He said, 'You have my best wishes anyway.'

So Alison went to work with her grandmother, who lost her fight a year later.

5

Monkwearmouth in Sunderland, March 1904.

The wind roared in from the sea, bitterly cold, and Francie caught a chill and took to her bed. Alison nursed her day and night and Michael Tarrant paid for the doctor to call every day. He examined the old woman but then took Michael and Alison aside and told them, 'This was one winter too many. She had bronchitis in early December, again in January, and she's not shaking this off.'

The two men tried to prepare Alison for the worst but she fiercely refused to accept it. There came a time when the old woman lay inert and woke for only a minute or so at a time to whisper, 'Bonny lass.' Then at the end she added, 'You've done more for me than my daughter and made these last few years happy. Bless you.'

There were tears in her eyes now and Alison dabbed at them gently with her handkerchief. Her grandmother went on, her voice weak and anguished, 'I'm ashamed to say this, but all these years I've told you that your mother would come back for you one day, and I was lying. I always knew she would never show her face again. I knew she cared for nobody but herself and she would serve you as she served me. I'm sorry.'

'Never mind,' Alison whispered. 'I think I always knew that.' And now her grandmother's words came as no surprise. She realised she had accepted a long time ago that her mother had abandoned her. 'It doesn't matter. Don't fret yourself. You've been a mother to me, all I could wish for.'

'Bless you,' said Francie again with a tremulous smile, and closed her eyes.

Michael asked after Francie's health every day. Alison thought that she and he had both had to face a loss, she of her mother, he of Esme, his wife. They had that much in common, that and their caring for Francie, her out of affection, he out of a sense of a gentleman's duty.

Alison was alone with her grandmother on the final night. She dozed in an armchair by the bed where Francie lay sleeping, all through the long hours. Until the girl woke and saw the old woman watching her. She whispered, 'I wish I could have left you more, bonny lass. Hold my hand.'

Alison took the thin gnarled fingers in her own.

Francie never spoke again and died just before the dawn.

Alison saw to the laying out of the body as her grandmother had taught her when Silas had died. Then she sought solace in routine, cooked Michael's breakfast and took it up to him and informed him of Francie's death.

He said gravely, 'I'm very sorry.'

She returned to the kitchen and found Cuthbert Price, the groom, sitting at the table drinking a mug of tea. He looked at her with his vacuous grin. 'You're late this morning.'

Alison thought she should slap his face but she was numb with grief and he was a fool. 'My gannie died this morning.'

'Ah?' He took this in slowly and finally offered, 'Still, she had a good innings.'

Alison said wearily, 'Your breakfast is in the oven.' He took his meals in the kitchen. 'Eat it and get out of my way.'

He obeyed, ate and then wandered off while Alison was working in the kitchen. She hurried down into town to tell the doctor and he returned with her and wrote out the death certificate.

Afterwards she paused to think what she had to do next. At once her grief leapt out on her again: Francie was gone.

But that brought to mind . . . She climbed onto a chair as she had seen her grandmother do so many times. She brought down the old tea caddy and opened it. There were some copper coins, an insurance policy and insurance payments book. The last two were what she sought. She concluded that Francie had spent her savings during those last weeks of illness; she had said she was sorry she had left little to Alison.

She heard a footfall behind her, turned and saw Cuthbert entering the kitchen through the green baize door leading from the house. She asked, 'What are you doing in here?'

'Just been up to see the boss and get my orders for the day.' He sidled past her, saying, 'He said he wanted to see you.'

'I'll go up.' Alison watched him leave by the door to the back of the house. Through the kitchen window she saw him cross the yard to the stable. She wondered why Michael had demanded her presence. To give her some order regarding the running of the house presumably?

He wanted to pay for the funeral but Alison would not allow that. Francie had paid in pennies for her life insurance policy. She defied Michael, saying, 'My gannie wanted to pay for her own funeral, not to be buried as a pauper nor from charity.'

Michael kept his temper and held his tongue. He saw that the girl, just fourteen, was exhausted and at the end of her tether. He left the matter to her but discreetly watched that the arrangements were properly made. He noted, approving, that Alison obtained receipts for the amounts expended, a total of just under £5. That was the amount paid out on the policy. Alison bought extra flowers with the few pennies she received in change.

He was not surprised that there was no alteration in his household routine. He had become used to Alison serving the meals that he liked, cooked as Francie had cooked them. He knew that she had taken over during the periods of her grandmother's illness, just as he had known that she was helping Francie long before that and before the episode of his wife's room. Now he decided it was only fair to pay her the same wages he had paid the old housekeeper. He told her this when she served him his breakfast on the day after the funeral.

'Thank you, sir,' said Alison dully. At fourteen she did not appreciate how well she was paid at three pounds per month.

He thought she looked listless and uninterested, but that it was hardly surprising after her ordeal. He added, 'There's too much for you to cope with in this house. You've done very well but you're still a child. I've consulted an agency and they've written today saying they are sending a lady for me to interview, to see if she is suitable to be housekeeper. She'll be here at ten tomorrow.' He picked up the letter, several sheets of it, from the breakfast table and glanced at it. 'A Mrs Clara Skilton.' He flipped through the other sheets. 'Her references seem to be in order. I expect she will fit the position.' He laid it down and looked at Alison. 'Of course, there will still be a place here for you.'

'Thank you, sir,' Alison said apathetically. In truth she had not got over her gannie's death, did not care who came to the house or what they did.

That changed the following morning. Alison had just cleared away the breakfast crockery and was about to start making beds, when the front door bell rang. It was one of the array of bells hanging on the kitchen wall; others connected to the back door, drawing-room, dining-room and so on. It jangled as its rusty wire was pulled. She glanced up at it, startled, because it rarely tolled, then she remembered: Mrs Skilton was due.

She took off her kitchen apron of rough canvas, walked through the house to the front door and opened it. The woman who stood on the steps was in her mid-twenties with mousy hair piled high under a flower-bedecked hat, a coarse skin and prominent bosom. She licked wet lips and smirked with cold eyes. 'Hello, dear. I'm Clara Skilton to see Mr Tarrant. You should be expecting me.'

Alison disliked her on sight but stayed impassive. 'Yes. Will you come this way, please?'

She led Mrs Skilton to the drawing-room, tapped at the door and heard Michael's deep, 'Come in!'

Alison opened the door, announced, 'Mrs Skilton, sir,' and ushered the woman into the room. Then she shut the door and left them to it.

She returned to her work in the kitchen but was no longer uninterested in who would be the new housekeeper. Now she was sure it would change her life. She could not imagine working with Mrs Skilton, did not want to. She realised that no one could take the place of her gannie so her time in this house was coming to an end.

Back in the drawing-room, Michael had made up his mind. Mrs Skilton had said she was a widow. He had accepted the statement although he suspected she had used the title in order to get the job and to show she was – available. He had noticed in Mrs Skilton several feminine wiles he had seen before in women he had brought to the house, admiring glances aimed at him and a shy lowering of her gaze under his. And she had said, 'I will be glad to wait upon you whenever you call.'

The message could not be more clear. Now he said, 'Your duties will be those of a cook/housekeeper, no more nor less, and I will pay you three pounds per month. I do not keep a large staff; there'll just be you and the girl. If you cannot manage all the work then leave some undone. I will not take on extra staff. This is not for reasons of economy. I could afford a half-dozen maids if I wished, but I don't want a lot of people about the place, except of my choosing. The – ladies – I may bring home will be my responsibility. I will entertain them – and *vice versa*. I may ask you to leave out a cold meal, but that aside you will not be involved. Are you able to agree to those terms?'

Three pounds a month and her bed and board! Clara Skilton's eyes gleamed. In her last place she had pleasured the master of the house and got neither credit nor payment for it. Michael looked a proper man but if he did not want her she did not care. There were plenty of fish in the sea. 'Those terms seem quite satisfactory, sir.'

Alison heard the bell ring where it hung on the wall but this time the jangling did not startle her; she was expecting the summons to the drawing-room and it was that bell that was ringing now. She took off her kitchen apron again and answered the call. She found Clara Skilton smirking and Michael on his feet and impatient.

He said brusquely, 'Mrs Skilton is now the housekeeper and will be moving in tomorrow. Will you be so good as to show her round? I am going riding.' And he strode out and left them to it.

Alison said, 'Shall we start on the top floor and work down, Mrs Skilton?'

Clara gave her a steely smile. 'Call me "Ma'am".'

Alison returned it. 'Yes, ma'am.'

'Thank you.' Again the false smile. 'Lead on, child.'

That annoyed Alison and she knew it was meant to annoy her, but she held her tongue and led the way. They toured the house and Clara made great play of wiping a white-gloved finger along window sills and ledges. She would follow this up with a shaking of her head and a pursing of her lips. Once she put her criticism into words. 'The place

has not been dusted for a long time. It seems my prede-
cessor was a little slapdash.'

Alison replied angrily, 'My gannie was dying, and then I
had to manage the place on my own.'

Clara said soothingly, 'Of course. I'm sure you did all that
could be asked of a child.'

Alison knew she had risen to the bait and saw the flicker
of triumph in the housekeeper's eyes.

They ended the inspection of the house with the kitchen
and servants' rooms. Alison's was last of all. Clara looked it
over, the bed and cosy rocking chair, and asked, 'This was
the housekeeper's room?'

Alison started, 'Yes, ma'am, but now it's—'

Clara cut her off. 'I will have this one.'

Alison was silent for a moment, her breath taken away.
She had not expected this. Then she explained, 'It was my
room as well. My gannie and me, we shared—'

Clara cut in then. 'That may have served for you and your
grandmother, but I will not share. We will find another room
for you.'

Alison was about to weep but they were tears of rage and
revulsion. She had a mental picture of Clara Skilton walking
through this house and having the ordering of her, Alison's,
days. The thought of Clara in this room, supplanting the
memory of her grandmother, that sickened her. She said
curtly, 'I'll save you the trouble. I'll find another room and
another place. You start here tomorrow, Mrs Skilton. For
now I'll thank you to leave my room.'

Clara gaped for a moment then outrage claimed her. 'Don't
you dare to speak to me like that, my girl!'

Now it was Alison's turn to cut in. 'Don't call me your
girl! I'm not your girl and never will be!'

'You're little more than a child.'

Alison knew that, did not know where this newfound

resolution came from but did not care. She knew she had aged and wanted no part of Mrs Skilton. She picked up the poker from the fireside and pointed it at the woman she hated now. 'Out!'

Clara backed away, frightened. 'You're mad! I'll tell Mr Tarrant—'

'Tell him what you like, but get out!'

Clara Skilton fled.

Now reaction set in; Alison's legs gave way under her and she sat down on the bed with a bump. The tears came and she let them fall, for Francie and herself, for the life they had shared and that was over now. After a time she found a handkerchief and dried her eyes. She would have to start again. She realised she still held the poker and wondered if she would have used it. She did not think she would have done, though she had been angry enough. Mrs Skilton had thought she would use it and that was what mattered. She set it down in the fireplace and went back to work.

Alison cooked and served Michael Tarrant's dinner that evening as usual. Afterwards, as she served his coffee and brought his bottle of whisky, she said, 'Excuse me, sir, but I wish to give notice.'

He was prepared. 'Mrs Skilton met me when I came back from riding. She told me about your – disagreement – and said you were leaving. You can't manage to work with her?'

'No, sir.' That was said with force.

'I see. And when do you wish to leave?'

'Tomorrow.'

His eyebrows lifted. 'Have you somewhere to go?'

'I'll find a place.' That was said with determination but she did not know where to start.

He guessed at that and sat silent for a moment, staring down at his hands spread on the table, thinking. Alison thought that he was looking older. She recalled Francie saying that Michel Tarrant was burning the candle at both ends and he would not make old bones. He was haggard now in the light from the oil lamp, his hair turned from coal black to silver. Alison judged him to be in his fifties now, from what she had learned over the years, and she was correct. But now he looked to be sixty and more.

He raised his head to fix her with his piercing gaze. 'To tell the truth, I've been thinking of sending you away. I've hesitated because I didn't want to hurt you and out of respect for your grandmother's memory. She was a good and faithful servant. But I think this is no place for a young girl like you. When your grandmother was alive it was different, but for you to stay on in this house now would not be right. It has a reputation and so do I. It would be wrong for yours to be besmirched and there would be plenty ready to describe you in hard words. Francie would not have liked that. Mrs Skilton is a different matter.' His lips twisted ironically, 'She knows she will be safe from me and won't care what people think.'

He drained his glass and reached for the bottle. 'So, you go with my blessing and I'll pay you a week's notice.' He dug into his pocket and handed the coins to her. 'I'll write you a reference and leave it in the hall so you can pick it up in the morning. No need for you to cook breakfast for me; Mrs Skilton can see to that and you can be on your way. And now, goodnight.'

'Goodnight, sir, and thank you.' Alison tucked the coins away in the pocket of her apron, picked up her tray and made for the door. As she opened it Michael called, 'A moment!' She paused, head turned to face him. He said gruffly, 'If ever you are in need of help I would be grateful if you would come to me.'

'Yes, sir. Thank you.' Alison closed the door behind her. She felt great pity for Michael Tarrant.

She returned to the kitchen and washed up, banked up

the fire and left all in order for the morning. Back in her room she assembled her few possessions. She did not have a suitcase but solved that problem by sewing up one end of each of two old skirts she had long since outgrown. That gave her two sacks. She packed one of them and went to bed.

She lay awake for some time, watching the play of shadows on the wall, the flickering flames of the fire that she was leaving to burn itself out. She saw pictures in the fire as she had done when sitting by it with Francie on cold winter nights. She pictured her grandmother in the glowing coals now, and Michael Tarrant – or was that his young nephew, Richard?

She remembered the night when she first came to this house. Bellhanger had been gloomy and forbidding and she had been apprehensive and afraid, rightly so as it proved, for she was about to be abandoned. But then she had found love and care here, and happiness through the rest of her childhood years. Now childhood was behind her, she was leaving her home and did not know where she would go. She had no one in all the world. She was only fourteen and her courage born of anger, that had flamed so strongly in the day, had deserted her now.

Alison cried herself to sleep.

6

Monkwearmouth in Sunderland, April 1904.

Alison woke to the sound of rain battering at the window. Through a crack in the curtains she could see a grey and lowering sky. The fire was only dead ashes in the grate and she could feel the chill of the room on her face. She lay still for a minute or two, thinking of what she had to do, then forced herself to face the day. She said aloud, 'This won't do,' as Francie had said so many times, a call for action.

She threw off the covers and jumped out of bed, shivering. She washed and dressed then cleaned out the grate and laid the fire ready for lighting. She stripped the bed and made it again with fresh linen. The used sheets she took down to the kitchen where she stoked the fire and breakfasted on tea and toast. Then she laundered the bedding and her own clothes and spread the former on the big drying frame that hung from the ceiling. The latter she ironed dry and packed in the second of the two bags she had made. She would air the clothes in her new place. She dared not guess where that might be.

Alison looked about her. All was left neat and clean, as her grandmother would have wished. She pulled on her coat and pinned a felt hat on her piled hair; she had put it up now, a schoolgirl no longer. She looked at herself in the mirror and saw a young girl entering adolescence, long-legged and gawky, flat-chested as any boy, wide-mouthed but with the corners turned down now, solemn. Frightened?

She stiffened and turned away. She was ready. She threaded the passages to the front of the house. It was silent

about her but Mrs Skilton should arrive soon and she wanted
to be gone by then. Her reference lay on the small table in
the hall as Michael had promised, an envelope addressed *To
whom it may concern.* There was another, labelled simply
Alison. She opened it.

Michael Tarrant had written, 'George Grindly runs a café
of that name in Dundas Street. Tell him I would be obliged
if he could help you, and show him this note. I think he will
find a place for you.'

Alison felt a flood of relief. It was tinged with doubt because
it might be that this George Grindly could not find room
for her, but there was hope where there had been none before.
She tucked the letter and the reference into her handbag,
picked up her home-made sacks and left the house. She
closed the front door behind her and paused for a moment
at the head of the steps. How many mornings had she washed
and whitened them? It was Clara Skilton's job now.

She ran down the steps and set out on the long road into
the town. The rain had stopped and a watery sun peeped
between hurrying clouds. Her new life had a direction now,
somewhere to go, and she stepped out light-heartedly.

Alison knew the town and Dundas Street where the shops
were and Grindly's café. She had passed it many a time,
though she had never set foot inside. Francie had said, 'Places
like that aren't for the likes of us; they're for folks wi' money
to spare.' Alison found a dozen people in the little café
despite the earliness of the hour – it was just turned nine.
They did not look to her to have money to spare, most being
men in overalls, eating a quick breakfast after starting work
at seven or earlier. Then there were a few middle-aged women
who might be cleaners, sitting over cups of tea.

A girl of eighteen moved slowly among the tables, waiting
on, and a man emerged from the kitchen door behind the

counter. He carried a plate holding a pie and some peas. He was a middle-sized man in waistcoat and shirtsleeves, a sacking apron about his waist. His sallow face held a day's greying stubble. Alison learned later that he was shaved two or three times a week by Mickey Hobson in his barber shop nearby. His thinning hair was oiled and parted in the middle with two little quiffs.

He handed the plate to the serving girl and she took it lackadaisically and moved to deliver it to a man in a painter's white overalls. Alison took her place before the counter and asked, 'Are you Mr Grindly, please, sir?'

He looked down at her and did not see a customer. 'Aye, and I'm busy. Did you want to order something?'

'No, sir.'

'Then don't waste my time. I'm busy, always busy.' He turned back towards the kitchen.

Alison said, 'I'm looking for a job. I—'

'I don't want anybody.' He was halfway through the door.

She called desperately, 'I have a letter from Mr Tarrant!'

He spun round in the doorway and in one stride was back facing her. 'Why didn't you say so? Let me have it.' He took the letter and the reference and read them slowly, his finger tracing the words, lips moving, speaking a word aloud here and there: 'Alison Bailey . . . I would be obliged . . . hard-working and honest . . . excellent character . . .' At the end he gave back reference and letter to the nervous and hopeful Alison. 'Aye, that looks all right. He thinks well of you and that's good enough for me. I can give you a job waiting on and helping in the kitchen, four shilling a week and your bed and board.'

Alison blinked at that, making a comparison. When she had been working as cook/housekeeper after the death of Francie, Michael Tarrant had paid her triple that amount, three pounds a month.

Something of this must have shown in her face because Grindly, mindful of his landlord's request, wheedled, 'If you're good enough and I keep you on I'll make it five bob a week.'

Now Alison reasoned that she did not know what wages were being paid in other places and anyway, she needed the money and a roof over her head. She smiled at Grindly. 'Thank you.'

'Righto!' He nodded approval. 'Now, when can you start?'

Alison had nowhere else to go. 'Now?'

'Good! We're always busy here. Come on, then.' He lifted the flap of the counter and she passed through into the kitchen. It was warm and small, with a table set against one wall and covered with a gaudily coloured oilcloth. In the opposite wall was a black-leaded stove and a sink. The third wall between those two was occupied by an old sideboard, ornately carved, backed by a huge mirror and with two doors at the front. In the fourth wall a flight of stairs led up to the floor above, while a door and window looked out on a back-yard and a line hung with cloths for washing and drying dishes.

A tall, merry-faced woman in her forties stood at the table kneading dough in a big earthenware bowl, a floured white apron over her brown dress. Grindly introduced her. 'This is Mrs Maguire, the cook. Dolly, this is Alison Bailey. She's going to wait on and give you a hand in here.'

Dolly smiled. 'Hello, canny lass.'

'Hello, Mrs Maguire.' Alison liked the look of the cook.

It was reciprocated. The grin widened. 'Folks just call me Dolly.'

Grindly butted in impatiently, 'Now then, we're busy here. Put your things in the cupboard in the corner, Alison, and do what Dolly tells you. You'll sleep in here. I'll sort out the bed for you later on.'

Alison looked around her furtively, thinking, *Sleep in here?* She did not like the idea. But now the waitress appeared in the doorway. 'There's a man wants a pork sandwich.' She stood there, waiting. She had an hourglass figure with an enviable bosom – at least it was to Alison, with her still boyish figure. She wondered how much of the hourglass was due to corsetry, and thought her a dreamy girl.

Grindly said, 'This is Una.' He introduced Alison and the girl smiled vaguely. He said, 'All right, Una.' She drifted back into the café and he continued, 'That's a pork sandwich wanted, Dolly.' Then he hurried after the waitress.

The cook rolled her eyes up comically. '"Pork sandwich wanted". He can see my hands are thick wi' flour. That man's always too busy to do anything, and that Una wanders about as if tomorrow would do.'

Alison said quickly, 'I'll do it.' She jammed her two sacks in the cupboard and hung her coat and hat on a nail in the door leading to the yard.

Dolly said, 'Bread is in the tin, pork in the larder.' She pointed to both.

Alison deftly carved the slices of pork off the joint and made the sandwich. She took it out to the counter and passed it on to Una, who drifted over to the customer with it.

When she returned to the kitchen Dolly nodded approval and grinned. 'I think you'll do, but you'd better put on an apron.'

Alison bound the apron round her waist. She spent the rest of the day between helping Dolly, or waiting on when Una was at lunch or on some other break. The cook chatted as she worked and Alison learned that she was the only one living in; Una and Dolly returned home after work was done for the day.

Dolly said, 'You'll be comfortable in here with the stove being on. You don't want to be upstairs with her.' The

Grindlys lived above the café and 'her' was his wife, Moira. 'She doesn't come down here very often but when she does it's to moan and find fault.' Dolly grinned. 'Most of the time she moans at George. She thinks she married beneath her.'

When the café closed that evening, the cook and waitress departed and Alison was left alone with Grindly. He looked in the larder. Alison suspected, rightly, that he was committing its contents to memory, because he went on, 'You can sort out a bite o' supper but don't make a pig o' yourself. I'll know if you do.'

There was a hammering on the floor above and he glowered up at the ceiling and muttered, 'All right, I'm coming.' He turned to the sideboard with its elaborate carving but numerous scratches, opened the two doors and set them wide. 'The bed is in here.' It was folded up inside like a concertina, an ancient affair with rusting springs, a thin mattress and bedding jammed in on top of it. He demonstrated how it was pulled out, creaking and dusty. 'There y'are. You'll be snug in there. But mind you're up and out of it and all cleared away by seven in the morning for the cook starting work.' He pointed to the clock standing on the shelf above the stove. There was more knocking over his head and his lips moved but Alison did not hear the words. He moved to the stairs but turned to say, 'I'll be going out later but not this way; I'll use the front stairs.' They ran down to a front door next to that of the café. Now he said, 'Goodnight, Alison.'

'Goodnight, Mr Grindly,' she called after his retreating back as he climbed the stairs. Then she sat down, slumping wearily on the foot of the bed. She had to make it, and her supper, but could not bestir herself now. She was lonely, missing her grandmother, and wondered if she had made the right choice in walking out of Bellhanger. But a few moments' thought, and a mental picture of Clara Skilton, dispelled that doubt. She straightened and told herself that life would not be easy here, but somehow she would make her way up. What would Francie have said? *You've got to get on with it.*

She stood up determinedly and began to make her bed. That done, she made a supper of cold beef and bread, sardonically recalling Grindly's warning not to eat too much. While she was eating she heard voices upstairs, a woman's shrill. 'Every night you're off to that pub and I'm left here on my own.'

Then Grindly's defensive whine – 'I've asked you often enough and you won't come.'

'No! Never! I won't set foot in one of those low class places. But they suit you down to the ground because you'll never be nothing! I should have listened to my mother, God rest her soul. "Common as muck", that's what she called you, and she was right.'

Alison heard the rapid clatter of his boots on the front stairs as he fled and the slam of the front door. She sighed, finished her meal and put on her nightdress. The boiler attached to the stove dispensed plenty of hot water from a brass tap and she washed herself and her underclothes. Those, and the washing she had done that morning, she hung around the stove. It only remained to turn off the gas light and crawl into bed. She approved of the gas and thought the light much better than the oil lamps still in use at Bellhanger.

She was worn out but lay restlessly awake for some time. The mattress was hard and the rusty bedsprings creaked and twanged as she tossed and turned. There was a faint but comforting glow from the stove but she was uneasy about the stairs coming down from the rooms above. Anyone could walk down into this room of hers; she could not lock any door against them. She had heard many stories of young servant girls being ravished, all of them true.

At that moment George Grindly lay in Una's bed, her nakedness pressed against his body, his hands caressing, hers fondling. She still wore the dreamy smile but moved urgently, cried out with him, sinking together.

Alison was dozing, hovering on the edge of consciousness, when Grindly returned home. She came fully awake with a start when she heard his boots on the front stairs. There was a wail from up there – 'You've come home to wake the neighbourhood!' But that was all she heard. No one crept down her stairs. Her eyes closed and finally tiredness claimed her and she slept.

By seven the next morning Alison was up and dressed and the kitchen all ready for Dolly when she should arrive. She could hear the clatter of the workmen's boots on the cobbles as they hastened to their work in the shipyards, the crying of the gulls. They were all sounds remembered from her childhood in the East End, before she went to live at Bellhanger in the country. In a way, and in this optimism of a new day, it was like coming home.

Dolly came in then and beamed at the girl waiting eagerly. She laughed, 'You've been busy, bonny lass. Well done.'

There came a cry out in the street: 'Milk-oh!'

'Quick! Give me that jug,' cried Dolly. 'I'll have to chase that milkman half-way down the street if I don't catch him now.' She seized the earthenware jug hurriedly handed to her by Alison and dashed outside. The girl watched from the kitchen doorway and saw the milk float holding the churn and drawn by an old horse. The milkman, red-faced and in blue and white striped apron, dipped his measure into the churn and ladled out milk into Dolly's jug. She paid him and returned to join Alison, as he shook the reins and the horse walked on.

Dolly laughed breathlessly. 'That's the first job of the day done.'

They cooked and ate breakfast together. Dolly grinned, 'Another day serving up the same old stuff: pie and peas or sandwiches.'

Alison asked, 'Don't you like cooking then?'

'I don't call that cooking,' said Dolly scornfully. 'Not a joint nor a casserole, just the same old stuff. That's all Grindly wants. I get bored stiff some days. It's a godsend to have you to talk to. As for that Una, she hasn't a thought in her head.'

They had just finished eating when Grindly came bustling down the stairs. 'Come on now, lasses, time we were at it. I'm going to open up.' He hurried past them and into the café. They heard him unlocking the door and drawing the bolts, greeting Una who lived in a furnished room further down Dock Street.

Dolly pulled a face. 'Another busy day.' Alison laughed.

As if on cue, Grindly reappeared, poking his head around the door to urge them, 'Busy day. Customer wants a cup o' tea and two slices o' bread and dripping.' He paused and saw Una was still lethargically shedding her coat and hat, so he ordered, 'Alison!' And ducked back into the café.

Her first customer of the day! Alison quickly spread dripping as Dolly poured tea, then carried the snack out to the customer. He proved to be a stocky little man in paint-smeared white overalls. He hailed her, 'Is that mine, bonny lass?' And as she set it before him he said, 'That was quick. Quicker than usual, anyway.' He glanced past her to where Una had now appeared in the kitchen and stood gazing dreamily about her. He looked back at Alison with a wry grin, 'That Una! You're new here, aren't you? What's your name?'

'Alison Bailey.'

He took a huge bite of bread and dripping and spoke through it, tapping his chest. 'Peter Robson. I'm a painter and decorator. I do a lot o' big houses, places like Roker Avenue and Ashbrooke. My wife died a couple o' years back.'

'Oh, I'm sorry,' said Alison sympathetically, and meant it, could see the little man's sadness.

He sighed. 'Aye, well, it's good of you. Anyway, since then I usually come in here for a bite o' breakfast.' Alison thought, *and company*. He shook off the mood like a dog coming out of the sea. 'I'd better get away to work.' He drained his cup, stood up and grinned at her. 'So if you want any decorating done, remember Peter Robson.'

'I will,' laughed Alison, though she thought it highly unlikely that she would need his services.

He left with a wave of his hand and she went back to her work in the kitchen.

It was mid-morning when they heard a heavy tread on the stairs. Dolly muttered, 'Oh, Lord, here she comes.'

Moira Grindly, heavy and sour, paused at the foot of the stairs, gazing about her at the kitchen. She was squeezed into a costume in black bombazine, rigidly corsetted, a handbag hanging from the crook of her arm, a too-small coquettish hat skewered to her piled hair. Her cold eye came to rest on Dolly. 'This floor needs sweeping.' Her double chin wobbled as she pointed at a small dusting of flour.

Dolly said, 'We'll see to it straight away, Mrs Grindly.'

Alison hastily reached for the broom and the cold eye shifted to her. She smiled nervously and Moira snapped, 'What are you laughing at?'

'I'm not!' Alison denied the charge. 'I was smiling.'

'Don't answer back or I'll have you out of here!' Moira glowered and Alison swallowed her protests. Moira charged, 'You're the new lass.'

'Yes, Mrs Grindly.'

'I'll be watching you. I insist on civility and cleanliness. I have standards, if he hasn't.' She shot a venomous glance towards the café where Grindly could be heard talking to a customer. Moira went on disdainfully, 'I was brought up to better than this, living over a café that hardly pays its way, scrimping and scraping. My father was foreman fitter at Buchanan's yard and don't you forget it.'

'No, Mrs Grindly.'

'Right. Now get on with your work.' Moira sniffed and crossed the kitchen, swept them with one final glare and passed through to the shop. They heard her hectoring Grindly, 'That lass is too slow to catch a cold . . .' Her voice faded.

Dolly said dryly, 'Now Una is getting it.'

The waitress entered now, dabbing at her eyes with a scrap of handkerchief. She said weepily, 'Pie an' peas, please.'

Dolly deftly put the food on a plate and consoled her. 'Look on the bright side; she's gone for the day.' And then, explaining for Alison's benefit, 'Today is Friday, when Moira goes to see her sister at Shields. She won't be back before tonight so we can all breathe easy till then.'

Una wiped her eyes and took the loaded plate out to the customer. Alison relaxed and smiled, feeling the easing of the tension in the atmosphere.

She asked, 'Doesn't this place pay then? Mrs Grindly said—'

Dolly laughed. '"Scrimping and scraping!"' She echoed Moira Grindly. 'Don't believe that, pet. This place is a little goldmine. He could make more money if he tried. He could do with somebody different to Una, but he makes plenty.' Dolly saw Alison's puzzled expression and explained, 'Moira doesn't know because she's too stuck up to come down here and see what goes on. He takes the money out of the till and puts it in his pocket. She only knows what he tells her.'

Alison, struggling with this insight into the life below the surface, said, 'I see.'

Dolly went on, 'And Una is his little bit of entertainment. You haven't seen him at it yet but I expect you will. He runs his hands all over her. He's careful, mind, never does it when the customers can see.'

Alison settled into her new job and grew to know the customers when she worked a shift waiting on. There was Mr Trench, the 'rent man', going about his work of collecting rents. This was not the man with pendulous cheeks that Doreen had said, so long ago, would have to whistle for his money. Mr Trench usually came in mid-morning for a cup of tea and a sandwich. His shiny suit sagged, the pockets filled with coins. He confided to Alison, 'Most of the rents I collect are for properties belonging to Mad Michael. That's Michael Tarrant. Have you heard about him?' Alison answered, tongue in cheek, that she had, but said nothing of her life at Bellhanger. Trench added, 'He might be mad but he's a good landlord, keeps his properties in good repair – or gets his agent to do it.'

Then there were the young men from the bank, and the lady manager of the dressmaker's shop, Miss Devenish, who rather disapproved of their freed-from-work high spirits. Then there was the foreman from the tram company, the women out shopping with a few coppers, and a few minutes, to spare. Alison wore a bright smile for all of them.

In the kitchen she showed herself quick to learn and Dolly commended her. 'You're a good little lass.' Alison in her turn found the older woman always helpful. They talked as they worked, sometimes about the food they were cooking and the dishes Grindly would not countenance, declaring, 'Keep it simple! We're too busy for fancy stuff!' And Alison told how she had been taught to cook by Francie, and Dolly approved, saying, 'You've been well trained.'

Alison also learned that Grindly's reiterated claims of being busy were just show. He liked to think he was organising his little work force and that the whole structure would fall apart without him. In fact, when he had occasion to go out it functioned perfectly, with Dolly and Alison doing most of the work. He found time to study the racing form and back a horse most days.

Alison got out on her day off. The café stayed open on Wednesday, early closing day for the shops, but Grindly let her out for the afternoon. She often walked down Dock Street then along the sea front. Sometimes she went window shopping in the town shops of Sunderland, in Fawcett Street, spending little or nothing because of her small earnings and her desire to save. She had not forgotten leaving Bellhanger with only a week's wages between her and the workhouse, would never forget.

It was on one of these outings to the shops, and when she was crossing the bridge over the river, that she saw a familiar face. Her thoughts were far away, recalling when she had crossed the bridge with her mother, going to be abandoned at Bellhanger. Then she suddenly realised she was staring into the face of the groom. 'Cuthbert Price! What are you doing here?'

He seemed more startled than she. His usual vacuous grin was replaced by a shocked gape, his mouth an O. After a moment he said, 'Hullo.' He seemed uneasy, not meeting her gaze, his eyes darting as if he sought a way out.

'I didn't expect to meet you,' said Alison. 'Have you brought Mr Tarrant in the carriage?'

He shook his head, his hair like straw sticking out from under his cap. 'Don't work there no more.'

'He sacked you? What a shame.' She was surprised. Cuthbert had seemed to be good with the horses.

'No!' He rejected that forcibly, blinking at her, then his eyes flickered away. 'I handed in me notice, I did.'

'So where are you working?' Alison asked, now concerned for him.

He shrugged. 'I'm out o' work.'

'I'm sorry about that. How are you managing?' She wondered if he was eating. She had a few coppers, maybe a shilling's worth, in her purse, if . . .

'I'm all right. Don't you worry about me.' He started to edge away.

Alison wished him well. 'I hope you find a job somewhere soon.'

'Aye. Thanks.' He hurried off without even a wave of his hand.

'Good luck!' Alison called after him, but he did not pause or answer.

She went on her way, but troubled now. She was sure there was something wrong with Cuthbert. It had seemed as if he was afraid – but of what?

Alison forgot about him as the days went by, all of them the same, saved from monotony by her growing friendship with Dolly. It countered the obvious dislike Moira Grindly felt for Alison. She had picked on the girl ever since their first meeting. The others suffered too, but Moira was careful not to say too much to Dolly, knowing she was a key member of the staff. As the cook said wryly, 'If I walk out she'd have to do this job.' And Una had some consolation because Grindly was quick to comfort her. Alison learned there was little chance of Dolly leaving because she was a widow with two young children and an aged mother to support.

As predicted, Alison came on Una and Grindly one day, locked in an embrace in a corner of the yard and out of sight of the kitchen. He was massaging the girl's breast and she had her arms around his neck and was panting, eyes closed.

Alison hurried away, shocked, and Dolly asked, 'What's the matter?'

She explained, blushing, and asked, 'Why does she do it? He's old enough to be her father. Couldn't she find a young man?'

Dolly raised her eyebrows. 'Who knows? Maybe she can't be bothered. And she's not much company.' Alison agreed with that, could not remember a conversation with Una lasting more than a few monosyllables. Then the cook delivered the clinching argument: 'Besides, Grindly has plenty of money, like I told you. That can be attractive to a lass like Una.'

It was not the last time Alison 'caught them at it' as Dolly phrased it, but in time she ceased to be shocked and passed on with a shrug.

The days and weeks ran into months; she grew and filled out. She had to buy new clothes as she grew out of them but by careful budgeting she was still able to save a little. Dolly looked on at this transformation of her ugly duckling and marvelled at the burgeoning beauty. 'You're going to turn the lads' heads, bonny lass.' Alison blushed shyly. She had seen the glances of the men and read them. She became wary of Grindly but if he took note he did not molest her and saved that for Una.

Alison had been working for Grindly for nearly two years when the day came. It began like many in March, grey, with rain blown in on the wind from the sea, save that it was Friday, when Moira Grindly was due to visit her sister. Before that a small boy came to the café fetching a note written on a scrap of paper. The ragged urchin, a badly-sewn patch on the seat of his shorts, gave the note to Grindly. 'The lass that gave me this said you'd gi' me a ha'penny.'

Grindly paid him his half-penny, read the missive in the kitchen then threw it in the fire and watched it burn, saying, 'Una won't be in today. You'll have to see to the serving, Alison.'

'Aye, Mr Grindly.'

He told the boy, 'You sit down. I'll have a job for you, later.' Then he went on with his bustling.

The lad sat by the fire and Dolly fed him tea, bread and dripping.

Moira Grindly clumped down the stairs at her usual time, glowered, carped, wrinkled her nose in disdain at the boy then demanded to know why he was there.

Grindly answered, 'He's going to put a bet on for me.'

Moira wrinkled her nose again, this time with disgust. 'Gambling! No wonder we're always short of money! My father never got where he was by betting on horses.' She finished, 'It's my sister's birthday so I'll be late back. You'll have to get your own tea.' Then she went off.

As the door closed behind her, Grindly ran up the stairs two at a time. He came panting down again a minute later with a folded slip of paper that he handed to the boy. 'Take this back to that young lady and she'll give you another ha'penny.' Then he added, as the boy made for the door, 'Run!' The messenger took to his heels, his patched seat disappearing out of the door. Grindly shot up the stairs again and Dolly exchanged mystified glances with Alison.

The cook whispered, 'What's going on?' But Alison could only shake her head.

They worked on, Dolly at the stove, Alison shuttling between café and kitchen. It was half an hour later that Grindly descended the stairs again. This time he carried a suitcase in one hand. He set it down by the kitchen table then passed through into the café where Alison was taking an order from a customer. He called, 'You come wi' me, lass!' Then he opened the drawer that served as a till, scooped out its contents and jammed them into his pocket.

Alison followed him into the kitchen. There he counted out two piles of coins, far more than he had taken from the till. He pushed a pile to each of them. 'There's a week's notice for you and a bit of a bonus an' all. I'm off. I have enough to buy meself another place for me and Una. I left a letter upstairs for Moira, given her this place an' all. She always said she knew how to run it better than me and now she can get on with it. There are the keys.' He tossed a bundle of them onto the table. 'Ta-ra!' He picked up the case, gave a flirt of the hand and was gone.

They gaped at each other then went to the door to look out. They were just in time to see him join a waiting Una. She also carried a suitcase. He took it from her and they hurried away along the street. Dolly said, low-voiced because of the customers sipping tea only feet away, 'They'll be getting a tram from Roker Avenue to the station and then a train.'

Alison was still aghast but seeing a number of things now. 'I used to hear him go out every night and thought he went to the pub. So did Moira, but he must have been spending his time with Una. And all the time he was saving up for today.'

'Fancy!' Dolly shook her head but agreed. 'I think you've got the right of it. We do see life. But I don't blame him for going, though I think he's making a mistake. He'll be running around his new place as he did here, and only Una will benefit.'

Alison whispered, 'What do we do now? He's paid us off.'

Dolly grinned. 'Go on working. I'm waiting to see Moira when she gets back tonight.'

It was dark when Moira returned. The café was shut but Dolly and Alison, all their work done, sat at a table in the window. Moira glared at them through the glass, pushed in through the door and demanded, 'What are you two doing in here at this time o' night? Where's George?'

'He went off earlier on,' replied Dolly blandly. 'He said he'd left a letter for you upstairs.'

'A letter?' Moira looked from one to the other. 'What d'ye mean, a letter? What is he doing writing letters? I suppose he's won wi' that bet he was putting on and now he's in the pub blowing his winnings!' She charged past them into the kitchen and they heard her clumping up the stairs.

Dolly said, 'Come on.' She led the way into the kitchen and they stood in breath-held silence until a howl, half pain, half rage, came from overhead. Silence again for some minutes, then the shoes clumped on the stairs again.

Moira stopped on the last step so she was looking down on them. Her face was suffused, her mouth set tight. There was no sign of tears or trembling lip. She showed her teeth and said, 'He's gone, but God help him if I ever lay hands on him! I'll be carrying on and there are going to be some changes made. Grindly said he paid you a week's notice. You can keep that money, Mrs Maguire, but I want you to stay on.' She glanced at the keys, lying on the table where Grindly had thrown them. 'Take a key for the front door. You can let yourself in of a morning and open the place.'

Now her gaze shifted to Alison and it was poisonous. 'You should never have been taken on.' She checked there, had been about to say that the letter Alison had brought from Mad Michael two years ago suggested she was one of his bastards. But caution stopped her, and instead she went on, 'I never wanted you, don't want you now. I'll thank you to be out of here by the end of next week.'

Alison felt Dolly stir beside her, saw her lips move, knew she was going to protest. But she knew Dolly's wages fed two young children and her aged mother; she needed the job. Alison put in quickly, 'I'd already decided to leave, Mrs Grindly, and I'll be out just as soon as I can.' She heard Dolly sigh.

Alison lay in her bed that night, watching the glow from the stove and looking into her future. It seemed bleak. She did not know what to do, where she could go. She hugged herself, knees pulled up and curled down small in the bed, frightened.

Young Richard Tarrant sat in the leather armchair in his digs, long legs outstretched to the fire. He smiled into the flames because this was a celebration. The polished table behind him was laden with books but they could wait until the morrow, his first day as a medical student. He was looking into his future and finding it exciting. He remembered, for the first time in years, the girl who had said he should become a doctor. He wondered what she would say if she could see him now? She was probably at some young ladies' academy or finishing school. He grinned. She was a funny little thing. What was her name? But it eluded him. No matter; he would visit Uncle Michael one day and look her up.

7

Monkwearmouth in Sunderland, April 1906.

～～～

Tuesday. She had searched for four days now. Alison plodded through the rain, seeking work and shelter. She had received offers of both but all had strings attached. In the case of some she had not liked the look in the men's eyes, in others she had recoiled from a room she could not inhabit, it being alive with bed bugs. She was hoping, but the hope growing faint now, for a living-in job, home and work in one, so she did not want to take a room on its own. But soon she would have to do that, take anything, because she had to be out of the café in three days.

Now the day was ending, the rain falling out of a darkening sky, the lamplighter hurrying from post to post with his long pole, bringing to life pool after pool of yellow light to splash on the glistening pavements and cobbles. Alison made her way back to the café, went in past the glower of Moira Grindly, standing at the counter, and sank down in a chair by the fire.

Dolly Maguire, lifting a tray of pies from the oven, glanced aside at her and clicked her tongue. 'No luck again?' she said sympathetically, reading Alison's despondent expression. 'And you're soaked. I'll make you a cup of tea. That will cheer you up.'

Alison laughed. 'I feel better already.' She took off her wet shoes and stockings, wiggled her toes in the heat from the stove and sipped the tea. 'I'll find somewhere tomorrow.'

'You'd better do it soon,' said Moira, passing through the

kitchen. 'I want you out of here. I have a new lass starting at the end of the week.' And then to Dolly, 'I've locked up for the day. See you tomorrow.' She clumped up the stairs.

Dolly and Alison exchanged wry grins. They talked on in low tones as the cook cleared up. She said, 'We're not doing so much business. Moira is waiting on but she's slow and she puts people off. Una was slow but always had a smile. Folks come in now, see Moira with a face like thunder and they don't come back a second time.'

'Maybe the new lass will be better,' suggested Alison.

Dolly sniffed. 'Maybe, but I doubt it. From what I saw of her when she came to apply for the job, she won't last long. Her mother came with her. When Moira starts picking at her I reckon she'll go back to her mother.'

Dolly set off for home and Alison cooked a meal and ate it, washed her clothes and prepared for bed. Worried, but weary from the cares of the day, her eyes soon closed. This little hovel – it was no better than that – seemed a cosy, secure place now she was about to lose it. She wondered at Moira losing business. As she drifted into sleep she thought, *even I could make a success of a place like this.*

Wednesday dawned bright and dry. Alison was up early, breakfasted with Dolly and was out hunting for employment and shelter before Moira came down. The wind off the sea had dropped and Alison tripped light-heartedly in the warmth of the sun, smiled into it.

At the other end of Dundas Street she came across a man wearing an apron who was loading furniture from a house into a horse-drawn pantechnicon. As Alison approached he shoved a chair into the van and returned to the house. She saw another man inside the pantechnicon, stacking the chairs and so forth in neat order. As Alison paused he took the pipe from his mouth to ask good-humouredly, 'Going to give us a hand, bonny lass?'

She laughed. 'I could manage a chair or two.' Now two men were carrying out a wardrobe and finding it a struggle. She added, 'But not that.' She looked from the men to the house, one of a terrace, its front door opening onto the street like so many others. She could picture the two rooms on the ground floor, the three upstairs. Her gaze was wistful; she knew she could never afford the rent of a house like that from the wage she was likely to get. Then something stirred at the back of her mind. She asked, 'Are the people inside?'

He grinned, 'Aye. And the rent man, come for the keys.'

He stared as she skipped past the wardrobe and entered the house. Alison glanced about her, eyes darting everywhere, seeing dust and faded wallpaper but no sign of dampness. There were voices upstairs, a woman squeaking, agitated, 'Mind how you shift that dressing table; it cost a mint!' But there was Mr Trench, the 'rent man'. She had often served him in Grindly's. He was fifty or so, in a navy blue suit shiny with age and pockets filled with chinking coins, as always. He had a brush and a pot of paste and was sticking a notice on the ground floor window: 'TO LET'. He greeted her cheerfully, 'Now then, Alison, what are you doing here?'

Alison asked, 'How much is the rent?'

He smoothed out the notice. 'Ten shilling a week.' He grinned, 'Are you thinking of taking it?'

As she had expected, she could not afford it. That was twice the wage she had been paid at Grindly's and she would not earn much more anywhere else. But while the 'rent man' was an employee and could not reduce the rent . . . She remembered him telling her about Mad Michael. 'Is this one of Mr Tarrant's properties?'

He jammed the lid on the paste pot and eyed her, puzzled. 'Aye. But what d'ye want to know for?'

Michael Tarrant! Alison recalled her last meeting with

him, when he had said that if ever she was in need of help
she should go to him. She smiled radiantly at the 'rent man'.
'I'm just curious.' She ran from the house and set out for
Bellhanger.

Her pace slowed as she drew near and she struggled against
looming doubts. Would Michael Tarrant remember her?
Would he care about her? Why should he help? And this
brick pile, that had become home to her as she grew up, still
had a grim aura. Its shadow fell about her, chill, like a shroud.
The weather was changing and clouds gathering. She passed
by the steps to the front door and walked around to the rear
of the house.

Her first knock on the kitchen door brought no one but
her second resulted in an irritated shriek: 'All *right*! I'm
coming!'

The door opened and Clara Skilton, mousy-haired, peered
out over her swelling bosom. She scowled at sight of the girl.
'Aye? What do you want?' Then she stared, because she had
not connected this darkly attractive young woman with the
gawky girl she had known for only a few hours. But now
she demanded again, and hostile, 'What do you want?' Then
she remembered more of their last meeting, when Alison had
threatened her with a poker. She stepped back hurriedly,
closing the door until her face showed through just a crack.
'Don't try to start your violence again,' she squeaked. 'Or
I'll send for the pollis.'

Alison smiled, seeing wry humour in this. She was frightened, not furious. 'I would like to see Mr Tarrant, please.'

'What for?' Clara challenged.

'That's my business and his.'

'Mebbe he doesn't want to see you.'

'That's up to him. Now will you tell him I'm here?' Alison
was losing patience. 'Or should I wait at the front until he
comes out? I have all day.'

Clara hesitated sulkily for a moment, hating to have to give in to this girl, but then she remembered Michael Tarrant's temper. She grumbled, 'Wait here.' And shut the door in Alison's face.

It opened again a few minutes later and Clara held it wide, said curtly, 'He'll see you.' And, as Alison entered, 'This way.' She led and Alison followed through the familiar passages. At one point Clara said, 'There's a lot of valuable things in here.'

Alison knew that very well and saw the implied slur on her honesty. She answered tranquilly, 'They'll be safe with me; always were.'

Clara tapped on the door of the drawing-room and announced, 'The lass asking to see you, sir.' And hissed as Alison passed in, 'He sees plenty like you.'

Alison pictured the girls she meant, and the naked young woman she had seen years ago, so she entered the room red-faced.

Michael Tarrant saw that she was flushed but put it down to shyness. He was taken aback by the way she had grown up. He tried to work out her age and calculated that she would be about sixteen. She was smartly dressed, though he guessed, correctly, that most of her clothes would be second-hand. He thought that Francie Bailey would be proud of her. But what did she want with him? He found he was offering her a chair.

She was surprised by that; they had always been master and servant and she had always stood in his presence. She was shocked at how he had aged in the past two years. His hair was white, his face deeply lined. But she concealed that with a smile.

He returned it. 'This is a pleasant surprise, but to what do I owe this visit?'

Alison started, 'There is a house in Dundas Street . . .'

She left half an hour later with another letter from Michael Tarrant, this one addressed to the estate agents. The rain had come while she was in Bellhanger and it poured down from a lowering sky, but Alison's spirits could not be dampened. Clara Skilton watched sullenly as she almost danced away from the house, and muttered, 'He's given her something.' She had listened and heard enough to know that much, though not the details. 'It wouldn't surprise me if she was a by-blow of his.'

Michael suspected no such conclusion. The thought had never entered his head. The girl had impressed him. She had convinced him she knew what she was talking about, that she could run a small business, had a deal of common sense and was hard-working. She had not asked him for money; she had some savings. He had agreed she could have the house for three months without paying rent. After that time she would pay twelve shillings a week, ten as rent and two more to pay off the arrears.

Alison presented the letter and claimed the keys to the house in Dundas Street by noon of that day. By nightfall she had moved her few belongings and bought a mattress and bedding, a few basic utensils. The previous tenant, she of the shrill voice, had cleared out the coalhouse, leaving only an empty bucket with a hole in the bottom. But Alison begged a battered wooden box from a grocer in Dundas Street and lit the kitchen fire with that. She made and ate a frugal meal of bacon and potatoes then retired to her mattress laid on the floor.

She lay and blinked drowsily at the last glow of the embers in the grate but her mind was still racing with thoughts of what she had to do on the morrow. This was her home and work now. She believed she could run a café but now she had to make a success of it, produce an income, a profit, and that before her meagre savings were exhausted. She had to keep down costs, could not employ anyone. She would have to do it all herself. Well, not all. She had an idea about that. Then she wondered if that was enough. Suppose she made a profit, a success – then what?

Suppose . . .

She slept with her dreams.

Alison woke early on Thursday, breakfasted on tea and bread and a scrape of margarine. She was waiting outside the dressmaker's shop in Dundas Street when Miss Betty Devenish arrived to open up. Betty was a straight-backed lady, greying and seeming fragile, but she ruled her shop with a rod of iron. She asked, 'Is everything all right?'

'It will be,' Alison smiled, 'but I'm going to open a café and I need some curtains.'

Miss Devenish stared in amazement. 'Open a café!' She listened while Alison told how she had been sacked and had taken the house. She pursed her lips. 'That Moira has taken her troubles out on you. And she always has a face as long as a fiddle.' Then she asked the girl, 'How old are you?'

Alison looked past her and answered, 'Eighteen.'

'You'll just about get away with that. But I remember when you started at Grindly's and you were just out of school and all arms and legs. Do you think you'll manage?'

'I'll have to. I'm not going into the workhouse.'

Miss Devenish caught her breath. 'No, you're not.' Then: 'When we shut tonight I'll come along and measure up.'

Alison spent the rest of the day scouring the town on both sides of the river for second-hand furniture. At the end of it she had bought six tables, all of them scarred and stained but sound and solid. She had also found fifteen chairs in similar condition, wanted more but she decided that would have to wait. With all of them she pleaded, persuaded, cajoled and threatened until the dealers agreed to deliver to her in the late afternoon. She took them in then and at that time a coalman with a loaded horse-drawn cart came by. He bawled, 'Coal! Tuppence a stone!' Alison ran to fetch the bucket from the coalhouse and covered up the hole in the bottom with some folded newspaper. She bought a bucketful of big 'roundy' coals that would make a bright fire.

That evening she talked curtains with Miss Devenish and later walked down Dock Street to a house that stood out from the rest with its gleaming paintwork. The front door was on the latch and she entered and walked along the passage to the door of the ground floor kitchen.

Stocky little Peter Robson answered her knock, stared then welcomed her. 'By, its nice to see you Alison. I heard you'd left Grindly's. Come in! Come in!' He held the door wide and waved her to a seat in an armchair by the fire, with its polished brass fire-irons of poker, rake and shovel winking at her in the firelight's glow. He sat opposite her and asked, 'So, how are you getting on? Glad to be away from that miserable Moira Grindly, I'll bet.'

Alison told him how she had rented the house and her plans. 'But the downstairs of the place needs decorating before I can open up. Will you do it?'

'Like a shot,' he agreed, 'but I work for a decorating firm. I'd have to do it at the weekend. How about that?'

'Fine,' Alison agreed, smiling. But now she came to the awkward part. 'I can't pay you, but I'll help and I'll give you your breakfast free until I've made it up to you.'

Peter sat back in his chair. 'No, lass, you won't have to pay me. I'll do it for nowt to help you out.' Then he grinned. 'But I'll take you up on the breakfast. It'll get me away from that Moira and her tak-it-or-leave-it attitude. Now then, I'll be round Saturday after I've finished work . . .'

They made their arrangements and Alison walked home with the feeling of having done a good day's work. She had not finished, but drew a chair up to one of her tables and carefully printed a card which read: ALISON'S COOK-SHOP CAFE OPENING SHORTLY.

She propped this in the front window and went happily to sleep – on the floor again but making a mental note that she must buy a bed on the following day.

On Friday she did, and saw it installed. The rest of that day she worked about the house. First she scraped the old wallpaper from the walls of the downstairs rooms. Then she scrubbed and cleaned, from top to bottom, inside cupboards and out.

In the evening Dolly Maguire called on her way home and found her on hands and knees in the kitchen, battling against stubborn stains. Alison had left the front and back doors open to dry the floor quicker, so Dolly was able to walk straight in. Alison sat back on her heels, her skirts kilted and wearing a coarse sacking apron. She pushed at a stray tendril of dark hair with the heel of a wet hand. 'Dolly!'

'I came to see how you were getting on.' The cook thought, *she's a little worker*. And asked, 'Can I give you a hand?'

Alison laughed. 'I'm nearly done, but you can make us a cup of tea if you like. The things are in the cupboard there.' She indicated it with a jerk of her head.

Dolly put the kettle on the fire to boil and made the tea. They drank it sitting at the table that Alison was going to use in the kitchen because it was the biggest. She talked of her plans and what she had done, listened as Dolly tendered advice but silently decided she would make her own mind up about some things.

Dolly grinned. 'Have you noticed Moira Grindly hanging around?'

'No.' Alison shook her head, mystified. 'Mind, I don't spend much time looking out of the window.'

'I'll bet you don't,' Dolly laughed. 'But our Moira has heard what you were up to and she's been along to have a look. She came back to our place fuming and said some rude things about you, threatened she would put you out of business.'

Alison wrinkled her nose, pulling a face. 'I can imagine. But we'll see.'

'Aye.' And Dolly asked, 'What have you bought so far?' The cook inspected Alison's utensils and read the lengthening list of supplies to be bought. 'You seem to have thought of everything.' And finally, as she left, 'I wish you all the best; you deserve it.' She sighed, 'I wish I was coming with you.' Then she laughed, 'If only to get away from Moira.'

Alison put an arm around her. 'I'd love to have you with me, but I have to do this on my own. I can't pay anyone, and I don't want to let anyone down if I fail.'

Dolly smiled and dabbed at her eyes. 'Thank you, but if ever I can help, just call.'

'I will.' But Alison was determined to succeed as she watched Dolly walk away.

On Saturday morning she went shopping again, this time for linoleum. After a long search she found a roll in a second-hand shop. It was worn and cracked but it would have to do. The dealer was muscular and jocular, with an eye for a pretty girl. She persuaded him to deliver it and he gave her a lift home on his cart. Arrived at the house she asked, 'Will you help me to put it on the stairs, please?'

'Put it—' He was lost for words for a moment, then, 'Next you'll be wanting me to lay it.'

'No, just put it in the stairwell,' Alison said sheepishly.

Now he grinned. 'Nivor mind, bonny lass. You take the front and leave me the heavy end.'

So they manoeuvred the roll to lie in the stairwell, out of the way of the ground floor. The panting dealer wiped his brow and admitted, impressed, 'You're stronger than you look.' Then, as he was leaving, 'Keep the place warm when you're laying that stuff. It won't crack so easily.'

'Thank you.'

Peter Robson came in the early afternoon and found Alison in her apron. He mixed his paint, as he had to in those days, and they worked together until the late evening, painting the woodwork and furniture, talking and singing. Then they started again on Sunday morning and spent the day papering the walls. In between whiles Alison cooked for the two of them. Finally they laboured in the heat from a big fire, cutting the linoleum to fit and laying it.

In the evening they stood side by side in the doorway, looking back to the kitchen, forward to the café, reviewing the finished work. Peter Robson said, 'That's not bad, though I say it myself. What do you think?'

A weary Alison breathed, 'Oh, Peter, it's lovely.' She threw her arms around his neck and kissed him.

He laughed. 'The curtains spoil it a bit.' Alison had taken them with the house, the departing, shrill-voiced tenant not wanting them.

Neither did Alison. She smiled at Peter. 'Miss Devenish promised to bring the new ones early tomorrow.'

The dressmaker was as good as her word. On Monday morning she arrived with the curtains she had made and she and Alison hung them. Betty Devenish looked from them to the freshly decorated walls and ceilings, the painted chairs and the tables covered with colourful oilcloth. 'You've been busy.'

'Thank you for making the curtains so quickly. They're lovely.' Alison laughed. 'I hope I'm going to go on being busy.'

Betty asked shrewdly, with twenty years' experience of running a shop, 'Do you think you'll be able to manage on your own?'

'I think so,' Alison answered bravely.

She was to remember those words.

The dressmaker departed and Alison addressed her final task before she could open. She sat down with pencil and paper and listed everything she thought she would need in the way of dry goods. Then she wrapped her shawl around her, picked up a capacious shopping basket and set out for the wholesaler. She chose Cadwalladder's because George Grindly had bought his supplies there.

Harold Cadwalladder was a vigorous fifty with a bemedalled watch chain looped across his paunch. He was busy but checked for a moment when Alison entered his store, as if about to speak, but then carried on serving a customer. Brian, his son, a smart young chap of eighteen, worked beside him. Alison waited patiently until it was her turn, then handed over her list. 'I'm Alison Bailey and I'm opening a café, Alison's Cookshop, in Dundas Street. Will you supply these, please?'

Harold let the list lie on the counter and scowled at her. 'Aye, I've heard about you. Where did you get the money to open a place like that, a young lass like you, on her own?'

Alison was taken by surprise and blurted out, unthinking, 'I don't see that it's any of your business, but a gentleman helped me.'

He pushed the list towards her. 'I don't want to get involved in that sort of business.'

Alison flared, 'It was honest, respectable business and don't you dare suggest otherwise! The gentleman was Mr Michael Tarrant of Bellhanger. Perhaps you would care to question him about it?'

Harold would not. He had taken his stand because Moira Grindly had said she would take her business away from him if he supplied 'that little slut'. Now he had to choose. From the corner of his eye he saw his son nodding, urging him, then holding out his hand for the list. Brian had never liked Moira.

Harold gave it to him and told Alison stiffly, 'The lad will see to it.' He had been bested in an argument by a slip of a girl and did not like it, would not forget. He turned his back on her.

Alison went away unhappily. She had won what she wanted but had seen his anger and resentment. She had made an enemy and it boded ill for their future relationship.

She carried home in her basket an advance supply of her groceries; the rest would be delivered. Back in Alison's Cookshop, she took down from the window the card promising to 'open shortly' and replaced it with another she had prepared. This read on one side: CLOSED. She propped it against the window to show the other side, which read: OPEN.

She worked as she had learned from Francie: 'Six days shalt thou labour and on the seventh do all thou can.' Alison worked from Monday through Saturday then on Sunday she prepared for the week to come. She cooked, waited on, acted as cashier, and when she closed for the day, she cleaned.

After a time she noticed several customers she had served in Grindly's were now coming to her. This was confirmed by Dolly, who came in for a cup of tea and said, 'We've lost some trade, and I can see some of them in here now.'

Peter Robson came regularly for his free breakfast under the terms of his agreement with Alison. When he had used up all his credit she extended it and he decorated the upstairs rooms. But first she cleaned all the old paper from the walls on one of her Sunday 'rest days'. Her trade kept on building. She paid off her debt to Michael Tarrant and now she planned to open one of those three upstairs rooms for service.

Dolly said, 'You're a success.'

Alison was cheered by that as she fell into bed each night, exhausted. But she knew this was only a beginning. She had a dream, an ambition, to forge a chain of 'Alison's Cookshops', selling simple food, well-cooked and cheap. She also intended to appeal to a wide clientele, with a range from soup and a roll through pie and peas to a casserole or hotpot or three courses if wanted. She would bury the last memory of the jailbird's daughter.

She did not know that men out of her past were about to enter her life again.

8

Monkwearmouth in Sunderland, July 1909.

'This'll do, lads! In here!' The speaker filled the doorway, his broad back turned to Alison. She stood at the till, a white pinny over her brown dress, taking payment from a customer. She had opened this new café, high on the sea front looking down on the beach far below, just a few months ago. She had an apartment upstairs, having moved out of her cramped quarters in Dundas Street. The café there, the original Alison's Cookshop, was now run by Dolly Maguire, with a girl to help her. She had been driven from Grindly's by Moira's sour bad temper.

Alison had found a good cook for this new branch of Alison's Cookshop, and a trainee manageress, Thelma Redfern, a girl of nineteen, her own age. Alison herself was, as always, waiting on, acting as cashier or cleaning – anything that needed doing. That included managing and that meant turning away undesirables.

Thelma, tall, slender and pretty, quick at her work, was hesitating now. She was uncertain, looking to Alison for a lead.

She marched towards the half-dozen young men now jostling in the doorway. She was aware of the startled and disapproving stares of the other customers looking on from behind their plates of sandwiches and cakes, their pots of tea and glasses of lemonade. Most of them had come off the beach and paused for a snack to stretch the day out into the evening. The sun was setting blood red over the land, darkness sweeping in from the seaward horizon. These were the people she catered for, literally. She did not want crowds of noisy and boisterous young men.

The leader turned as she came up. He had a shock of rumpled black hair and his wide shoulders filled his Norfolk jacket. Alison had to put her head back to look up at him. For some reason that annoyed her, or was it his confident grin? He began to say, 'Can we have a table for—?'

One of his friends coming behind him, red-faced under a battered bowler hat, stumbled. His legs tangled and he had to be saved from falling by another. He guffawed.

That was enough for Alison. She snapped, 'No, you can't have a table! I do not wish for your custom and I'll thank you to leave.'

That wiped away the tall young man's grin and for a moment he looked down at her, perplexed by her frosty reception. The waitress confronting him was a dark-haired girl with a wide mouth, lips tight-pressed now. Her slender body was wrapped in a crisp white apron over a brown dress, but it was her huge dark eyes that struck some chord of memory that eluded him. He explained, 'We're celebrating Paddy's birthday.' He indicated the red-faced one. 'We just want some tea and a bite to eat. If you—'

Alison was sure they had done their celebrating in public houses. She did not wait for him to finish. 'It doesn't matter what you want. I won't serve you.'

The others were restless behind him. The red-faced Paddy called, 'What's going on?'

The tall young man was becoming angry now. He tried to step around Alison. 'I'd like to speak to the manager.'

She took a pace that put her in his way, so he had to stop to avoid walking into her. 'I am the manageress. I have a legal right to refuse to serve you and I'm exercising it.'

He was staring now, the elusive memory now captured.

It had been seven years and she had been a skinny twelve-year-old. He recalled the face, but the name? It came: 'Is it Alison Bailey?'

That startled her. He knew her name? Then who –? She answered him, 'Aye, it is.'

He thought she was not skinny now and that she was still at a loss. He reminded her: 'Richard Tarrant. We met on the beach years ago. I was staying with my uncle, Michael Tarrant, as I am now.' His grin returned. 'I was in a spot of trouble at the time.'

Now she remembered him and that he had a propensity for getting into trouble, a boy running wild. And now a wild young man. 'Aye, I remember. And you don't appear to have changed. I haven't changed my mind, either. You may as well take your friends out of here, or I'll call a pollis.'

He was very angry now, had replies on the tip of his tongue, but he could not hurl them at this girl. He turned and said shortly, 'The lady refuses to serve us, lads. We'll have to look elsewhere.' He shepherded them out into the street. Some grumbled but only because they did not see why they were being turned away. Paddy grinned at her disarmingly and tipped his bowler. Then he stumbled again as he went out of the door.

Alison followed and stood in the doorway, watching them trudge away. She felt a qualm of conscience. Had she been too harsh? But then she saw the approving expressions on the faces of her customers and was reassured; she had done the right thing. She turned to go back to her work and tripped. The doormat had curled up and that had caused her to stumble. She wondered, had that been the reason for Paddy's near fall, and not 'celebrating'? She had a moment's doubt again but shrugged it off. The incident was in the past and she was unlikely to see any of the young men again.

Richard Tarrant might visit his uncle as often as he liked.

Alison had no reason to go to Bellhanger now. She was grateful to Michael for the chance he had given her, and always would be, but he moved in a different world. As did Richard. She intended to be a part of that world one day and already had a reputation in the town as a young businesswoman, but she would choose her friends and Richard would not be among them.

He was striding along with the other young men he had met while staying with his uncle, students or training in the professions. He joined in the conversation and joked with the others but he was still remembering his brush with Alison. He recalled that he had never gone to her home but to him the fact that she owned the café proved that she came from a moneyed background. Doubtless she was one of those New Women wanting the vote and to be seen as making her own way in the world. So her father had set up his daughter in business.

Richard nodded to himself, thinking that was it. But he also thought she was too prim and proper by far. He would not go back to her café, to tender an apology or ask for one. Then he grinned because he did not think that would worry Miss Alison Bailey.

Paddy said, 'What are you laughing at?'

'Me.'

And they turned into the Blue Bell, where the publican allowed them to cook sausages on a shovel held over the fire.

Oliver Crawshaw came lusting a few weeks later, his intention to add another to his list of conquests. Thelma said, 'There's only that nice toff left now.'

Alison smiled. She remembered the 'nice toff'. He had eaten in her café once before, on a quiet mid-week evening. Beside supplying the usual snacks, she had built up a trade in three-course meals; her two cafés called Alison's Cookshop were known for them, simple food well cooked. He was tall, though long in the body and short in the legs so he had an apelike look. But he was fleshily handsome, powerful and bulky in his expensive, well cut suit. He was carefully shaved save for a wide silky moustache he stroked with the tips of his fingers. His dark hair was cut by a good barber and neatly combed. He had talked vaguely of 'working late in my office' and Alison had judged him to be a professional man, the kind the café was attracting now.

Oliver had looked at the money paid for working in the shipyards and the toil needed to earn it and decided there must be an easier way. He had started in his chosen career by stealing any article he thought he could sell, like fruit from a market stall, but he had grown into a professional thief. He had links with a number of receivers and stole what they could market. He was successful.

Alison did not recognise in him the small boy who had bullied her so long ago. Nor did he connect the frightened little girl with this nubile young woman, the object of his lust. He knew her name was Alison Bailey, had made it his business to find out, but he had known the girl in the play-ground as Alison Grant.

'That's all right, Thelma,' Alison said. 'You can go home and I'll lock up when he's gone.' The cook had already left.

Thelma shrugged into her coat and Alison escorted her to the door, let her out and turned the key but left it in the lock. As she walked back past the late diner she smiled and said, 'We're closing now but finish your coffee. Call when you're ready to go and I'll let you out.'

He smiled, showing big teeth. 'Thank you.'

Alison went back to the kitchen and sat down at the table where she was counting the day's takings, her back to the door. She worked quickly, humming to herself, recording the figures in her ledger with a pen and bottle of ink. She regarded fountain pens as expensive and unnecessary in her business. Then she became aware of a looming presence. She twisted round and found he had quietly come up behind her.

Suddenly frightened, she challenged him: 'What are you doing in here? I said I'd come and let you out.' She started to rise but he set his hands on her shoulders and forced her back onto the chair.

He leaned over her and she smelt the pomade on his hair. He purred, low-voiced, like a big cat, 'We should try to know each other better, Alison. We haven't been introduced but I can do that now. I'm Oliver Crawshaw, worth a few bob and ready to spend it on a nice girl like you.' That had worked in the past.

Alison tried again to rise but he held her. Her heart thumping, she demanded, 'Let me go, please. I don't wish to be introduced to you, Mr Crawshaw.' Now the name, as she spoke it, came like an echo out of her past. There had been an Oliver Crawshaw, leader of a howling, deriding mob. She burst out, 'You were at school in the East End! I remember you too well!'

'School?' His fingers on her shoulders bit into her cruelly, holding her as in a vice. 'I don't remember any Alison . . .' His voice trailed away, then he laughed unpleasantly. 'Aye, I do! There was a lass, but it was Alison *Grant* and she was the talk of the place because her father was sent to prison for manslaughter. No wonder you changed your name to Alison Bailey. You didn't want to go through life as a jailbird's daughter!'

Alison sat stunned, humiliated and deeply hurt. This monster had accidentally manoeuvred her into giving away her secret. Her cheeks flamed.

Oliver was going on, taunting and jeering, 'Don't worry. It doesn't matter to me what your old man got up to. It's you I want. You're a lovely package of charms and I want to see more.' He thrust one hand inside the top of her dress.

Alison's humiliation and hurt had changed to bitterness and boiling fury. Why should she be treated like this by a onetime schoolyard bully? She snatched up the pen from the table and drove its nib into the hand still gripping her shoulder. Oliver yelped from the pain of it and pulled his hand away. She seized her chance and kicked out, shoving the chair backward and into his middle. He grunted, face contorted from the agony of that. Freed from his grip, Alison ran around the table to the drawer that held the cook's kitchen knives. She yanked it open and grasped a long carver. Oliver had started in pursuit but when she brandished the knife it gave him pause.

He jeered, 'You wouldn't dare use that.' But it was said with uncertainty. He took a step forward but Alison lashed out with the knife. The blade flashed past his face and its point slashed a hairline across his jaw. He cursed and retreated, put a hand up to the wound and stared at the blood on his fingers. 'You bitch!' But he kept on retreating and she followed him. Out in the café he turned and ran, turned the key in the lock and fled into the darkness.

Alison slammed the door and locked it, then walked back to the kitchen on shaking legs. She saw the pen lying on the floor where it had fallen from Oliver's hand, and picked it up with trembling fingers. She sat down on the chair with a bump and there she stayed for some minutes, steeling herself to recover her composure. She saw the nib of the pen was bent and after a while she was able to replace it with another taken from a drawer. She stubbornly returned to her task and finished her paperwork.

She climbed the stairs to her apartment above and lay in her bed with the window open, listening to the sea breaking below. She found it soothing. She had made up her mind she would not let this incident – and she was determined to regard it as such – spoil her life. She would not be left alone with a customer again, but she would not go to the police. She shied away from telling her story to a stolid constable and she did not want bad publicity. There would always be those who would say, 'She must have led him on.'

She finally sank into unconsciousness in the early hours. It was some days before she slept without bad dreams.

Oliver Crawshaw slowed to a walk after his first flight from the café. He staunched the trickle of blood from his cheek with his handkerchief, cursing the while. Then he shouldered through the doorway of a crowded dockside public house where smoke hung like a pall, and sought out Cuthbert Price. The former groom sat on a bench in a corner with a half-pint of beer in front of him. He was pallid and thin, eating only rarely when Oliver fed him. His corn-coloured hair was matted and dirty. He looked up hopefully when Oliver appeared by the table. Cuthbert slid along the bench to make room for him.

Oliver asked, 'How long have you been here?'

Cuthbert squinted through the smoke at the clock above the bar. 'Couple of hours.'

'I've been with you all that time.'

'What?' Cuthbert blinked at him.

'You heard what I said. If a pollis asks you if I was in here with you all night, you say I was.'

'Ah,' Cuthbert nodded. 'Aye.'

Oliver gave him money, satisfied. 'Fetch me a large whisky and get yourself something to eat.'

Cuthbert ventured, 'You've cut your face.'

'I did it shaving.' But it was because of the hairline wound inflicted on him by Alison that he did not want to go to the bar. It would not do for the barman to notice it.

Left alone, Oliver thought about the girl who had fought him off. Bad-tempered, stupid little bitch! He raged inside, knew she had beaten him but swore he would have his revenge some day. He would make Alison Bailey pay.

Cuthbert brought the whisky then hurried out to a butcher, still open, just a few doors away. He returned eating a huge pork sandwich. Through a full mouth he mumbled, 'Ta, Mr Crawshaw. Have you got any work for me?' Oliver had taken him along on some of his thieving expeditions, when he had needed another pair of hands. But Cuthbert had to be closely supervised because if left to himself he would steal trinkets that were almost worthless, simply because they were there.

'Not at the moment.' Oliver put him off, and advised, 'You'd be better getting a job with horses again.'

'I've tried.' Cuthbert shook his head mournfully. 'A lot o' people have gone over to using motor cars and I don't know nowt about them. I went up to Bellhanger today to see if that Mr Tarrant wanted somebody but he's got a feller comes in from a livery stable every day, doesn't want a groom living in any more. I offered to work in the house but he wouldn't have it. I suppose he was worried I might smash some of his vases and things. The owd lass that was there, she once told me they were worth a mint o' money.'

Now he had Oliver's attention. He swallowed what was left of his whisky and gave the glass to Cuthbert. 'We'll have another. And then you can tell me about this Bellhanger.'

A week later he collided with Clara Skilton, seemingly by accident, as she was returning to Bellhanger with a basket of shopping hooked on her arm. He burst out of a doorway and knocked the basket aside, scattering its contents. 'Oh, dear! I'm sorry! My fault. Please let me help you.' He insisted on taking the basket from her and then picking up the items and replacing them.

'Kind of you, I'm sure,' murmured Clara. She took in his good suit and homburg, the bulky strength of him. She was glad that on this summer day she had put on a dress of white muslin and broderie anglaise that showed off her bosom.

Oliver weighed the basket in his hands and pursed his lips. 'That's heavy for a young lady like yourself to be carrying. Allow me.' He called, 'Cabbie!' And the cab he had engaged earlier, and told to wait, came up with a clatter of hooves and jingle of harness.

Clara allowed herself to be persuaded, demurred but only faintly. 'It's nice to meet a gentleman like you, sir.'

'You're welcome, miss. I'm always glad to oblige a lady. But if I may introduce myself: I am Vincent Featherstone, at your service.'

'Clara Skilton.' She lowered her eyes modestly. 'Mrs Skilton. I am a widow.'

'I'm sorry,' he said solemnly.

Clara smiled bravely. 'My husband was in a good way of business and we loved each other dearly, but he died some years ago and almost his last words to me were: "I don't want you to mourn, Clara. Life is for living."'

'I fully agree,' Oliver lied earnestly. 'I am in the same situation. I lost my dear wife over a year ago. I am a commercial traveller for an enginering firm and I live in lodgings. It's a lonely life.' It was his turn to smile bravely. 'Perhaps we could keep each other company? I was thinking of going to the Empire Theatre tonight. I hear it is a good show. Would you do me the honour of accompanying me?'

Clara would. She had served Michael Tarrant's dinner, and been dismissed for the evening, in good time for the last performance at the Empire. They had seats in the circle and afterwards 'Vincent' escorted her to supper at the Palace Hotel. Clara was impressed. She peered about her at the other couples, many of the men in black evening dress with starched white shirts, the women in silken gowns. Clara whispered, 'They're all dressed up to the nines.'

'No better than you, my dear,' he replied.

She preened herself. Then, 'Look at that couple coming in now. They must be important.'

He knew who she meant, the tall man, handsome and well-dressed with curling yellow hair, the woman blonde and blue-eyed, but the eyes hard, the lips too thin. He said, 'That's Julian Baldwin and his wife. He is the manager of Baldwin's shipyard.' He saw he had made an impression and later he improved on it when he took her back to Bellhanger in a cab.

It was the first of several outings, a campaign planned by Oliver but Clara was aware of the moves in the game. Early on she caught a look in his eye as he surveyed her ample charms. She knew what that look meant and was not averse to his attentions. He awakened her hunger. It had been a long time . . . Normally she saw no one but Michael, and the people she passed while out shopping, or on her time off. But she had her mirror, and read the glances cast her way by the men who were out of work or between shifts and standing on the corner. She knew that she was desirable to some and now it gave her a shivering thrill to know this muscular man wanted her.

Oliver knew what he wanted and was playing a part. Inevitably there came a night when he did not leave her at the back door of Bellhanger but went to her room with her. He brought with him a bottle of wine, the fire was warm and soon she was spread, voluptuous, on the bed. He pulled off his clothes, genuinely lusting now and she moaned with pleasurable anticipation, cried out when he took her.

Later, when she lay drowsily blinking at the flames in the grate, he said, 'This chap Tarrant, does he know what he has hidden under those dust sheets?'

'I doubt it,' Clara sneered. 'He never looks. I'm left to clean all the bloody things.'

'Then he wouldn't miss a few of them, would he?' Oliver said. He ran his hand over her body and she wriggled sensuously. He went on, 'We could share it and he would never know. Are you game?'

She was game for anything now. Clara said thickly, 'Aye.'

The following evening Oliver padded about the house, shoeless and silent, with one of the new electric torches. With Clara at his elbow to help he inspected what was under the dust sheets that lay ghostly in the night, and made his choice.

When they came to the locked room that had been Esme's he asked, 'What's in here?'

She shrugged. 'Don't ask me. It's locked and he has the key.'

That did not hinder Oliver. He fished in his pocket and produced a tool of his trade. The lock was a simple one and he picked it in less than a minute and opened the door. No one had entered the room since Michael had found Alison in there, trying on Esme's dress. He had resolutely cut himself off from the portrait of Esme and the clothes that had once been hers. They would no longer torment him.

Oliver glanced at the items of furniture and shrugged them off as useless to him save for one chair he thought was a nice piece – and the picture. He looked at the portrait of a woman, his eyes slitted, and thought, *she's a nice piece an' all*. Her shoulders were bare, her bosom thrusting. She smiled at him with green cat's eyes that promised and tempted. Oliver thought, *she'd give a man a night to remember*. He said, 'I'll take the picture.'

'I think that's his wife, Esme, what run away,' said Clara.

'I don't care who she is.' He wanted her, hanging on his wall if no other way.

He returned a week later with a steam-driven pantechnicon and parked it by the kitchen door. A faint red glow leaked out from around its furnace door. Oliver had decided on a moonlit night and it was almost bright as day. He did not fear them being seen. Now Michael Tarrant hired a groom to come in from a livery stable to care for his horses and there was no one in the room above the stables to wake and give the alarm.

Oliver drove and Cuthbert Price sat beside him. They jumped down and another man clambered out of the back of the pantechnicon. He was big and burly and grumbled, 'That was a rough ride in there.' His mouth looked to be full of teeth like fangs.

Oliver said, 'Never mind; we're there now, Sharky.'

The big man stretched his frame. 'Bloody good job.' Sharky Spraggin had been given his nickname beause of his shark's tooth grin.

Clara opened the kitchen door to them and hissed, 'He's drunk most of a bottle o' whisky, he's got nobody in with him and he's dead to the world.'

'Good lass!' Oliver kissed her and started to turn away.

'I've been thinking,' said Clara, worriedly. She was neither drunk nor impassioned now, a frightened woman in the cold moonlight. 'Suppose he takes it into his head to look under one o' these sheets some day, finds his stuff missing and some tat there instead. He'll blame me.'

Oliver had been expecting this. 'You just say you know nothing about it. That it must ha' been done before you came. He can't prove otherwise.' He patted her cheek and smiled confidently. 'Don't worry, just trust me. I won't drop you in trouble.'

Clara believed him because she wanted to.

They went to work. First they unloaded the pantechnicon and lined up its contents handily by the kitchen door. There were pieces of furniture, pictures or ornaments, set out in the order of the numbers chalked on each, 1 to 22.

Oliver and Sharky carried piece number 1 into the house, a battered and scarred old desk. Cuthbert followed with a chair. They moved almost silently, socks pulled on over their boots. Clara went with them, carrying the list Oliver had given her, identifying, locating and numbering each piece he had ear-marked. They stole through the rooms and passages that were lined with sheeted furniture like spectres in the moonlight. Clara whipped off the sheet covering an antique escritoire and the old desk took its place under the sheet. They brought out the escritoire, loaded it into the pantechnicon then carried piece number 2 into the house.

So they went on, methodically, until all the old articles or pieces of cheap furniture they had brought were in the house. The pantechnicon was full of those they had taken out. There had been one hitch when Cuthbert had brought out the wrong painting but Oliver had cursed him softly, venomously, and set the matter right.

Last to go in, and carefully wrapped by Oliver, was the portrait of Esme.

Now he closed the rear doors of the pantechnicon and ordered his helper, 'Stoke her up a bit.' Cuthbert obediently climbed up into the cab, opened the furnace door and started shovelling coal into the flames. Oliver paid off Sharky, giving him two sovereigns.

The big man offered, 'D'ye want me to come with you and drive, give you a spell?'

Oliver shook his head. 'I'll be all right.' He knew Sharky was trying to wangle a bigger cut and Oliver wasn't having any.

Sharky shrugged philosophically and pocketed his fee. He drove a coal lorry for a living and supplemented his wages from petty crime such as this. The two sovereigns he had made this night was more than he was paid for a week, and he wasn't coated in coal dust. He said, 'I'm off, then.' He strode away into the night.

Oliver smiled at Clara, 'You can go back to bed now.' And he added, 'I wish I was coming with you.'

She took his hand in hers. 'I wish *I* was coming with *you*.'

That did not suit his book. He soothed, 'It might make Tarrant suspicious. Better that you stay and I'll come back for you as soon as I can.' Then he cursed as Cuthbert dropped the shovel and it clanged like a bell on the cobbles. Oliver strode to pick it up and ground out, 'Do you want to wake the bloody neighbourhood?'

'Sorry. It slipped out o' my hand.'

'Never mind.' Oliver swallowed his anger, told himself there was no one to hear anyway. 'We're off now.'

He swung up into the cab with Cuthbert, sat behind the wheel and drove the pantechnicon away round the side of the house. He waved a hand at Clara where she stood outside the kitchen door, then he passed from her sight. She sighed, went into the house and locked the back door. Now she would have to wait for him to bring her share of the proceeds of the robbery and take her away to a new life. She wondered if he would.

Oliver was not in any doubt. He obtained a good price from a London fence, paid Cuthbert a few pounds and left him to fend for himself in the capital. The rest of the money he put in his pocket. He could see rich pickings in London.

He wrote to Clara, enclosing a postal order, and giving an address for 'Vincent Featherstone'. It was that of a newspaper and tobacconist's shop, an accommodation address. He meant to keep in touch with Clara because there was no knowing when she might be useful again. There were a few more pieces in Bellhanger that might fetch a good price.

He rented a house and hung the portrait of the temptress where he could sit and devour it of an evening. He soon became as familiar with the dark beauty as with any other he had known.

Alison was wiping down oilcloth-covered tables in her sea-front café but a part of her mind was busy with plans for yet another Alison's Cookshop. She was jerked back to the present when she glimpsed the tall figure from the corner of her eye. She turned quickly to face him where he stood in the doorway but then saw it was not the man she had thought. This was one of her regular customers. He was older, not so tall nor so broad, not like Richard Tarrant at all, in fact. She had not seen him since they had parted in anger and there was no reason that she should ever see him again.

She told herself it did not matter and went back to her work and her plans. She had seen an advertisement for the Voluntary Aid Detachments. This was an organisation set up to enable women to help in time of war or emergency and they were recruiting girls for various tasks. Alison would not volunteer to cook, nor as a clerk, because she had enough of cooking during her time at work and of paperwork in the evenings.

But nursing . . .

9

Monkwearmouth in Sunderland, April 1914.

Alison saw Julian Baldwin for the first time that Easter weekend. The Voluntary Aid Detachments were holding a recruitment drive in Mowbray Park. She was present as a member of four years' standing, in her blue dress with white starched collar, cuffs, cap and apron. With Thelma and four other girls she was giving demonstrations of dressing wounds and splinting limbs. The Territorial Army, a company of the Durham Light Infantry, was also recruiting and had supplied a dozen grinning khaki-clad privates to act as casualties.

Alison and Thelma were explaining what they were doing but aware that there was some giggling among the other girls. They all came from wealthier backgrounds and Alison regarded them with amused tolerance. They had needed to learn a lot. Simple tasks like making a cup of tea had previously been done for them by servants.

Alison recited, 'Now in the case of a broken arm, a splint may not be needed and it will be sufficient to put it in a sling to give it support until the casualty reaches hospital. Can I have a volunteer, please?'

The sergeant of the Durhams ordered, 'Right! Private Stothard! You come and help this nurse.'

A young man stepped out from the soldiers still waiting. He was a bare inch taller than Alison, with brown eyes and a round face that gave him a boyish look, but a firm jaw.

Alison smiled at him. 'What's your first name?'

He returned the smile, shyly, thinking what a pretty girl she was. 'Simon.'

Alison continued her discourse for the benefit of the spectators. 'The sling can be made from a large square piece of cloth.' But there was a prickling of memory. 'Fold it across the middle to make a triangle.' She demonstrated, but murmured to Simon, 'Did you go to school in the East End?'

'Aye, I did.'

She went on with her demonstration but between each point she made they carried on their low-voiced conversation. 'Do you remember a little lass called Alison?' And as he stared at her, puzzled and thinking back, she recalled for him: 'A lad called Oliver Crawshaw was leading a gang that were baiting me—' She stopped there, hesitant. Tell him they were baiting her because of her father being in prison, a murderer? No. She went on, 'You stood up to him so I could get away and hide.'

His frown of concentration cleared: 'I remember.' He recalled the reason for the bullying but said only, 'And that was just about the last I saw of you.'

'I went to live in Monkwearmouth with my gannie.' Her fingers were deft as she bandaged his arm.

'And now here you are, a nurse.'

'Only a VAD. I'm really a café manageress.' She did not wish to boast. In fact she now owned four cafés, two of them in Sunderland itself. 'What do you do when you are out of khaki?'

'I'm a draughtsman in Baldwin's.' That was one of the biggest shipyards on the Wear. He did not add that he was highly thought of there and earmarked for advancement.

Alison patted the neat bandage. 'There you are. You're good as new.'

He laughed. 'Thank you.' Then, smiling shyly, 'Maybe we could meet again. I mean, to talk over old times, take a walk by the sea.' Then adding hastily, 'I don't mean to be too forward.'

'You're not.' She smiled at him. 'Sunday afternoon?'

'Aye,' he agreed eagerly. 'Where—'

'Mackie's clock?' That was a well-known rendezvous. 'About two?'

'That's fine.'

He went off to join his comrades and Alison took on another 'patient'.

At the end of the day the VADs had signed on another twenty recruits. They were packing up their display stand and their various dressings and splints when Alison looked up and saw the tall, imposing figure of a man walking by some thirty yards or so away. He was well-dressed, with a mane of curling yellow hair combed into waves. He was staring at her intently and their glances locked for a second. Then the woman on his arm said something and he turned away to look in the direction of her pointing finger.

Alison asked Thelma, 'I wonder who that couple are? They're both dressed in the height of fashion.'

'That's Julian Baldwin of Baldwin's shipyard, and his wife,' said Thelma. 'My father works there and once pointed him out to me.'

Alison said nothing more, left it as a casual remark, and they turned back to their work. On the way home – she now had an apartment above one of the branches in the town – Alison thought about Simon Stothard and how he had stood up for her so long ago. There were unhappy memories there, and thoughts of her father. They had been with her all through the years. She had been busy, working all day and every day in pursuit of her dream. There had been no boys or men, though many had tried.

But in odd moments of rest, lonely at night before sleep or in the dawn as she awoke, then she had thought of her father. She had never ventured to seek him out, afraid of what she might find. There was the memory of her mother's condemnation: 'He killed a feller! God knows what'll happen to us now. Not that he'll care.' And Francie's advice: 'Forget about him. You have a life of your own.' Both made her wary. So she had lived her life as Alison Bailey. The little girl, Alison Grant, had been left in the past.

Now there was Simon. She was looking forward to Sunday. With four cafés doing well she could relax a little, couldn't she?

But at the back of her mind there was that piercing glance from Julian Baldwin. It would not leave her.

On Sunday she and Simon talked and walked all the way to the fishermen's cottages at Whitburn, and back again. It took them all afternoon and then he offered to take her to tea at Alison's Cookshop on the sea front. She accepted, tongue in cheek. But then he recognised Thelma, the manageress, who was on duty that day and greeted Alison. He put two and two together and said, still disbelieving, 'You're *the* Alison?' And when she nodded, smiling, he turned red and admitted, 'If I'd known how important you were I wouldn't have had the nerve to ask you out.'

He looked boyish with his flushed, round face and Alison laughed, but kindly. 'Then it was a good job you didn't know.'

That was the first of several outings. Simon took her to the Empire Theatre and to shows of the new moving pictures. Alison made sure those more expensive recreations were kept to a minimum; she suspected she had a great deal more money than he did and his pride would be hurt if she offered to pay her share.

Then he obtained permission from his foreman to take her into the yard to see its workings. Alison said, 'I didn't know they allowed visitors in.'

He replied casually, 'They don't, as a rule.'

Alison thought, *he's tactfully showing me that he is somebody in here, bless him.*

She endured many blushes and comments of, 'Aye, aye, bonny lass!' An attractive girl was a welcome but unusual sight in a shipyard and the men showed their appreciation. She was fascinated to see the partly built ship on the stocks, the steel wall of the hull towering over her like a cliff. And walking underneath it she saw that it was flat-bottomed. 'They all are,' bellowed Simon through the deafening din of the rivetting hammers. Alison clapped her hands over her ears.

Out from that clamorous steel cavern, she lowered her hands and laughed, 'I think I'll stay in my own business and leave you to build the ships.'

He smiled proudly. 'I can't see women ever building ships.' Nor could Alison, but they were both to be proved wrong.

They stood side by side at the top of the yard near the offices. Simon said regretfully, 'You've seen it all. I'll see you home now.'

'Don't you have to work?'

'We're nearly finished for the day. The men are packing up.'

Alison could see them climbing down from the staging around the hull, putting away tools and pulling on coats, picking up the tin cans that had held their tea.

A voice said behind them, 'I see we have a visitor.'

They turned and found Julian Baldwin smiling down at them. He wore a suit of Harris tweed, well cut and pressed. He carried his cap in his hand, his yellow hair neatly combed into waves.

Simon said hastily, 'I have the foreman's permission to show this lady around the yard, Mr Baldwin.'

'That's all right, Stothard.' Julian waved a hand in generous acceptance. 'A lady like this is always welcome.'

Simon explained and introduced, 'This is Miss Alison Bailey, the proprietor of the Alison's Cookshop restaurants.'

'Julian Baldwin.' His hand gripped Alison's and held it for a long moment as he said, 'I know the restaurants, of course. Quite an achievement for a lady as young as yourself. I must try one some day.'

'You will be welcome.' Alison let her hand stay within his. He was looking into her again and she could not look away.

He finally released her. 'Until then.' The words were almost drowned out as the shipyard siren blared to signal the end of the working day and the gates swung open to let the men leave. But Alison heard him, and both of them knew that other messages had passed though none were spoken.

Simon escorted her back to her apartment. They crossed the bridge in one of the electric trams, clanging and noisy with chatter, crowded with workmen on their way home. The streets teemed with them. Alison had a seat but Simon had to stand. They were passed by Julian Baldwin, driving back to his big house in Ashbrooke. His Vauxhall motor car with its fluted bonnet was open-topped and Julian drove himself, his uniformed chauffeur sitting beside him.

They descended from the tram in Fawcett Street and Alison remembered a horse-drawn tram when she had been with Francie so many years ago. She and Simon walked the last yards to her apartment. She answered absently when Simon made some remark, her emotions and thoughts in turmoil. She had never felt like this before. But with every stride she told herself that her feelings for Julian Baldwin could only bring her hurt.

Simon said, impressed, 'I was surprised he knew who I was.' He did not know that his foreman had mentioned his emerging talent more than once when talking to Baldwin. 'He's a pleasant chap to talk to.'

Alison asked, casually, 'What's his wife like?'

'A bit stuck up, I think.' Simon grinned. 'I've seen her when she's come into the office to meet him. She's always dressed up to the nines, very smart, but we didn't talk. To her, I'm just one more draughtsman.'

Alison managed a smile. She could almost feel Francie's presence, warning – or accusing? She told herself she would get over this.

Fate was against her. A week later she was passing Binns, the big department store, when a woman emerged. She was fashionably dressed in a silken gown and wide brimmed hat with ostrich feather. It sat on piled and carefully coiffured blonde hair. She crossed the pavement to a waiting motor car, a silver Rolls Royce. A liveried chauffeur, his hand to his cap in salute, held open the rear door. The woman was followed by a shop walker in black jacket and striped trousers, carrying a stack of packages. She ducked her head to enter the car and he delivered the packages to the chauffeur, then took a step back and gave a little bow. 'Thank you, Mrs Baldwin.'

Julian's wife! The woman had passed close by Alison, she had seen her face, the blue eyes narrow, lips thin and with a cruel twist. The car pulled away and she was left with a memory of a cold, distant beauty.

That evening she met Simon and they walked in Mowbray Park. It was as they stood by the lake, hidden in the dusk, that he proposed. Alison was taken by surprise. There had been embraces and stolen kisses but she had not thought of marriage. She was in his arms but gently pushed away from him. 'I didn't know you felt so strongly. I feel honoured, you're a fine man and one day you will make some girl very happy. But I'm not ready to marry.' She had plans for more restaurants, to expand with branches of Alison's Cookshop in Newcastle.

He stepped back a pace. He had heard the finality in her voice and now said heavily, 'There's no chance you will change your mind?'

Alison shook her head. 'I'm sorry.' She offered, 'We can be friends.'

'No.' That was final, too. 'That would be – painful.' He walked with her, out of the park and along Fawcett Street to Alison's Cookshop and her apartment. There he said, 'Goodbye. I won't trouble you again.'

Alison kissed him. 'I'm sorry, Simon. I wish you all the best in life.'

Then he was gone, walking out of her life. That caused her pain but she knew she could not give him the love he wanted and deserved. She missed him.

Then one evening she was acting as cashier in the sea-front Cookshop, the manageress having an evening off. Alison turned around from serving a young couple with toasted tea-cakes and saw Julian Baldwin standing just inside the doorway, his cap in his hand, watching her. She felt the colour rise to her cheeks but went to meet him, smiling. 'Hello. Where would you like to sit?'

He returned her smile, glanced about him, then nodded to a table at the back, away from the window. 'That will do.' He sat down with his back to the wall.

Alison handed him a menu. 'And what would you like?'

He grinned up at her. 'Young Stothard said you owned these places. Or was he exaggerating?'

Alison laughed, in control of herself again now. 'I do and he wasn't. But I do whatever needs doing, like taking your order.'

'Very well.' He scanned the menu and ordered cheese on toast and a cup of tea.

Alison walked back to the kitchen, conscious of his gaze following her, realising this was why he had sat where he did, so he could watch her. She prepared the snack herself and brought it to him.

'Thank you.' He smiled up at her. 'If you are the owner then you can keep me company. Will you?'

She hesitated, then told herself it was a quiet evening. 'All right.' She sat down opposite him.

'I've been working late at the yard,' he explained. Then he went on to tell her about the ship he was building, the problems encountered and the solutions he had found. Alison thought he sounded like any man talking about his day's work, except he was the boss. She asked questions when he said something she did not understand, and he seemed surprised then impressed. 'You really take things in very quickly. I'm beginning to see why you are so successful.'

He also asked questions. Alison had to break off now and again to take payment from customers. After her return from one of these visits to the till he asked, with that disarming grin she was beginning to know, 'Are you and young Stothard walking out? Or should I mind my own business?'

Alison said ruefully, 'No longer. That's all over.'

He did not press her for details but went off at a tangent. 'I thought I saw you with the VAD nurses the other day. Am I right?'

'Yes.' He wanted to hear why she had joined, whether she liked it, why she had chosen nursing. 'Because I wanted a change from cooking and serving food and I can't drive.'

He laughed. 'That's logical.'

He left soon after that. She accompanied him to the door and saw his Vauxhall with its fluted bonnet standing at the kerb. Alison wondered why he did not drive the silver Rolls Royce. She was not to know that he used the Vauxhall because it attracted less attention. He drove away with a wave of his hand. When she turned back she saw the waitress watching, awed. Alison grinned at her, 'We're getting the carriage trade now.' But she did not explain further.

The following day was different. Alison looked in at the Cookshop in Fawcett Street and found the manageress and the waitress both labouring with heavy colds, streaming eyes and red noses. She sent them home and turned to herself, waiting on and acting as manageress. Late in the afternoon a large and raucous woman entered with a brood of four noisy children. She ordered jam and bread, tea and lemonade. Twenty minutes later they left the table a mess of jam, crumbs and butter, with more of the same littering the floor. It also became obvious that they had walked where horses had preceded them – the evidence was there.

Alison, silently raging, set to with a pail of hot soapy water and disinfectant. She was scrubbing furiously when she heard a woman say in cultured tones, 'See if you can find a waitress, Dickie.'

Alison sat back on her heels and used the heel of the hand holding the brush to wipe away a damp tendril of hair from her brow. Her new customers stood over her. The woman was in her early twenties, cool in a cotton costume in pale lime green and a straw boater. The man towered behind her and he was staring down at Alison incredulously: Richard Tarrant.

He said, 'Oh, no. I don't believe it.'

The woman looked at him enquiringly. 'What is it, Dickie?'

He said wryly, 'I'm sorry, Delia, but this lady and I have met before.'

'You mean this – person?' She smiled, amused.

Alison was sure that he was laughing at her. She slammed the brush into the pail and water sprayed over all of them. Then she jumped to her feet and demanded of Richard, 'Why have you come here?'

Delia was dabbing ineffectually at the lime green costume.

He gave her his handkerchief and bestowed a hard look on Alison. 'We were going to have tea but I didn't know you were here. I suppose you were sacked from the last place.'

'No. In a way I was promoted for maintaining a good class of customer. I own this place, too.'

Now he remembered how he had concluded her father had set her up in business.

Delia had recovered her cool poise. 'May we go, Dickie, please? This is hardly the Savoy.'

Alison smiled, 'You are free to leave.' And to Richard, 'Off you go, Dickie, and take this – person – with you.'

Delia's face crumpled and she hurried to the door, still clutching Richard's handkerchief. He started after her. He had caught the irony in Alison's use of 'Dickie' and now he turned his head to say evenly, a judgment without anger, 'You sound like a spoiled brat.'

He left Alison open mouthed. She watched him stride away with the girl on his arm and thought, outraged, *spoiled*! How dare he use that word about her! She turned her back on him and returned to her scrubbing. *Spoiled*!

He was calmer now but not sorry for what he had said. This episode had only confirmed his opinion of her as the daughter of well-off parents who had funded her business. The scrubbing had merely been a pose, as Marie Antoinette had played at being a shepherdess. He turned his attention back to the lithe and lovely Delia.

Alison travelled to Newcastle to inspect two properties she thought might be suitable for another branch of Alison's Cookshop. The city was a familiar landscape of a river lined with shipyards, like Sunderland. She spent the afternoon and the early evening there then ate dinner at a hotel near the station. It had been a disappointing day, neither property proving satisfactory. She shrugged mentally, put it behind her and set about enjoying her meal. It was pleasant to be served without serving, to eat without cooking, to be treated with respect by the head waiter. She grinned, thinking: *better than scrubbing*!

In that time of relaxation the thoughts of Julian Baldwin intruded, as they often did now. From carefully casual enquiries she had learned that he was respected as manager of Baldwin's, one of the biggest yards on the river. He was thirty-four, ten years older than herself. His wife was Pamela and they were without children. She had learned none of this from him. He had got into the habit of calling in the evening for a snack. He would ask her to join him and she would drink a cup of tea and they would talk. It was mostly about his work or what was going on in the town – or what Alison was doing. She had come to look forward to his visits.

Alison tried to suppress these thoughts but they would not go away. She finished her meal and left the restaurant. She was passing through the foyer as a couple were settling their bill. The clerk was saying, 'Thank you, sir. I hope you and your good lady have enjoyed your stay.'

Alison paused and feigned interest in a picture, watched them walk to the door, saw the doorman open it and heard him say, 'Good day, Mr Griffith, Madam.'

Alison did not recognise the man, had only a fleeting impression of raffish good looks, but she knew the woman. Pamela Baldwin clung to Griffith's arm and gazed up at him adoringly. The cold beauty Alison had seen before was now lascivious.

She let them go, stood staring sightlessly at the picture, trying to take in what she had seen. Pamela Baldwin was having an affair. She was being unfaithful to her husband. How could she betray him like that? Alison felt sorry for him. She walked out of the hotel and sought out her train back to Sunderland. It had proved to be a bad day. She had not found the premises she needed and was now burdened with a secret she did not want.

The following evening Julian came to her Cookshop. She found it hard to listen and talk, knowing what she did. He eventually noticed and said, smiling, 'Have you something on your mind? I think you've hardly heard a word I've said.'

'I'm sorry.' She searched hurriedly for some excuse and seized on a snippet of conversation she had had with another VAD. Julia Firbank was a young woman, daughter of a wealthy man, who drove her own motor car. She had said, 'Why don't you buy a car and learn to drive?' Alison had laughed but had later given it serious thought. A car would be more convenient than jumping on and off trams – provided she could control the beast.

Now she said, 'I'm trying to decide whether to buy a motor car and learn to drive, but I'm not sure if I can do it.'

He laughed. 'I'm sure you could. Suppose I took you out in my car and let you have a go on some quiet country road, clear of other traffic?'

Alison thought that was a generous offer by a generous man. How could his wife deceive such a man and take a lover? She smiled at him. 'Thank you. I'd like to do that.'

So she soon found herself at the wheel of the Vauxhall, Julian by her side, on an empty stretch of the coast road to West Hartlepool. She was nervous and erratic at first as they trundled back and forth but he was good-humoured and patient, helpful with his hand on hers. Soon she was relaxing, gaining control of the car, speeding up. She was flushed and laughing when he finally took over the steering and said, 'That's enough for one day.'

He took her out on several further occasions and she learned quickly. Until he said, smiling, 'I can't teach you any more. You can drive us into Hartlepool and we'll have dinner to celebrate.' When she looked down at the dustcoat she was wearing in the open car, he laughed and reassured her, 'This place is used to motorists. You'll be fine.'

She proudly followed his directions, dextrously manoeuvred through the mostly horse-drawn traffic and parked outside the restaurant he indicated. She discarded the dustcoat at the door and it was taken by the waiter with a little bow. Alison saw that the staff knew Julian and she thought, *he's been here before.* With his wife? She tried to thrust that thought aside and to match his mood. He was light-hearted and attentive, ordered a bottle of wine and toasted, 'To a new driver.' He raised his glass to her. 'You've done very well.'

And they dined well, to leave in the evening and drive back along the road to Sunderland with Julian at the wheel. He had put up the hood and it was cosy in the car. Alison was happy and relaxed. The darkening sea lay on their right hand, pinpricked by the navigation lights of vessels steaming off the coast.

Julian slowed and turned into a narrow track looking out over the black water laced with the silver of the surf. He switched off the engine and in the silence said softly, 'Isn't it lovely?'

Alison nodded. 'Mm.'

He put his arm about her and turned to kiss her. She said, 'No,' but she was taken by surprise. He sensed that uncertainty and pressed his lips to hers again. His hands began exploring. She knew this was wrong and pushed away from him, snapped, 'No!'

He slumped back in his seat and said quietly, 'I'm sorry. I thought you – cared for me.'

'I do,' Alison confessed. 'But you're a married man.'

'Married!' He laughed harshly. 'It's a marriage in name only. There is no – affection. We pretend in public but it's a sham.' He faced Alison and said bitterly, 'She trapped me, said she was expecting my child and so we married. But it

wasn't true. She only wanted a husband to show to the world.'
He paused, then said low-voiced, 'She takes lovers. I've
charged her with it and she hasn't denied it.'

Alison knew Pamela could not, but she said nothing of
that; she thought Julian was suffering enough.

Now he said, 'I'll take you home.' He drove out onto the
road, then added, 'I'm going to see a solicitor about a divorce.
I can't go on like this.'

Alison huddled down in her seat, cold inside. She wanted
to comfort him but was not sure what passions that might
arouse. They drove in silence until he set her down at her
apartment. Before she got down from the car he said, 'I'm
sorry if I upset you. It's just that –' There was a catch in his
voice, then he went on, '– but I love you.'

'I know,' said Alison huskily. She admitted now that she
had suspected as much. And the way she had been thinking
about him had been a clue to her own emotions. She said
no more but fled from the car to her door as if she did not
want to be seen. Inside, she stood with her back to the door,
heart beating. Her whole life had changed. When would she
see him again?

He stayed away for a week. Night after night she looked
for him but he did not come. Then, at last, he was there,
striding in and his eyes seeking her. He saw her and his face
lit in a smile. She went to meet him, took his order and
brought it to him, then sat opposite him, all as had become
routine – save for the thumping of her heart.

He hardly sipped at the tea, did not touch the food. His
smile had gone and he ran a hand through the golden waves,
tousling them. He said gravely, 'I've had a hell of a week;
couldn't stop thinking about you.'

Alison could sympathise but stayed silent.

'I have to go to London on business. The Admiralty want
to talk to me about contracts.' He flapped his hand,

dismissing the importance of the business. He looked into her eyes, pleading, demanding, promising. 'Will you come with me?'

She loved him. Alison was sure of that, had never felt this depth of emotion before. Francie was forgotten. Would she go with him? Need he ask?

The woman was dark-haired, green-eyed. She wore a silken gown that clung and slid on her body. She moved long-legged across the foyer and disappeared into the hotel lounge. Oliver Crawshaw could hardly believe his eyes because he was sure he knew her, that she was the woman he had seen in the portrait he had stolen from Bellhanger. He had it still, kept it so he could stare into the eyes looking back at him, bold and inviting.

He left his hat and walking cane in the cloakroom, then followed and looked around the lounge, seeking her. He acknowledged that this was not the Ritz but it was ornately comfortable and expensive, a favourite haunt of his. It smelt of money to him and that was an odour he savoured. He was successful; his lounge suit was well cut with narrow legs to the trousers, his white collar was high and stiffly starched, his boots a shiny glacé kid. He looked a man of means. There was nothing to suggest he lived on the proceeds of crime.

His gaze took in the native Londoners, who had come in to dine in the restaurant and were now taking coffee. Then there were the residents of the hotel, up from the country or the provinces, bent on seeing the sights or a show. And then there was the woman. She was a resident, a woman alone. She had taken her seat at a table and now looked up and found his gaze on her. She returned it, looking him over, lazily, hungrily. He felt a stirring of excitement.

He crossed to stand over the chair at her side and asked, 'May I?' He saw she had aged, was a woman of forty or more but with barely a line to show for it. She was slender, her bosom straining at the silk, desirable.

'You are . . . ?' She smiled up at him and extended her hand.

'Oliver Crawshaw.' He bowed over it. He saw she wore a wedding ring; that only added a little more excitement to the planned seduction. And was she the woman of the portrait?

'Esme Tarrant.' She indicated the chair. 'Please.'

Michael Tarrant's wife! He knew the story of how she had run away, learned it from Clara Skilton who had picked it up from local gossip. He took his seat, a waiter brought coffee and they made small talk. Esme asked, 'And what do you do, Oliver?' In her considerable experience, all men liked to talk about themselves.

'I'm in furniture.' That was vague, a standard response.

'And what are you doing in London?' She had recognised his North Country accent.

'I live here in London. I have a house.'

'So do I.' She smiled at him. 'I'm just staying the night here.' And seeking a man – with money. She had plenty but would always take more. She did not need the money, but the man . . .

She played him for another half-hour and he knew it and enjoyed it, the excitement building on itself inside him. She finally rose to her feet, dispensed with decorum and came straight to the point. 'Give me five minutes. I'm in two-oh-four. I have no maid to help me.'

He watched her walk away towards the lift then he sat down again. After five minutes he went to room 204 and she was waiting for him.

10

London, June 1914.

It was Tuesday, a fine evening, and Richard Tarrant was walking back from St George's Hospital, where he was a doctor, to his rooms in Knightsbridge. The traffic was slow-moving, hooting taxis and motor buses creeping along with horse-drawn cabs and hansoms. The odour of petrol fumes mingled with the ammoniac smell of manure.

He saw the couple come out of Hyde Park and cross the road ahead of him, threading their way through the vehicles. At first he thought he had made a mistake, but he quickened his pace and when he was closer he was no longer in any doubt. He had come up with them just in time because at that point they turned into a hotel. The doorman greeted them. 'Good evening, Mr Baldwin. Good evening, madam.'

There was confirmation. Richard stood still, watching as they passed through the doors held open for them. He was shocked. The doorman turned, saw him and asked, 'Can I help you, sir?'

'No, thank you.' Richard shook his head and walked on. He could not believe it of either of them. He had met Julian Baldwin a year ago. Richard had been staying with his uncle when Michael had said, 'I have an invitation to attend a launch at Baldwin's yard. They send me these things from time to time because I was once in the business, but they don't interest me now. Would you like to go?' Richard had taken Delia. Julian was their host, with his wife Pamela, and Richard had not liked the way he held Delia's hand, nor his ogling of other young girls when he thought Pamela could not see. Richard had watched him, and taken an instant dislike.

And now? He had not suspected something like this. And while he and Alison Bailey were always at odds when they met he had never doubted her morals. He told himself that there might be some explanation. He doubted it but in any event the affair was none of his business.

They had arrived on Monday evening. Julian took a cab to the Admiralty on Tuesday morning but returned at noon. He said he would be doing this each day. Alison would spend the morning in Hyde Park, then they would meet again for lunch and spend the rest of the day together.

On Wednesday morning Julian kissed Alison before he climbed into his taxi and called to the driver, 'Take me to the Admiralty!'

Alison watched the cab pull away, then started to walk towards the park, deep in thought. She was uneasy now. She had come to London because she was in love with Julian, wanted to comfort and support him. He had proved passionate but somehow – uncaring? They always seemed to go where he wanted, did what he wanted. He said little and spoke only vaguely of his business with the Admiralty. Wasn't that odd if it was so important? He never talked of their future.

'Excuse me.' The voice came from a tall figure looming at her side. She turned her head and saw with surprise that it was Richard Tarrant. He said, 'Can we talk?'

Alison kept on walking. 'I don't think we have anything to talk about.'

He strode along at her side. He had cursed when he saw her again, was sure he would be sent packing if he involved himself, but had decided he had to speak. 'I saw you with

Julian Baldwin a minute ago, and last night. I think you may end up in serious trouble.' He was talking of adultery and they both knew it but skated around the word.

'What business is it of yours?' Alison challenged him, red-faced.

'I don't want to see you hurt.' That was said instinctively and it was true.

Alison was not impressed. 'I don't need your advice and you're mistaken. We are to be married. But I will warn you: that Delia will ditch you as soon as some other man takes her fancy.'

Richard, incensed, snapped, 'That is a slanderous remark.'

Alison said only, 'Ha!' She swung away from him to cross the road.

He stalked on, fuming, telling himself he should have held his tongue and saved embarrassment.

It was too late anyway; the damage had already been done.

Julian poked his head out of the window of the cab to call to the driver, 'I've changed my mind. Never mind the Admiralty.' Instead he was taken to a club he knew where he could pass the morning playing cards and drinking. As he paid his fare he did not see the cab pull in behind his own, nor its passenger get down, but he looked round, irritated, at the tug on his sleeve. The man smiling at him was fleshily handsome with a silky moustache, big-bodied and long-armed. He wore a checked suit and carried a walking cane.

Oliver Crawshaw had seen them arrive on Monday evening. He had moved into Esme's house and he had brought her out to the hotel to dine. He was waiting for her to emerge from the ladies' cloakroom when Julian registered himself and Alison as 'Mr and Mrs Baldwin'. Oliver had licked his lips. He had watched the hotel and learned Julian's routine. Today he had hired a cab, waited for him to emerge and followed him.

Now Julian demanded testily. 'Yes? What do you want?'

'You don't know who I am.' That was a statement.

'I don't give a damn who you are, either.' He tried to step past but the man put a restraining hand on his chest. Julian glared. 'What the devil—'

A wink. 'The point is, Mr Baldwin, I know who you are and who your friend is. And I know where Mrs Baldwin is and she wouldn't like to hear about this little jaunt.'

'What! How dare you!' Julian brandished a clenched fist.

Oliver took a step back and lifted the cane. 'This thing is loaded with lead so don't try any rough stuff.' He eyed Julian and saw him hesitate. He went on, 'Anyway, that wouldn't shut my mouth, so why don't we just talk this over like gentlemen?'

'Suppose I call a policeman?' Julian looked around as if seeking one.

Oliver was ready for that. 'I'll deny it. Your word against mine, remember. Suppose I sue *you* for slander? How do you fancy that?'

Julian glared, frustrated, his bluff called. 'What do you want?'

'Let's see how much you've got,' Oliver said, businesslike.

Julian took out his wallet and opened it. Oliver's fingers dipped in quickly and extracted the banknotes inside, some twenty pounds. He jammed the wad in his pocket. 'There y'are. All settled.' He smirked at the fuming Julian. 'Now we can forget the whole affair and live happily ever after. I'll bid you good day, sir.' He flourished the cane in salute and strode away.

Julian's money was in a Sunderland bank but he had an arrangement with a London branch for trips to the capital. He walked there because he had no money for a cab. His anger simmered but as he walked it cooled. He told himself it was all over and he could forget the whole affair, as that bounder had told him.

Oliver strolled back to Esme's house. He had thought of making further demands of Julian at a later date but decided against it. There was always a chance he might go to the police. So instead Oliver wrote a letter to Mrs Baldwin and signed it, '*A friend*'.

Esme came up behind him and purred in his ear, her hands busy, 'What are you grinning about?'

'I've just made a few quid. I thought I'd take you out to lunch, and after—'

She put a finger to his lips. 'Now.'

Thursday evening. Julian and Alison were to travel north the following day, but after that – what? Alison's uneasiness was increasing. She had not forgotten the savage exchange with Richard two days earlier. The memory of it haunted her and her anger with him remained. But that was not all. Julian made passionate love to her every night, but afterwards – she felt used.

They went down to dinner. In the passage outside their room a vase of flowers had been knocked from its stand. An old cleaning woman knelt, sweeping up the mess with a dust pan and brush. As they emerged she climbed creakily to her feet, tall and thin, grey hair in a bun. She bobbed in a little bow or curtsey before scuttling away. Alison was reminded of her 'Gannie', Francie. She stood by Julian as the buttoned page boy in his pillbox cap operated the lift. It was a disturbing reminder. She had not thought of Francie lately. What would the old woman think? Alison could see her in her mind's eye, hear her: 'I didn't bring you up to go on like this! You're taking after your mother!'

In the restaurant Julian escorted her to her chair. Other women were watching him. Alison had seen this before, knew he was a handsome man, but now she saw he was looking around before he took his seat, relishing the glances.

He pulled up his chair and now he found a smile for her, then began to study the menu. That was when the woman appeared at their side. She wore a light raincoat, open over a day gown. She smiled at them both but there was no mirth in it. The cold, distant beauty was a raging fury now, the cruel mouth a white-lipped slash. Pamela Baldwin said, 'It seems I'm just in time for dinner. May I join you? Or maybe not.' Julian was gaping, winded by her appearance. She concentrated her glare on him. 'I received a letter this morning, signed by "a friend". It said I would find you here with this trollop. And here you are. You said it was business and I thought I could believe you this time.'

She switched her malevolent gaze to Alison, pitying. 'You love him, I suppose?' She did not wait for an answer but laughed unpleasantly. It stilled conversation in the room. The head waiter looked across at them, worriedly. Without turning her head she snapped, 'Get out and settle your bill. There's a taxi outside. Wait in it for me. The hotel will send on your things.'

Julian walked out with never a glance at Alison.

Pamela went on, 'I don't suppose he told you about the others. Did you think you were the first? And did he tell you his name was Julian Blenkinsop and I made him change it to mine? I wanted to keep the Baldwin name alive. I own Baldwin's yard. Without me he has no job. I keep him because I need a husband, but I won't have him playing games behind my back.'

'Keep him!' Alison was angry now. Julian was the cause but she snapped back at Pamela because she was there. 'You're welcome to him.'

Now the manager arrived in his tails, the head waiter hovering at his elbow. 'Ladies, please.'

Alison said coldly, ignoring Pamela, 'You can please me by showing this person to the door.'

'I'm going.' A baring of teeth in a wolfish grin. 'I have what I came for. Enjoy your dinner.' Pamela strode from the restaurant.

The manager coughed and said discreetly, low-voiced, 'I think it will be best if Madam—'

Alison did not wait to be told but broke in, 'I'm not hungry.' She gave him a dazzling smile. 'I'm sorry you've been troubled.' With that she rose and walked out, head held high.

Julian had carried the key to their room. Alison asked at the desk in the foyer and found he had left it there as he slunk out. The young clerk on duty stared wide-eyed as he gave it to her. She realised the tale would have gone all round the hotel, staff and guests would all be sneering at her. She found a smile for him, too. But she had a sudden flash of memory, of a little girl in a school yard hounded by a circle of jeering children accusing her: '*Jailbird's daughter!*'

She had to get out. There was no question of her staying in their room. It was littered with his clothing and there was the bed she had shared with him. She could not sleep there. She did not call for a maid as 'Mrs Julian Baldwin' would have done, but packed for herself, Alison Bailey. Downstairs again she called for a taxi and the porter loaded her case aboard. She tipped him with a smile and told the driver, 'King's Cross Station, please.'

As the cab pulled away the porter watched her go and said, 'I don't care what they say, she seems a good sort to me, not like some we get.'

'You're right there,' the doorman agreed. 'Not like that bloke who was with her. I reckon he used her.'

That was the word in Alison's mind: used. At the station

she found she had just missed a train but did not mind; Julian and his wife would have been on it. She caught a night train but did not take a sleeper for she knew she would not sleep. She sat in a corner seat, staring at her reflection in the window as the train pounded north through the darkness. Used. She could see Francie's anguished face, hear her voice: *My poor bairn*! *What have you done?* Alison had shown a smiling public face when she was humiliated but she did not need to now. The tears ran down her face unchecked and unnoticed by the others in the carriage.

What she had thought was her love for Julian was now dead. Her emotions now were shame and anger. Shame at how she had been duped by Julian, seduced. Anger with the 'friend' who had written to Pamela Baldwin. She thought she knew who that 'friend' was: Richard Tarrant.

The train delivered her to Newcastle in the cold dawn of Friday. She caught a local train to Sunderland and almost crawled into her apartment, physically and mentally exhausted. She had arranged to be away all week so no one expected her back until Saturday. She boiled kettles and filled a hip bath then cleansed her body, as if washing away the last trace of him. The sunlight streamed through her window but she burrowed down in her bed and closed her eyes. She slept with the tears still wet on her cheek.

The pounding on her front door woke her. Peering bleary-eyed at the clock on the mantelpiece she saw it was late afternoon. Who could it be? The knocking came again. Alison cried, 'All right! I'm coming!' She shoved her feet into slippers and pulled on a dressing-gown, opened the door and saw Clara Skilton standing there. Alison stared. What had brought the woman here?

Clara said, 'He wants you.'

11

Monkwearmouth in Sunderland, July 1914.

'Who?' Dazed from sleep, for a moment Alison could only ask, 'Who wants me?'

'Him. Tarrant.' Clara enlarged, exasperated, 'Mad Michael.' She was clearly not in the best of tempers.

Nor was Alison and she resented Clara's tone. She was wide awake now and snapped, 'I wasn't expecting you, let alone a message from Mr Tarrant. So I'll thank you to be civil. And how did you know where to find me?'

Clara scowled, but realised this was not the young girl she had driven out of Bellhanger ten years ago. She said sulkily, 'He had an address of a café in Dundas Street. I went there and they told me you lived here.'

That would be the original Alison's Cookshop, managed by Dolly Maguire. Alison nodded. 'I see. So why does Mr Tarrant want me?'

'He's poorly, doesn't know where he is or who he is for most of the time.'

'You mean delirious?' Alison said, alarmed.

'That's right. The doctor says its a fever, wanted him to go into hospital or get a nurse to live in, but he wouldn't have that. Wouldn't have me, either. "Fetch that Alison Bailey", he said, though I don't know what you can do for him that I can't.'

Alison thought: *a little kindness*? She asked, 'How did you get here?'

'Walked till I got to the tram stop.' That was said as if the answer was obvious. How else might she have come there?

'I thought you might have the carriage.'

Clara sniffed. 'There's no groom now, just a feller comes from a livery stable of a morning and finishes mid-day. He's no use.' He was happily married and had spurned her advances.

'See if you can find a cab.' Alison thought Michael Tarrant must be very ill to ask for her. She couldn't recall him asking for anyone's help before. And she was indebted to him. The money he lent her had been repaid but she still owed him for the faith he had shown in her. 'Bring it back here and I'll be ready in ten minutes.'

Clara went without argument. She realised their situations had changed. The former kitchen maid was now a businesswoman who casually ordered cabs and lived in a well furnished flat – she had seen that much from her position at the door.

Alison made a hasty toilet and breakfasted on toast and tea as she packed a bag. She was ready when Clara returned with a cab. They did not talk as the horse trotted up to Bellhanger. The morning sunshine had gone, black clouds were driving in from the sea, carrying a spit of rain. Alison saw the house looming dark, recalled her first visit when but a child and she had been virtally orphaned. She wondered what it held for her now.

They got down from the cab at the back door of the house and Alison paid the driver. Clara was waiting, only to be told, 'I can find my way.' She shrugged and went off to her room. There she penned a letter to Oliver Crawshaw. She wrote to him regularly, hoping that he would return some day as he had promised. He sometimes replied, usually by registered post and enclosing money. Clara told herself it was because he still cared. He looked on it as insurance; she would not inform on him if it would mean she lost a source of income.

Clara was not an educated woman and wrote in an untidy scrawl with little punctuation. She related how Michael Tarrant was ill '. . . and likely to snuff it. If he does go what about you know what suppose they find whats missing.' She paused for thought, chewing worriedly at the pen, thinking of the old, worthless furniture hidden under dust sheets. She went on: 'Now hes got that lass as used to be kitchen maid here to come and nurse him I think she might be a byblow of his.'

She walked down to the pillar box through the pouring rain to catch the last post, hoping for an early reply, some reassurance that would lift this load of worry from her shoulders.

Alison made her way through the remembered passages, the sheeted furniture like ghosts in the gloom as the rain lashed at the windows. She thought that at least they would be cleaned on the outside, and that there had been precious little work done inside. Francie would have been appalled.

She found Michael in his bed. That room seemed to have had a perfunctory cleaning. She wondered: in anticipation of her coming? He lay still, his eyes closed. She had not seen him since she had repaid the loan she had from him, eight years ago, and Alison was shocked. His face was unshaven, hollow-cheeked, his body was skeletal, shrunken, his hair grey – a dirty grey, that should have been white. It had not been washed. A water carafe and a glass stood on a bedside table but both were empty. Alison gave Clara the benefit of the doubt there; Michael may have emptied the glass while she was fetching Alison. But she could have washed his hair. And the fire was nearly out.

Was he conscious? Feverish? She went to him and laid a hand on his brow, testing. His eyes opened and he stared up at her. She saw recognition and he smiled and said hoarsely, barely a whisper, 'Alison. Bonny lass. You came.'

'Aye, I'm here,' she said softly. 'I've come to make you better.'

'Too late now.' His head moved slowly in negation. 'I don't care, but I'm glad you'll be here.'

'Don't talk like that,' Alison ordered stoutly. She raked the dead ash out of the grate and shovelled coal onto the embers. 'Now you lie quiet. I'll fetch you some water and something to eat.'

She went down to the kitchen, washed out both carafe and glass and quickly inspected the larder. She was not impressed. Clara returned from posting her letter, standing a dripping umbrella by the stove to dry. Alison ordered, 'Cut up some vegetables and I'll make some broth out of that ham shank.'

Clara bristled. 'I don't have to take orders from you!'

'I'm giving them during Mr Tarrant's incapacity. I don't want to ask him to choose between us, but I will if I have to.'

Clara swallowed that, albeit reluctantly. She knew she had a good job – and she had a profitable sideline in diverting household expenses into her purse – and did not want to lose it. She set to work, sulkily.

Alison added, 'And I want some clean bed linen and towels, hot water and hot bottles.' Then left Clara to it.

She found a blazing fire in Michael's room now, propped him up on pillows and helped him sip some water. During the next hour she set the broth to cook and gave him a blanket bath, as she had been trained to do as a VAD nurse. Then she packed him round with hot bottles and dosed him with aspirin.

He was as helpless as a child, with only a tenuous grasp on the present. Sometimes he knew Alison but at others he confused her with Francie, or called for the long-dead Silas to saddle his horse. In the gathering dusk and by lamplight, with Clara's enforced assistance, she changed his bed linen and nightshirt. The housekeeper pointedly averted her eyes at that stage. Alison dismissed her and went on to feed Michael with broth. He ate little but thanked her. 'That was good.' Soon after he drifted into sleep.

Alison found a room at the back of the house, dusted it and made up the bed with clean linen. Then she put in a hot bottle to air it. She would not use the room that had been hers and Francie's, now occupied by Clara.

The doctor, Pennington, visited that evening and found Michael in one of his lucid periods. His patient woke, seeming to sense his presence, and submitted sleepily to being examined. The medical man said jovially, 'You're much improved, Mr Tarrant. I see you have a nurse.'

Michael smiled. 'A good one.'

But outside the sickroom Pennington shook his head and pursed his lips. 'He is better; temperature's gone down a bit. But he's very frail. I just hope this fever doesn't turn to pneumonia.' He glanced at Alison. 'Are you a qualified nurse?'

'I've trained with the VAD for five years.'

'Um.' He was not impressed, regarding VADs as amateurs, but he nodded and they discussed treatment. He left, saying, 'You seem to be on the right track. I'll call in tomorrow.'

The next day dawned with a clear sky and bright sunlight. When Dr Pennington called he found Michael a little further improved after a good night. Alison had watched him constantly and he was always sleeping peacefully. After breakfast she had shaved him. That improved his appearance but somehow it emphasised his frailty.

Pennington told Alison, 'I think we can be cautiously optimistic. It looks as though he's going to pull through.'

Alison smiled her relief.

In London, Oliver had paid an early morning visit to the

newsagent who was an accommodation address for letters
to his alias, 'Vincent Featherstone'. Now, at home and seated
at breakfast, he opened and read the letter from Clara. He
looked across the breakfast table to where Esme, in a silk
dressing-gown that outlined her figure, sat drinking coffee.
'I have some news for you.'

Her eyebrows lifted, disinterested. 'Oh?'

'Your husband – Michael Tarrant—'

She put down her cup. 'What about him?'

'He's very ill.'

'Who says so?' She put out her hand for the letter.

'A little bird. His housekeeper.' He withheld it.

'Why can't I see?' she pouted.

'You don't need to.' There were a lot of things he had not
told her, and would not, because he doubted her loyalty.
Besides: 'I don't read your post. And I've told you all that
matters.' He glanced at the sheet again. 'She says: "He's
likely to snuff it".'

Esme was interested now. 'Is he, by God!'

The fine summer day ran on into a clouding dusk with a
chill wind coming in from the sea. Alison sat in Michael's
room sewing buttons onto some of his shirts. He lay in his
bed, dozing. She heard the clatter of horse's hooves and went
to the window that looked out to the distant sea. Peering
out, she saw the cab halted below at the front door, the horse
with its head nodding, and heard the jingle of its harness. A
woman got down from the cab. She was foreshortened from
Alison's viewpoint, her face largely hidden by the wide-
brimmed hat, but fashionably and expensively dressed in a
cream tailored broadcloth suit with an ankle-length skirt.

Her voice rose up, addressing the cabbie, commanding,
'Take the case in, please.' He had climbed down from his
seat and now carried the large suitcase up the steps. The

woman paid him. Alison saw Clara at the head of the steps now, presumably summoned by the ringing of the front door bell. That commanding voice now demanded, 'And you are?'

'I'm the housekeeper, Mrs Skilton, ma'am.'

'I am Mrs Tarrant. I'll thank you to have my luggage taken to my room and I want to see my husband.'

She was lost to sight as she entered the house, followed by Clara lugging the heavy suitcase. The cab wheeled around and headed back to the town.

Alison could scarcely believe it. Michael Tarrant's runaway wife had come home after more than twenty years! She turned away from the window. Michael still dozed. She went to him but hesitated for a moment. Should she wake him? To prepare him to meet again the wife he had loved and lost for a lifetime? Alison squeezed his thin hand where it lay on the quilt and said softly, 'Mr Tarrant.'

He woke slowly, blinking, and said in a drowsy murmur, 'Alison?'

'Your wife is here.'

'No.' His head turned on the pillow in negation. 'No. It was you in her clothes when you were just a little girl. I thought you were her.' He stopped then, the half-dream as he came out of sleep dissolving as he became aware. 'My wife? Esme? Did you say she was here?'

Alison did not need to answer. The door was thrown open and Esme swept into the room. She cast one quick, assessing glance at Alison then went to sit on the side of the bed. She took off hat and gloves, saying as she did so, 'I came as soon as I heard, caught the 11.45 out of Kings Cross. There's no need for you to worry now. I'll look after you.'

He struggled to sit up and gasped out, 'You left me more than a lifetime ago for another man and he was just the first. It's ten years since I admitted to myself that you would never come back, that I knew I didn't want you back any longer.

You'd ruined my life. The drink had got me and I couldn't give up. Now you've come to destroy what peace of mind I have now.' His voice had risen, querulous. His head shook in negation and anger. 'I don't want you!'

Esme's smile remained fixed. 'Poor darling, he's delirious, quite hot.' She laid her hand on his brow, testing.

He brushed it away with a feeble gesture. 'Damn you! Get out of here and leave me alone!' But the effort was too much for him and he collapsed back onto the pillows.

Alison went to him quickly, holding his hands, soothing.

Esme clicked her tongue. 'It seems I got here just in time. I'll leave you to stay with him while I settle in. Then I'll take over the care of him.'

Michael relapsed from that moment. He tossed and turned restlessly, muttering all the while, mostly incomprehensibly, but sometimes, 'Go away . . . don't want her here . . . Alison, *Alison*!'

She tried to calm him but to no avail. Esme appeared at intervals to lean over his bed and croon, 'There, there, try to sleep, my love.' He turned his face away from her.

Alison protested, 'I think your presence is upsetting him.'

'Nonsense,' Esme replied curtly. 'But what are the terms of your employment here?'

'I am not employed.

'So you really have no business in this house.'

'Mr Tarrant asked me to attend on him.'

'Before I arrived and when he was not in his right mind. Now I am in charge.' Esme paused to let that sink in, then went on, 'But you seem to be fond of him and so you may stay.' She had decided Alison would be useful.

It proved her idea of taking over his care consisted of her organising Alison and Clara to take turns watching over him day and night. 'And I will help when I can.'

That suited Alison. She thought the less time Esme spent with Michael the better he would be. She agreed to stand watch through the night, a full twelve hours, and it seemed to last twelve months. Michael was restless, tossing and turning, and she had to replace his covers several times. Whenever he recovered consciousness he was wandering in his mind. She was glad to see the grey dawn, but it brought no relief. It seemed Esme had to go into Sunderland to shop. She had the groom from the livery stable harness the horses to the carriage then paid him to take her into the town for the day. She informed Alison, 'I'll take luncheon while I am there but I'll return this evening for dinner. Call on Mrs Skilton if you need any assistance.'

When Alison sought that assistance Clara whined about the work she was being asked to do: '. . . helping you wi' him on top of everything else. Her ladyship give her orders, wants a five course dinner when she comes in and then there's the washing up . . .' Alison was glad to be rid of her.

The day dragged out as long as the night. Michael was disturbed by Esme's brief visit before she left. Dr Pennington called, examined his patient, shook his head over the temperature reading and left unhappily. Michael was restless throughout the day and Alison could not rest. To make matters worse, in the evening a storm roared in from the sea, low, leaden clouds driven in on the wind out of the north-east. Lightning forked down at the house and a clap of thunder shook it. Michael woke with a cry but Alison quietened him and he slept again. After Esme had eaten her dinner, she and Clara visited the sickroom and found him sleeping and Alison red-eyed and weary.

'More like a winter's day than a summer one,' Esme smiled. She whispered, 'Mrs Skilton and I will share the night duty. You must have a good night's sleep.'

Alison said, 'He has been restless, and there's the fire—'

'No need for you to worry,' Esme assured her. 'Mrs Skilton will make it up quietly and watch over him.'

After thirty-six hours without sleep, Alison was ready to obey. She made a scratch meal from the leftovers of the dinner, too tired to do more than pick at the food. She pulled on her nightgown and fell into bed.

Clara carried out her duties with ill grace, but did make up the fire with more coal and replaced the coverings when Michael threw them off. In between whiles she dozed, snoring, in an armchair. It was midnight when Esme shook her and she woke, guiltily agitated and mumbling, 'Just resting me eyes.'

'That's all right,' Esme calmed her. 'I've made a pot of tea. Come down and have a cup.' And, as Clara glanced towards the bed where Michael lay, 'He's sleeping soundly; don't worry.'

Clara was ready to be persuaded and accompanied Esme to the kitchen. The housekeeper thought it odd that this lady should make tea for them and sit in the servants' quarters, but was not disposed to question her. She sipped at her tea and complained about the storm raging overhead. She did not offer to go when Esme said, 'I'll just make sure he is all right.' Clara sat on, luxuriating in the warmth from the stove.

Esme entered Michael's room quietly and paused a moment to be sure he was asleep. There was only one shaded lamp but that was sufficient for her to see he lay supine, his eyes closed. He had been restless, one corner of the bed-clothes tossed aside. She saw the fire had burnt down because Clara had not replenished it before going to the kitchen. Esme left it. She moved light-footed, like a cat stalking her prey. She came to the bed and slid the bedcoverings from the unconscious man as if he had shaken them off onto the floor. She added the hot bottles, now barely warm, left him lying in only his nightshirt and prowled from the room as silently as she had entered it. In the kitchen she assured Clara, 'He's fine.'

Alison had slept despite her unease at leaving Michael, unease because she doubted the competence of either Esme or Clara. That prickling of distrust woke her in the small hours to stare up into the darkness, listening to the rumble of the storm passing away. She thought that might have woken her but felt that something was wrong. She rose from her bed, pulled on a dressing-gown and jammed her feet into slippers. She hurried through the dark but familiar passages, lit only once by lightning, accompanied by distant thunder. She opened the door of Michael's room, looking first for Clara or Esme to be sitting by the shaded light. She saw neither, but then turned her gaze on Michael. He lay naked save for the nightshirt, his fingers plucking at the sheet on which he lay, as if trying to pull it over him.

Alison stifled a cry and ran to him. Her swift hands found his limbs cold, his body like marble. She rescued the sheets and blankets, spread them over him but knew that was not enough. She remembered her childhood and Francie warming her in bed. She slid in beside Michael, loosened her dressing-gown and wrapped him in with her, his cold body pressed against the warmth of her own.

That was how they found her. This time Clara remembered she had not built up the fire or changed the hot bottles. She filled fresh ones and went with Esme to the sickroom. They opened the door and Esme exclaimed. She had expected to find Michael chilled, probably fatally so, but now . . .

Clara cried, 'She's in bed with him!'

'Get out of there, you harlot!' Esme crossed the floor, raging. 'Are you trying to kill him?'

'I'm keeping him alive!' Alison whispered. 'Don't wake him! He'd thrown off all his bedding. He was freezing and it was the only way to warm him.' She slid out of the bed, took the fresh bottles from Clara and put them in her place.

Esme fumed, 'Impossible! We had only left him for a few

minutes to fetch those bottles. You thought you saw your chance to wheedle something out of him, thought we would be downstairs for a long while! You brazen trollop!'

This was an outrageous lie. Alison knew Michael had been in her arms for half an hour or so. And how long before that had he lain uncovered?

But Clara was nodding agreement. Esme's lie was to her advantage, saying she had not left her post.

Alison's heated reply was low-voiced but clear: 'Don't call me a liar or a trollop. I'm neither, but you ran off with another man.'

'Get out of here and stay out,' hissed Esme. 'I won't have you in this house.'

Alison would have liked to go, but Michael had asked for her and she believed he still wanted her. Besides, an ugly suspicion was surfacing in her mind, born of the lying of these two. She had assumed Michael had thrown off his covers as he had before, though he had never been stripped completely. Now she was not so sure that it had been an accident.

'I'm staying,' she said firmly, 'and if you try to force me out I'll make a row about it.'

Esme glared, but conceded. 'Very well, but from now on you'll keep out of his bed.'

'I only did what was needed and if needs be I'll do it again. I leave him with you but I'll be back.' She walked out, clutching the robe about her. She dressed and returned to the sickroom to tend Michael. He was warm from the hot bottles Clara had brought and sleeping. Alison hoped she had come on him in time. She sat in a chair by his bed, sharing Clara's vigil, and prayed for him.

Michael survived another twenty-four hours but never recovered consciousness. There was no knowing if his exposure to the chill night air had killed him or if it had been a natural progression of his illness.

Dr Pennington thought the latter and signed the death certificate accordingly. Alison did not tell him of the events of that fatal night, nor of her suspicion. It was no more than that and she had no proof; it was her word against those of his wife and his housekeeper.

Arkenstall the solicitor read the will. He was into his sixties, his pointed beard mostly grey, and he peered through wire-rimmed spectacles. They learned that Michael had left £100 to Alison but nothing to Esme. The rest of his estate went to his nephew, Richard Tarrant. He had written to Arkenstall saying that he was extremely busy at St George's and could not attend but he would like Mrs Skilton to continue as housekeeper to look after the property.

'It's a disgrace!' Esme raged at Arkenstall when she was left alone with him. 'I was his wife for more than twenty years and he leaves me not a penny! He was out of his mind, you could see that, a raving lunatic! I'll contest the will!'

The solicitor eyed her with distaste. He knew all about her running off all those years ago. 'You will certainly lose your case and be reported in the newspapers. Michael Tarrant was as sane as I when he signed that will. That would be my evidence and that of his doctor. He was an eccentric but honest man who suffered greatly, and it will do you no good to seek to besmirch his reputation.'

Esme swore she would have her revenge but went back to London and Oliver.

Alison threw herself into her work, starting with a visit to the original Cookshop in Dundas Street. She was pleased to see it full, with a lot of men from the tram company's depot drinking mugs of tea. But Dolly Maguire, standing behind the counter, was not her usual cheery self. She greeted Alison with a muttered, 'Do you see who we've got in here?' She gave a jerk of her head.

Alison looked in the direction indicated and drew a quick

intake of breath. Moira Grindly sat at a small table tucked away in a corner but she was barely recognisable, had lost weight so the rusty black bombazine of her dress hung on her, and her face was haggard. Two badly wrapped brown paper parcels lay by her feet that were stuffed into scuffed and cracked old shoes.

Dolly whispered, 'She came in and said she was going to the workhouse and could she have a cup of tea for old times' sake. I didn't charge her.'

'No,' Alison answered instinctively. 'You can't do that. But what happened?'

'Her place just lost business,' Dolly sighed. 'I heard gossip from people who left it to come here instead. She couldn't keep staff; the young lasses wouldn't work for her. She told me she had to close, couldn't pay the rent and had nowhere to go. She got a room in Society Lane but couldn't pay the rent there either.'

Society Lane was an alley where the rent of a room was only a few pence. Alison reflected that she had known that situation of having nowhere to go, but she had been young and faced and fought it with the confidence of youth, though she remembered she had not felt very confident at the time. Moira Grindly, on the other hand, was a woman in her fifties.

'I'll talk to her,' said Alison. 'Bring some breakfast over for her.'

'Aye, I will,' Dolly responded eagerly, having guessed what Alison's reaction would be.

She left Dolly, crossed to Moira's table and sat down beside her. 'Hello.'

Moira blinked at her dully, 'Alison, isn't it?'

'Aye, it is.'

'You've got a nice place here.'

Alison nodded. 'I hear you've had some bad luck.'

'Nowt else but bad luck since he deserted me,' Moira said

bitterly. She was talking of George Grindly, her husband. 'I lost my own place and couldn't find work at my age. They only wanted cleaners and the money wasn't enough to pay my rent and feed me.'

'Do you think you could work in a place like this?'

'Waiting on, you mean?' Moira seemed unsure.

'No, I mean in the kitchen.' Alison did not want her dealing with customers.

'Oh, aye, but where? I nearly asked Dolly if she needed somebody in the kitchen but she seems to have two good lasses here.'

'I have another place on the sea front. You could work in the kitchen there, and sleep there at night.' Thelma was manager there now and living in the apartment above. Alison thought that would be better than trying to fit Moira in with Dolly. Both would have memories of when the roles had been reversed, Moira being the employer and Dolly the cook. It was only later that she realised that Moira would be sleeping in the kitchen as Alison had done when she went to work for George Grindly.

'Ee! I'd love that!' Moira had no hesitation now. 'When can I start?' Then the tears came and she seized Alison's hand. 'You're a canny lass. I'm so grateful.'

Dolly brought her breakfast now and Alison gently disengaged her hand. 'Eat up now and afterwards we'll take a tram down to the sea front.'

Alison introduced Moira to Thelma and saw her settled in, made sure she would be comfortable but also made it clear that the young lass was in charge. She had a quiet word with Thelma alone. 'Moira's had a hard time but a lot of it was her own making. She's been used to giving orders but she is not to do it here. If she tries, tell me or Dolly.'

As she rode back into town on the tram, Alison looked back on recent weeks with a mental shudder. She resolved to put behind her the disastrous affair with Julian and the loss of Michael. She told herself that she had come a long way from when she had been abandoned by her mother so long ago. She owned four Cookshops and could do a good turn for someone like Moira. And she planned to open another soon with the bequest from Michael. Life was good and would be better.

So she dreamed and planned.

Then Gavrilo Princip assassinated the Archduke Franz Ferdinand, Britain was plunged into war and everything was changed.

12

London, April 1915.

———————

'Nurse!'

'Nurse!'

'*Nurse!*'

'Ower here, bonny lass!'

Alison, scurrying between patients, heard that last call in a North Country accent and acknowledged it with a quick turn of the head. 'I'll be there in a minute, Geordie.' She knew the young soldier in the Northumberland Fusiliers. The long ward held sixty beds and in each was a wounded, and sometimes dying, man. It was a long hut in the grounds of a big hospital on the outskirts of London and Alison had been serving there for six months. Dolly Maguire had been left as overall manageress of the Cookshops for the duration of the war. That had been when it was thought it would be 'over by Christmas'. Now the armies were locked in a war of attrition in the mud of Flanders and no end in sight.

Alison was a bustling figure for most of each day, dealing with bedpans, sweeping a floor, dispensing tea, making beds, changing dressings. She had not become used to the smells of disinfectant and gangrenous wounds but had trained herself to ignore them. As she had learned to blank out the cries of pain or the squeaky strains from the wind-up gramophone, so they would not affect how she did her job.

She sometimes reflected wryly how life had changed for her. She was no longer the young businesswoman, giving orders. Now it seemed everyone gave orders to her. She lived in a hostel a mile from the hospital, sharing a dormitory with five other girls. She rose at six every morning to walk to the hospital, to breakfast before going on duty for a twelve-hour day. She had to be always smart in her ankle-length blue skirt. White collars, cuffs and long apron were stiffly starched. For this she was paid £20 per year.

She always found a smile for the men. That was not easy when she was changing the dressings on fearsome wounds and they were in agony. It had been known for a new nurse to faint when helping with the task for the first time. Alison had come close to it. She often thought back to the days of her training before the war, when she had given demonstrations in Mowbray Park. She thought of Simon Stothard and wondered how he was. Had his battalion of the Durham Light Infantry gone to Flanders? Had he been wounded like one of these men? Was he – but she would not think of that.

On her weekly half-day Alison would take a clanking tram down into London's West End, to see some of the sights, window shop and finally treat herself to tea in a café. She would grin to herself as she found she was watching the service and how the place was run – a busman's holiday. On a day at the end of April she sat at a table near the window, sipping at her second cup and looking out at the rain that pattered on the glass. Her mood was bitter. She had lost a patient, a young man, and she had fought for his life. And Dolly had written giving all the local news but including, in all innocence because she knew nothing of the affair, a *Sunderland Daily Echo* cutting about Baldwin's shipyard building a destroyer. That reminded Alison of Julian's treatment of her and added to her bitterness.

Then she saw Richard Tarrant. The passing crowds made a wall of umbrellas and hurrying figures, heads bent against the rain, but for an instant they parted and she caught a glimpse of him. His tall figure stood out, partly because he was in mufti – a well-worn tweed jacket and battered trilby, a hat that was an old friend – when the streets teemed with men in uniform.

Alison shot from her seat and ran out, shoving money at the open-mouthed waitress on the way. Richard was lost in the crowd again but she could see that awful hat bobbing above the other heads. She set off in hot pursuit, swerving through the pedestrian traffic. Coming up with him, she caught at his arm and swung round in front of him, planted herself in his path and so stopped him dead.

He stared, startled, then recognised her and smiled. 'Good Lord! I didn't expect to see you.' He was glad to see a face he knew and a pretty one. She was flushed from her chase and he found her very lovely, a girl to gladden the heart and he needed cheering. 'I heard from the solicitor, Arkenstall, how you had cared for my Uncle Michael. Thank you.'

'I did it for him,' Alison said curtly. 'He was good to me and it was the least I could do. I don't want your thanks but we have some unfinished business. You'll be glad to know you were right about Julian Baldwin; he had made a fool of me. And no doubt you'll be delighted that your letter to his wife brought her down on me and showed Julian as he really is. I suppose I should be grateful but it was hardly the act of a gentleman.'

'Letter?' Richard was bewildered. 'To his wife? I wrote no letter.'

'Of course you did.' She was contemptuous of the lie. 'Why try to talk your way out of it? You virtually condemned me when you saw us. Who else could have written it? You were the only person in London who knew me. Or did you get your lady friend to write it? What was her name? Delia.'

He reacted angrily to that. 'Delia did not and would not. She is a lady.'

Alison thought: *is*. She noted the use of the present tense and concluded: *so he is still seeing her*.

'And I'm not a liar,' Richard said bitterly. He had also lost a patient. He was now a captain in the Royal Army Medical Corps, in mufti because he was on leave from the front. He had come back on a hospital train, caring for a seriously wounded brother officer. He had visited the young second lieutenant, in the Royal Herbert Hospital at Woolwich, on every day of his leave. This morning he had learned the boy had died of his wounds.

Now he said coldly, 'I warned you about Julian because I thought it right. I didn't like doing it and I regretted it. I certainly did not write any letter.'

That gave Alison pause. He spoke with sincerity and she found she wanted to believe him, but there was the cold logic: who else could have written to Pamela Baldwin?

Now there came an interruption. This girl was also pretty and well dressed under an umbrella. She wore a smile but it was vapid. She held out a white feather to Richard and trilled, 'We don't want to lose you but we think you ought to go. You should be in uniform.'

He held the feather, for a moment taken aback. Then he started, 'As a matter of fact—'

Alison had heard of this practice but had not seen it before. She snatched the feather and rammed it into the girl's upswept tresses. 'You nasty little bitch!' And, as the girl gaped at her, 'I've a mind to slap your face! Now get out of here before I do it!' Alison spun her around and thrust her on her way with a spread hand in her back. She stumbled into a gutter, splashed out of it and scuttled away with a dripping hem flapping wetly about her ankles.

'I'm sorry,' Alison apologised to Richard on behalf of her sex.

'No need to be.' He shrugged. 'As I was about to explain,

I hold the King's commission. I am in mufti because I am on leave from France and I will soon be sailing to the Dardanelles. Now, you've made your feelings clear and I think we've said enough, so if you'll excuse me.' It was not a request. He circled her as she moved to let him pass, and strode away.

'Good luck,' she called after him, involuntarily.

He did not stop, let alone turn, but he raised his disreputable hat. Now she recalled she had seen hats like that on the heads of officers in mufti and told herself she should have guessed. Had she been wrong?

It was too late now.

She returned to the hostel because she was due to start on night duty that evening.

Alison served thus, from eight p.m. to eight a.m., for a month, tending to patients who could not sleep from the pain of their wounds, or writing or reading by the light of a shaded lamp. At the end of it she was granted a weekend off, so on Saturday morning she slept for a few hours then packed a suitcase and set off for Kings Cross Station. She would go home for Saturday and return on Sunday evening. It was not much but it would be a rest from the ward and the hostel.

Alison walked into the station and came face to face with Simon Stothard. She might so easily have missed him in the milling crowds of civilians and many soldiers. Some of the latter had just come from the Front, their uniforms mud-stained, boots plastered with great lumps of it, and carrying their rifles slung on their shoulders. Their smell of wet serge mingled with the station odour of coal smoke and steam. The clamour of voices rose to the high vaulted roof with the sighing of engines and clanking of couplings.

Simon wore the brand new uniform of a second lieutenant in the Durhams and looked older. The boyish round face had now thinned. They stopped to avoid collision, with scarcely a foot between them. Alison could reach out and touch him, and did. 'Simon! I'm so glad to see you!'

The expression of surprise on his face changed to one of pleasure. 'I didn't expect to meet you. I heard from Dolly that you were nursing in a hospital down here, but London is a big place.'

So he had been asking after her. Alison realised that she was very important to this young man. She smiled at him. 'I see you are an officer now.'

'Yes.' He shrugged deprecatingly. 'Battlefield commission.'

And he wore the ribbon of a decoration on his chest. Alison knew something of these matters now. Was that the ribbon of the Military Cross? 'You must have been very brave.'

He grimaced. 'I was very frightened.' It was clear he did not want to talk about that and he changed the subject. 'Are you here to catch a train?' And then, wistfully, 'Or are you meeting somebody?'

'No, I'm not meeting anyone. Are you?'

He shook his head. 'I'm on my way back to France but my train doesn't leave Victoria till tomorrow. I thought I'd stay in London tonight and see a show.'

So he could watch the lovely girls on stage. Alison had seen the faces of the men at the matinées she had gone to, their looks of longing. There would be no girls where he was going. 'What a lovely idea.'

He hesitated, then blurted out, 'Would you like to come?' He added anxiously, 'If you aren't doing anything else.'

'I'm not. I'd like to go to a show with you, please.'

The porter waiting behind Simon made an exasperated noise. 'Nah then, Guv. I can't stand here all day! Lor love a duck, I've got work to do.'

Simon laughed. 'Add this lady's case to your load.'

The porter obeyed and wheeled both Simon's valise and

Alison's suitcase out to a waiting taxi-cab. Simon tipped him and gave the name of his hotel to the driver of the cab. As they settled down on the worn leather cushions he said, 'I have a room booked there, but what about you? Where are you staying?' Then he remembered, 'You were going to catch a train, weren't you? Going home?'

'I changed my mind. Your idea sounds much better.' Alison laughed happily. 'I'll see if they can find a room for me.' It seemed as if she had not laughed for a long time. But she cautioned, 'You'd better drop me and then go round the block. They may be suspicious if we register together.' She saw his face redden and she went on quickly, 'I'll see you in the foyer in half an hour. We can have some tea.'

So they did. The room the hotel found for Alison was small and poky and looked out on an alley. The receptionist was apologetic. 'We are very busy this weekend.'

Alison smiled at him. 'I quite understand.' Doubtless he kept his best rooms for his 'regulars'.

They had tea in the hotel lounge. Alison had not packed an evening dress, not imagining she would need one. But she changed out of the drab blue VAD uniform into an ankle-length, lilac-and-white-striped cotton dress with court shoes and silk stockings. She went down to the foyer again and explained to Simon, standing to greet her, 'The dress rules for theatres have been relaxed because of the war.' She had learned that from the matinées she had seen.

There was no need to apologise to him. He stared, admiring. 'You're lovely.' Alison felt the blush creeping up from her throat and said hastily, 'Shall we go?'

They saw *Chu Chin Chow* and in the darkness of the theatre his hand stole out to hold hers. Afterwards they ate supper in a restaurant. Alison offered, 'I'll pay half.'

Simon was indignant, would not hear of it, so she changed her tack. 'Then I'll order the wine.' She doubted if he knew

what to order. A shipyard draughtsman would be ignorant
of wines. Alison had learned because she thought she might
have a demand in the Cookshops one day.

They took a cab back to the hotel and in its closeness he
asked, 'Can I come with you and — and talk?'

Alison thought of her room, so hole and corner, and said,
'I'll come with you and — chat for a while.' She stumbled
over the excuse. He took it at face value.

They employed the same tactic to pass separately through
reception. Alison went to his room and he opened to her.
She entered and turned to face him, a yard between them,
and he was tongue-tied. He stared at her, desolate, and she
went to him, slipping out of the lilac-and-white-striped dress.

Alison woke early, dressed and left him sleeping as she
returned to her own room. They met again at breakfast. Now
she did not care what the people in the hotel thought of their
relationship. Simon was adoring but not talking of leaving.
Then he grinned, 'I'm the junior rank in here. I can see three
colonels, a couple of majors — and blow me if that isn't a
brigadier-general on the Staff in the corner.' He indicated
with a jerk of his head with its neatly trimmed brown hair.
In the night she had run her fingers through it, her body
arching.

Alison looked where he indicated and saw the brigadier-
general, a man in his forties, immaculately uniformed with
the red tabs on his lapels that marked him as a staff officer.
She stared. The head waiter chanced to pass then and she
called him and asked, 'I think I've seen that lady before, the
one with the officer. Can you tell me her name?'

He smiled. 'That's Brigadier-General Bulloch and Mrs
Bulloch.'

Alison feigned doubt. 'No. Now I look — there's a strong
resemblance but she is not the lady I knew.'

He went away and they ate without appetite, talked a lot

and said nothing. Until Simon said, 'I must go to pay my bill and catch my train.' He thrust back his chair.

Alison said, 'I'll join you in a minute.' It was as if some signal had sounded. Two of the colonels were also leaving the restaurant, and Brigadier-General Bulloch was on his feet. Alison waited until he had gone, then she rose and crossed to his table. The woman sitting there looked up and Alison said, 'Hello, Delia. Or should I say Mrs Bulloch?' And as the girl stared, face frozen, Alison went on, 'I see you're wearing a wedding ring. I suppose it's like a flag of convenience. I'm surprised to see you here. I talked to Richard Tarrant the other day and he gave you a good reference, said you were a lady, but I bet he didn't know about Bulloch. And I also bet the brigadier is not the only one.' She saw Delia flinch and knew that had struck home. 'Richard is a good man and you've been unfaithful to him.' She had said that on the spur of the moment, but now realised she believed it of Richard. Despite all their rows she knew in her heart he was a good man, that he had not written that letter to Pamela Baldwin. He was too good to be hurt by this. 'You should mend your ways or leave him alone.'

The brigadier was returning, looking from Delia to Alison quizzically. Alison smiled at him. 'I thought we had a mutual friend but I was mistaken.'

She walked out to the foyer, settled her account and fetched down her case. The scene just ended had upset her. She had gone through it before when Julian Baldwin had seduced her and betrayed her. Then she had been aware of her own guilt and she had paid. She had not hurt anyone except Pamela, who had already been unfaithful to Julian. This time she was in the right, there was no hypocrisy in her denunciation of Delia, but it gave her no satisfaction.

She climbed into a taxi with Simon and he told the driver, 'Victoria Station.' He held her in the cab as it wound through the streets. Alison clung to him, knowing they had little time left. She would not marry Simon but as long as this war lasted she would be there for him because he needed her.

The heart-rending taxi journey ended, she saw him onto his train and made awkward conversation until it pulled out. He hung out of the window, waving until he was lost to sight. Then she could go back to the hostel, feeling emotionally drained and exhausted, knowing she would have no peace of mind from now on; she would always be tensed, waiting for the telegram. She knew the average life expectancy of an infantry subaltern in Flanders was only six weeks.

No telegram came – she realised that would have gone to his mother as his next of kin. Two weeks after Simon's leaving, Alison received a letter from his commanding officer. He regretted having to inform her ... fine young officer ... had asked him to notify Alison. He wrote that Simon had been killed instantly, had not suffered. She hoped it was true, though she knew they always said that.

Enclosed was a short note written by Simon, mud-stained where it had rested on some makeshift table in a dank dugout. He said she would only receive this if he was killed. He wanted her to know that those few hours they had spent together were the happiest of his life.

Alison wept for him.

That day there was a clean new sheet of paper on the hospital notice board. It stated that VAD nurses were needed in Mesopotamia. Alison applied.

She was going on duty a few days later when she came on a party of soldiers setting up a searchlight on a stand. She paused to watch. She knew why it was there; London was now suffering from air raids by German Zeppelins, the big airships. So a ring of guns and searchlights was being erected around the capital.

The corporal in charge glanced around and saw her

watching. He was young, like his men, fresh-faced and neat. He grinned at the pretty girl in nurse's uniform, put a fore-finger to his cap in informal salute and offered, 'She's a ninety-centimetre searchlight.'

Alison could see it was a searchlight, but, 'Why ninety-centimetre?'

He explained, parrot fashion, as if from the drill book he had used in training, 'A searchlight is just a big mirror reflecting a point of intense white light. The mirror in this one is ninety centimetres in diameter. The point of light comes from two carbons in the barrel of the searchlight. An electric current is passed through these, but when they are parted the current arcs, producing the point of light.' He stopped there and grinned. 'One of the blokes on the light parts them when I shout "Expose!" and we light up the Zeppelin. I hope.'

Alison laughed. 'Thank you for the explanation.'

'Give us a kiss, then,' he asked cheekily.

Because of the patients she cared for and grieved for, she planted a smacking kiss on his cheek, to his surprise, and with his hand to the place he watched her walk away.

Alison did not laugh for long. She and the hospital had not experienced an air raid and she dreaded the possibility. This was a new and terrible form of warfare, with death raining down from the sky. Some preparations had been made, orders issued on how a warning would be given – by whistle blasts – parties organised to keep watch on the roof for fires. She still felt totally unprepared to meet this threat.

Alison came off night duty a week later and saw an unpleasantly familiar face from her past. The man was climbing down from an expensive motor car that was parked in front of the hospital. He was moustached and held a smoking cigar in one plump hand. He wore a well cut suit, had put on weight but there was no mistaking that big-bodied, long-armed figure. Oliver Crawshaw saw her and paused, then grinned as he recognised her. 'I didn't know you in that get-up. A nurse! Well, I'm damned.'

'You will be,' said Alison curtly. She glanced about her.

Oliver said comfortably, 'Don't bother looking for a policeman. When we had that falling out over a bit of slap and tickle, that was five years ago and no harm done. There's no use dragging it up now. Nobody would be interested in some tea shop waitress complaining after all this time. Besides, I'm a respectable patriotic businessman, contracting to the Army and the government. That's why I'm here today: business. I have an appointment with your Mr Digby.'

Alison knew Percy Digby, albeit only slightly. He was portly and balding with mutton chop whiskers framing his pouchy face with its double chins. He always wore striped trousers, black jacket and spats, and a tight tie with a stiff wing collar. She had a vague idea that Percy Digby was the man who bought supplies and equipment for the hospital and that he had an office in the main building. She also knew him as one of those who stood on the roof to watch for incendiary bombs if there was a Zeppelin raid. Alison was another, if she could be spared from her other duties.

Oliver was going on, 'And anyway, to top it all there's a chap ready to swear blind I was with him that night and nowhere near you.'

Alison could see a bitter truth in what he said. Frustrated, she went to pass him.

He laughed. 'You're in no position to moralise after your fling wi' that Julian Baldwin.' Alison stopped in her tracks, head turned to stare at him. He went on, 'Julian was a bloody fool anyway. I got into him for twenty quid and he believed I would keep quiet. He didn't know I owed you for what you did to me with that knife, but I hadn't forgotten, so I wrote to his missus and dropped the pair o' you in it.' He grinned, gloating, and put the cigar in his mouth while he took off his driving gloves.

So this man had disrupted her life for a second time! At first he had tried to take her body, then he had shamed her and it was he who had set her at Richard. Alison raged inside, reached out and snatched the cigar from his mouth, reversed it and jammed its glowing butt against his forehead, grinding, then tossed it away.

Oliver howled, 'You mad bitch!' He clapped a tender hand to the angry red place on his brow.

Alison walked away. She thought that he could complain if he wished but she doubted if he would. Oliver would not stir up trouble that might involve him.

He had already come to that conclusion, even as he cursed her. His forehead stung but it would heal without a mark in a day or two. He shrugged it off, but with a mental note that he would settle with Alison Bailey one day. He walked into the hospital, thinking that he had told the girl he had an alibi for that time when he had sought to take her by force. That was true, but he wondered briefly now where Cuthbert Price might be. Oliver had brushed him off soon after they arrived in London five years ago, having no further use for him. As he had no use for him now.

Cuthbert was in London's opulent West End. After Oliver discarded him he had been successful only in escaping jail. He had lived, or more accurately existed, on the proceeds of petty crime. Now he was facing a choice. He was ragged, dirty, unshaven and penniless, had begged for his food for the past week and had not eaten for two days. He could go on like this, living in the gutter, pleading with an outstretched palm or . . . He knew he was not a brave man, had no desire to fight for his country, let alone die for it. But hunger won.

He stepped out of the gutter and walked into the Army recruiting office.

Oliver sat in Percy Digby's office in the hospital main building and asked, 'Why did you want me to come here at this time o' night?' He grinned with false bonhomie and made great play of taking the gold watch from his waistcoat pocket, opening it and peering at its face. 'It's time hard-working chaps like us were in bed.' He thought of Esme, waiting for his return, and lost some of the bonhomie. His big body filled the chair like a great ape. He glowered at Digby and now demanded, 'So, what's it about?'

Percy would not meet his eye. He muttered, 'It's got to stop.'

'What has to stop?' Oliver asked, but knew the answer.

Digby shook his head and his double chins wobbled above his wing collar. 'This – arrangement of ours. It can't go on any longer. People are asking questions, making comments. They're complaining that the stuff I'm buying from you is below standard.'

Oliver said with contempt, 'You're not going to take that sort of thing from a few nurses.'

'Of course not.' Digby shared his contempt for them. 'But it isn't just nurses. Some of the surgeons have complained. Two have even suggested there might be something underhand going on.'

Oliver had to stifle a grin. Underhand? Their 'arrangement' was all of that. Digby was paid to buy good supplies and equipment at a reasonable price. Oliver bought them from the cheap end of the market and sold them on to Digby. They both took a share of the profit.

'Anyway, it's becoming too risky so we can't go on with it.' Digby sat up straight, his hands splayed on his desk. He tried to look determined. 'I wanted you to know as soon as I'd decided.'

'You can't stop,' said Oliver. 'There's too much money involved.'

'I don't care about the money,' Digby said quickly. He had feared the conversation might take this turn.

'You've cared enough to take it until now.' Oliver's glare was malevolent.

Digby's eyes shifted frantically; he was frightened now.

Then there was an interruption that saved him. Whistles shrilled in the corridor outside and he jumped to his feet.

Oliver also stood. 'What the hell is that?'

'Warning. Air raid,' Digby gabbled. 'I have to go on duty.' He seized his opportunity and ran from the office.

Oliver cursed and followed. He had not finished with Digby.

Alison heard the whistles and they set her heart thumping. She ran to the main building, passing the searchlight crew who were gathering around their light, the corporal bawling orders. She climbed the flights of stairs winding up through the hospital, emerging at last on the roof. The steep-pitched inverted Vs of the tiles lifted on either side of her but there were timber walkways for the use of workmen when moving about on the roof. There was also a platform at one point and here she found Percy Digby.

He was clinging to the railing round the platform, still breathing stertorously from his ascent. He nodded curtly at Alison. 'Ah! There you are, nurse. I think everything is in order.'

'Yes, Mr Digby.' She thought there was precious little to be in order, just half a dozen sandbags and two buckets filled with water. These were intended to be used to put out incendiary bombs and fires.

Digby gradually recovered his breath as they waited and watched. Others had climbed the stairs and were occupying similar platforms. Alison and Digby could see them as black silhouettes against the dark blue of the night sky. A moon showed fitfully through scattered clouds.

They heard the sharp bark of gunfire from the direction of the coast and Digby muttered, 'Somebody can see him.'

There was a lull, all of them straining their eyes, then a ragged shout went up, excited but fearful: 'There he is!'

The huge silver airship suddenly emerged from the concealing clouds and Alison saw the frightening length of it, saw something fall from it. It seemed to pass right overhead and she could see the gondola that held the flight crew hanging beneath it. The Zeppelin passed in seeming silence, the sound of its engine covered by the racketting gunfire all around them. But she heard the explosion, saw the leap of flame at the end of the roof, realised a bomb of some sort had hit the building. She stared down the valley between the two pitched roofs and saw flames there still.

Digby shouted, 'Incendiary! I'll see to it! You wait here and watch for others.' He picked up one of the sandbags and started along the walkway leading towards the fire. He cut a strange figure in his striped trousers, spats showing white in the darkness. Then he was lost in the gloom.

So was the Zeppelin. Alison peered about her but the airship was hidden in the clouds again. Lacking a target, the gunfire had stopped. In the silence she could hear the voice of the searchlight corporal, faint with distance, raging. She wondered what had angered him, then realised the light had not lit up the Zeppelin; some member of the searchlight's crew had blundered and would be on a charge in the morning.

Now a single gun fired. Alison jumped at the shock of it and whirled around. The Zeppelin was returning, sliding out of the cloud cover, passing right overhead again. She turned once more as the corporal shouted and this time she heard him clearly: 'Expose!' The searchlight crackled into life and pointed its long finger of a brilliant white beam at the sky and the Zeppelin. It also provided a background of light for figures moving at the end of the roof where the bomb had fallen. Alison made out the portly shape of Percy Digby. She thought he was throwing sand on the flames but now another silhouette appeared, seemingly from another walkway, to come up behind Digby. This one was big-bodied and short-legged with long arms. She thought, *Oliver Crawshaw!*

She wondered – how had he come to be on the roof? But that did not matter now. He was grappling with Digby. Alison ran along the walkway towards them, shouting, 'Stop!' That was lost in the din of the gunfire. The struggling figures were there for a second or two, then Digby fell off the roof, thrown from it by Oliver.

Alison ran on, horrified by what she had seen. The Zeppelin had moved on and the searchlight beam followed it. The roof was plunged into darkness. She had to slow her pace and watch where she trod. She stopped at the end of the roof and peered about her cautiously, but there was no sign of Oliver. She concluded he had run off along one of the walkways. There would be no finding him now but she would see he was hunted down and paid the price for this murder.

Alison saw the incendiary bomb that Digby had smothered with sand. His prompt action had prevented the fire spreading. It was dead now but would have to wait until it cooled before it could be moved. She peeped over the end of the roof but saw only a black chasm. Digby's body would be down there. He could not have survived a fall from that height. Nevertheless, she ran down the stairs, breathlessly reported to a surgeon what she had seen, and went with him and two porters to look for Digby.

They searched for him by torchlight and found him lying

on a tarmac roadway. The surgeon examined him and said, 'Dead on impact.'

Alison told her story to a policeman, Inspector Davies. He was an elderly man, brought out of retirement because of younger policemen having gone to the war. He had a hatred of suffragettes and 'clever women'. He seemed reluctant to believe Alison. 'Are you sure about this – attack? Could he have just fallen off the roof? This was going on in the middle of an air raid. And why d'you suppose this Mr Crawshaw should commit murder?'

'I don't know,' Alison confessed.

Davies pursed his lips, unimpressed. He put away his notebook and said grudgingly, 'Thank you, Miss. I'll deal with this.'

Alison was left to ponder on what the outcome might be. She also realised, belatedly, that as Oliver had murdered Digby then he might just as easily have thrown her off the roof. She shuddered.

He had reached the same conclusion much earlier, as he ran down the stairs to make his escape. He cursed because he had not settled with that bloody girl. He had had his chance up on the roof, could have done for her for good. It had been her shrieks and her charging at him that had caused him to flee. She was a thorn in his flesh.

He left the hospital without being seen, its corridors darkened because of the air raid. He had gone there by cab but he walked away; he did not want any cab driver to remember him leaving at this time. The man he wanted to see lived a mile away in a large suburban house. By the time he arrived outside it the air raid was over. He knew Theodore Stamford's ways, picked his way through the garden and up to the french windows of the study. The curtains were drawn but he put his eye to a crack between them and saw Stamford sitting in a leather armchair before the fire.

Oliver rapped on the glass with his knuckles. Stamford turned to look towards the windows and half rose then paused, uncertain. Oliver rapped again, impatiently and harder. Now Stamford came to the window and dragged back the curtains. Seeing Oliver, he opened the window and invited, 'Come in. I wasn't expecting you, or anybody else for that matter.' He glanced at the clock on the mantelpiece.

Oliver shoved past him. 'Digby kept later hours than you do.' He went to stand in front of the fire, looking down on the other man, who had returned to his armchair.

'Digby?' Stamford's brows arched in interrogation.

Oliver did not answer him. The room suggested strength with its darkly polished, leather upholstered furniture. The walls were lined with leather bound books that had never been opened. Oliver thought it was like Stamford: all show. He was tall and distinguished in appearance with a firm jaw and wearing a silk smoking jacket.

Oliver said, 'If the police come asking questions you tell them I was here with you for the last two hours. Tell them you let me in the way you just did; that's why your staff didn't see me.'

Stamford's smile disappeared. 'Steady on, that's perjury. I can't—'

'You will,' Oliver cut in on him, brutally. 'We're all in this together, you, me and the rest. And don't try to oil out of it like Digby did. You can't get on and off when you like. It's not a bloody motor omnibus.' That was because Stamford was involved in the same swindles.

He asked again, his jaw not so firm now, 'Digby?'

'He had an accident.'

Stamford asked, fearing the answer, 'What sort of – accident?'

'Fatal.' Oliver let that sink in, saw the colour drain from Stamford's face at the implied threat. He knew he had his man and said, 'I knew I could rely on you.' He left as he had come, by the french windows.

Inspector Davies told Alison, 'I've questioned Mr Crawshaw and he wasn't near the hospital that night. It's borne out by a business acquaintance of his, so I think you may have been mistaken.' Alison made to speak but he held up a hand. 'This unfortunate death occured at night, when the light was bad and fluctuating and you were probably highly strung by the events around you.' He smiled stiffly.

'You mean I imagined it.' Alison was flushed and angry.

His smile stayed in place. He had discussed the case with his docile, worshipping wife and daughters the previous evening. 'The poor girl was overwrought, of course, being out on the roof in the middle of an air raid! But that's how there are sometimes miscarriages of justice, with people swearing as to what they *think* they saw.'

Now he said, 'You certainly did not see Mr Crawshaw.'

Alison gave her evidence at the inquest but the coroner was more sympathetic to the Inspector, a man of his own age and convictions as regarded women. His verdict was, 'Death by misadventure.'

Alison came away from the hearing bitter and angry at this lamentable failure of justice. Oliver Crawshaw had escaped again. During all these weeks Richard had been at the back of her mind, emerging now and then to give her a sense of unease. She thought of him now. He had also suffered from a miscarriage of justice. She had been wrong in blaming him for the letter written to Pamela Baldwin. He had been right when he warned her against Julian.

Now she lay in her bed in the hostel, listening to the breathing and small noises of the other four girls who shared it. She wondered about the other times they had ended up in a blazing row. As children they had played together so surely they could get on now? But she could remember altercations even then. She could not sleep for the memory of his wry grin and tall figure.

One thing was certain, he was due an apology. With that decision she turned over and slept.

She posted her letter to him, entrusted to the Army's post office to forward, the next day. Two weeks later she sailed for Mesopotamia and the port of Basra.

13

Sunderland, September 1915.

'*Fire!*' The shriek came a second after the explosion and rang through the prison kitchen. It had been steamy and clangorous but was now filling with smoke. Matthew Grant, Alison's imprisoned father, had just entered. He was grey-haired, not tall but broad and powerful in the drab prison uniform. He saw the blaze from an oil stove that had blown up. Now a wall of flame ran across from wall to wall. The prisoners working in there fell back from the heat of it, crowded to get out of the door. Matthew fought clear of them, let them go. He could see there were men on the other side of the flames, trapped with no way out.

Matthew knew his way around the kitchen; he had had plenty of time to learn. There was a pile of empty sacks by the vegetable store and a sink filled with water for washing the cabbages and potatoes. He dumped an armful of sacks in the sink, soaking them. Then he wrapped one about his head, leaving a crack to enable him to see and tucked the others under his arm. He took a deep breath and ran at the fire. There was a second of infernal flame, sucking the air from his lungs, but then he was through.

There were three men in the fire trap, two prisoners and a warder, all of them cowering back from the heat and coughing on the smoke. He shoved sacks at them and bawled, 'Put them on! Like this!' He showed them, coughing himself now, lungs burning, eyes smarting and weeping. They were ready. He coughed, 'Come on!' They hesitated. The wall of flame was leaping higher. He knew if they did not go now they would die in there.

He seized the front of the warder's jacket, shouted, 'Now!' And ran at the wall. Again that airless heat but then they were out of it, coughing and eyes watering but with the fire behind them. Matthew thrust the warder towards the door and the safety beyond it, turned and looked for the other two and saw them still trapped, afraid to make the passage through the flames.

His sack was smouldering. He tossed it aside and plunged another into the sink, wrapped it about him and charged at the fire once more. This time he stumbled and almost fell in that hell, knew the awful fear of being burned alive, but recovered and ran on and into the smoke-filled trap. The men he had come for were crouched against the wall, as far as they could get from the fire. Desperate, he grabbed one with each hand and set out – for one last time; he knew there would not be another chance.

They were small men and weak. He was able to hustle them through the fiery curtain against their will. When one tripped and fell he dragged him along like one of the sacks, disregarding his shrieks. Out of the fire, he shoved them ahead of him to the doorway and into the blessed open air. They went down on their knees, heads hanging, and breathed it.

All of them were taken to the prison hospital, but none were badly burned, due to Matthew's swift and determined action. He had served twenty years of his sentence and in gratitude they set him free, gave him a few shillings and a train ticket to Sunderland. He thanked God for his deliverance. He had not been a religious man but in twenty years he had learned to pray for his soul and his sanity, not always in that order.

He returned to Sunderland in trepidation but hope. He

stepped down from the train on his fiftieth birthday. When he had gone into prison he had left a wife and a daughter to survive as best they might. He had never received a letter from them. He set out to find them, starting with the rooms where they had lived, in the East End of the town. The old neighbours had died or gone away and no one knew where Doreen and her daughter had gone. He wandered about the town, without hope now, but doggedly asking, asking.

He came closest when he met Billy Middlemiss on the Monkwearmouth shore of the River Wear. Billy came out of the Pear Tree, a public house, wiping his mouth on the back of his hand. Matthew was passing and Billy stared, then called, 'Is that you, Matt?'

'Aye.' They shook hands, Billy awkwardly, not sure what to say.

He settled for speaking his mind. 'By, lad! It's grand to see you. How are you getting on?'

Matthew explained how and why he had been released from prison. He did not say he had been innocent and Billy would not have believed him because he had also been in that London pub when Matthew fought with Sean Rafferty, and killed him. He did tell Billy of his search for his wife and daughter.

Billy shook his head. 'I don't know where they went.' He stopped there, but had obviously been about to say more.

Matthew pressed him. 'If you're keeping something back, Billy, spit it out. I want to know.'

Billy admitted reluctantly, 'I heard Doreen had done a flit – with another feller.' Matt took this in. Now he knew what he had suspected, why he had never had a letter. Billy saw he was hit hard, and tried to console him. 'You're better off without her.'

So there was more. Matthew said, 'What else, Billy?'

Billy sighed. 'Sean wasn't the only one. There were two or three other fellers I knew of.'

Now Matthew faced his worst suspicion, that he had fought to disbelieve. Sean Rafferty had only spoken the truth. Matthew had served twenty years for nothing.

He thanked Billy heavily and went on. Now he was trying to find his little girl, now become a woman, and afraid of what he would find.

In the end he had to give up the search for the time being. His few shillings now reduced to pennies, he had to work. The German U-boats were sinking ships and drowning their crews every day. Seamen were desperately needed for the new ships being turned out of the yards on both sides of the River Wear. He signed on in a vessel carrying coal to Argentina and sailed for Buenos Aires.

'Fire!' The shouted order came down on the wind to Captain Richard Tarrant where he crouched in the trench. A split second later came the *crack*! of the 18-pounder field guns of the battery close by. A landing on the Gallipoli peninsula had been made months earlier. The intention had been to force the straits of the Dardanelles and knock Turkey, Germany's ally, out of the war. The attempt had failed. Now there were orders for evacuation and that could be a disaster. This was the season for storms that could make embarkation difficult, if not impossible.

Richard was on his way to tend to a badly wounded man who was trapped by a fall of earth and could not be taken to the Casualty Clearing Station. As the shells whined away towards the Turkish lines he started to make his way forward along the support trench. It had rained for the past week and he waded through mud that came up to his knees. The trench was under fire from the guns of a Turkish battery, detonations of falling shells shaking the earth and showering him with dirt. He kept on, breathing the soldier's prayer: 'Not in the face or the guts, Oh Lord.'

He found his patient. A group of soldiers were furiously digging in the entrance to a dugout. This was a cave in the side of the trench, walled and roofed with timbers. A direct hit had collapsed it and the man was trapped between two of its timbers. The diggers stopped work and drew back to let Richard enter the cave they had reopened. He crawled into the narrow, low-roofed passage, his shoulders scraping each side, his head bumping on the ceiling of earth.

'Now then, old chap, let's see what we can do for you.' He tried to sound confident, encouraging. His patient did not reply so he used his torch, then sighed and backed out into the air again. He told the waiting men wearily, 'He's gone, I'm afraid.'

One of them said, 'He hasn't said anything for ten minutes.'

And another, 'Well, you tried, sir. Thank you.'

Richard made his way back to the Casualty Clearing Station, a collection of khaki tents, their roofs marked with huge red crosses, joined by pathways of duckboards laid on the mud. Rain was falling again, soaking him, filling the pools between the duckboards. He squelched into the little tent in which he lived and sat down on his camp bed.

An orderly poked his head in at the open flap to say, 'There was a letter for you when the post came up, sir.' He passed the envelope to Richard.

'Thank you.' He took it eagerly and turned it over in his hands. He saw with disappointment that it was not from his guardians; he knew their writing very well and did not recognise this. Nor was it from Delia. He rarely had a letter from her and tried to blame the postal service. This was not her erratic, let's-get-it-over-with, impatient scrawl. It was a firm, bold hand. He opened it and glanced at the signature, was surprised to see it came from Alison Bailey. He remembered their last meeting. Surely she was not resorting to the mail to upbraid him for some imagined wrong?

He sighed and commenced to read. 'Dear Captain Tarrant, I owe you an apology . . .' His eyebrows lifted and he went on. She told how she had learned the true sender of the letter she had attributed to him, expressed her regret and concluded, 'I hope we may meet again in happier circumstances and forget the petty quarrels of the past. I pray for your safe return.'

He read it again. He thought she had not found it easy to write. It was a stiff little note from a stiff-necked little – He grinned. But she had written it and wished him well.

The orderly appeared at the flap of the tent again. 'Wounded coming in, sir.'

'Right.' Richard tucked the letter away in his pocket. He would write a reply when he had time.

The rain had become a deluge, beating on the roof of the operating tent as he worked into the night. As one man was treated and taken away another replaced him on the table. Richard first realised the danger when he noticed that the duckboards on which he stood were submerged, would have floated away if his weight had not been there to hold them down. The tent was flooding. He ordered, 'We have to get out of here and find some high ground!'

It was a nightmare manoeuvre, moving the wounded men in the pouring rain and through the mud. Dugouts filled with mud and water and became watery graves for the men sheltering in them. Trenches became rivers and men had to swim for their lives. Horse-drawn ambulances were overturned and handcarts washed away. Richard and his orderlies fought for the wounded and saved most of them, but for some it was one privation too many.

After twelve hours the storm abated and Richard crawled

into a capsized ambulance to sleep. In the grey light he tore a page from his notebook and wrote. 'My dear Alison.' He paused, thinking, *My dear?* Why had he written that? A little too affectionate? Would this prickly girl think it presumptuous? But he was weary to the point of exhaustion. He let it stand, went on to thank her for writing and echoed her hope that they would meet again in better circumstances. He looked around the inside of the ambulance, filthy from the storm, still blood-stained, and thought, *that should be easy*.

He slept and later returned to his swamped and mud-caked tent. He found an envelope, miraculously dry in his writing case, and posted the letter. He sent it to the only address he knew, that of the Alison's Cookshop on the sea front. He thought she would receive it there or it would be forwarded.

It was all for naught.

Some weeks later, Moira Grindly woke in the kitchen of the Cookshop where she slept and heard a letter fall inside the front door. Curiosity sent her to examine it and she saw Richard's name and military address on the reverse. Moira had been glad to take the job and shelter Alison had offered her, but was not grateful, resenting the necessity. She always remembered that she had once had the ordering of Alison. Now she looked at the letter and curled her lip. 'Some man of hers. She's officers' baggage.'

She tore the letter to shreds and threw the pieces in the flames of the stove.

Like many another man at that time of danger and tension, Richard was thinking with a part of his mind of a woman. It was not Delia but Alison who occupied his thoughts. He wondered if she had received his letter and whether she would reply. Not that it mattered to him, of course. But it was her face he could not get out of his mind.

On Gallipoli the night evacuation of the peninsula was almost complete. Richard had volunteered to stay until the last, to attend to any wounded if the Turks attacked. So far, it seemed, they had not realised what was going on, though a three-quarter moon made the night near as light as day. He stood outside the temporary Casualty Clearing Station he had set up behind the beach. He looked out on a flat, oily sea. The steamers that were the transports lay offshore, while lighters swarmed along the water's edge and ferried the troops out to the ships.

It was time to go. They had suffered heavy casualties in this ill-fated expedition. In these final days Richard had seen men tending the graves of the comrades they had to leave behind them, carefully lettering in the part-worn, painted names, raking the mounds. Now the last of the riflemen were coming down. There was a mist on the crests of the hills and threading down into the valleys. The men came out of it silently, in single file, rifles slung over their shoulders. They moved like wraiths down to the lighters. Flames sprang up from the bonfires of abandoned stores being destroyed.

Richard led his party of orderlies down to the shore by the light of the flames. A lighter, packed with men standing shoulder to shoulder, took them out to a waiting steamer. He climbed aboard and as the ship got under way he turned his back on Gallipoli.

It had been a nightmare experience. There had been 200,000 casualties, dead, wounded and sick.

The ship carried him to Alexandria and there he was given two weeks' leave, mainly spent eating and sleeping. He finally received a letter from Delia. It was light and thin and he fingered it with a sense of foreboding. There was only a single sheet of stationery, with the name of the hotel at its head.

Delia said she was sure he would understand, she was fond
of him and they could always be friends, but she had fallen
in love with a brigadier general who needed her.

Richard thought wryily that it sounded like a bloody funny
patriotism. He found he was not surprised, and didn't care.
He had thought he loved Delia, but now . . . He tore up the
letter.

His colonel sent for him. 'Richard! You're being posted
to Mesopotamia. I think you will be busy. The Expeditionary
Force there has fought its way up almost to Baghdad, but
now I hear they're pulling back.'

Richard thought, *not again*. He had just come from the
evacuation of Gallipoli, was now threatened with another
withdrawal.

He wished he had had a letter from Alison.

Mesopotamia. December 1915.

She thought of him. Alison was reminded of Richard when
she saw the captain in the Medical Corps, briefly, in the
crowd of soldiers flooding into the town of Kut el Amara
on the bank of the River Tigris. But then she saw this captain was shorter, older, harassed. She felt a pang of disappointment, then told herself not to be such a fool; the last
she had heard of Richard he had been bound for Gallipoli.
He had not replied to her letter but she supposed his might
have been lost. Or he was nursing old grievances, though
she found that hard to believe. Still, she had offered an olive
branch. It was nothing to her if he did not accept it.

Now she was a part of the Expeditionary Force fighting
the Turks in Mesopotamia. She was tired, dirty, wet,
hungry and thirsty. The stifling heat of the summer had
given way to cold and the rain that fell on her now. The
Force had fought a battle, and won it, only twenty miles

from Baghdad, but had then had to retreat as Turkish reinforcements came up. Alison had been told they would make a stand at Kut el Amara, roughly half-way between Baghdad and Basra.

She had brought downriver a score of wounded in a *maheilah*, a native craft converted to an amphibious ambulance. Bow and stern rose high like those of a Viking ship and her prow was painted like an illuminated manuscript. But the tall mast and triangular sail had been taken out of her and the well boarded over to make a continuous deck. Alison thought of the vessel as Noah's Ark.

A launch had towed the Ark this far but then left them to return upstream. Alison's orders had been to put her wounded ashore in the hospital but she had found it full to overflowing. The twenty wounded men were her responsibility and she would not leave them here. She had a map, taken from an officer who had died. She looked at it again now, but only to confirm what she remembered of the country, learned during the earlier advance when she passed this way. Kut lay in a bend of the snaking river. Alison knew she had to get her charges out of there. But how?

There was a tugboat approaching the shore now, big paddle-wheels in their boxes, one on either side, churning the water of the river. Her hull was scabby with rust but her name was lettered on her stubby bow in paint of red and gold: *Maid of Wallsend*. She towed two open lighters packed with weary troops. They turned thirsty faces up to the rain; water had been in short supply for some time.

As Alison watched despairingly, the tugboat slid in to the jetty and those big paddle-wheels thrashed in reverse, slowing her. She rubbed against the jetty and stopped. The lighters drifted in with the last of the way on them and men on bow and stern caught the mooring lines thrown to them. Alison thought it had been neatly done. Once the lighters were

secured to the jetty the troops began to disembark. Alison
wondered . . . ?

Private Tweddle, long and lugubrious and the senior of
the three medical orderlies, came bustling to say breathlessly,
'I've got to get these wounded ashore and into the hospital.'

'It's full,' Alison told him, her eyes on the tugboat.

'That don't make no difference,' Tweddle argued worriedly. 'My orders was to put 'em ashore here.'

'Your orders were to take them to a place of safety in Kut,'
she contradicted him.

'Aye,' he admitted, 'and that's what I'm going to do.'

'There isn't a place of safety in Kut. If you put them
ashore you'll be responsible for anything that happens to
them.'

He hesitated, uncertain now, as Alison had known he would
be if she mentioned responsibility. He passed it to her. 'So
what are we going to do?'

'You wait here.' Alison hurried through the rain to the
tugboat. There were Arabs working aboard her and there
was a gangplank – literally that, a plank not a foot wide –
reaching from the shore to the deck. Alison edged along it
cautiously, only too well aware of the brown flood waiting
for her below. Safely across she asked of the nearest Arab,
'Captain?'

'No,' said a voice behind her. 'I am.'

Alison turned. A head was poked out of the wheelhouse
window, a brown, leathery face with watery blue eyes topped
with flyaway, wiry grey hair bushing out from under a man's
cap. But this was a woman's face, an old woman who
reminded Alison of her grandmother, Francie Bailey. This
one was smaller but the likeness gave her confidence to go
on. 'Have you got another tow?'

'Who are you? And what's your business?'

'Alison Bailey. I'm a nurse. I—'

'I can see that! Damned great red cross on your apron.'
She swung down out of the wheelhouse to stand on the deck,
the top of her head barely reaching Alison's shoulder. She
wore a white cotton dress, grey and stained with age, like
her man's cap. She held out a hand grimed with oil and soot.
'Winnie Tunstall. And we're both from the same part of the
world, from what I hear.'

'Monkwearmouth in Sunderland,' Alison agreed.

'I was born and bred in Newcastle,' Winnie nodded, keen
eyes weighing up the girl. 'So why are you asking if I have
a tow? As it happens, I haven't.'

Alison explained about the wounded. 'I want to take them
down river to a hospital there.'

A man came stumping aft, short and stocky on bowed
legs, in a navy blue jersey and trousers held up by a four-
inch wide leather belt under his jutting belly.

Winnie introduced him, 'This is Jimmy, my engineer. He's
from Shields but apart from that he's all right.' And to him,
'Alison here wants me to tow a *maheilah* full o' wounded
down river.'

'That sounds like a good idea to me,' he said dourly.
'Johnny Turk is on his way.'

'Aye,' said Winnie. 'That's what I was thinking.' She
explained, 'My man brought this tug out from the Tyne
thirty years ago. When he died I took over as skipper. Jimmy
has always been our engineer.' And, severely, 'It's a
respectable arrangement, you understand.'

Alison murmured that she had no doubt of it and hastened back to the worried Private Tweddle. 'We're going to
be towed by that tugboat.'

He said uneasily, 'Are you sure it'll be all right?'

'My responsibility,' said Alison, and he accepted that with
relief.

An hour later the *Maid of Wallsend* was butting down-

stream with the Noah's Ark in tow. Alison had come up onto
the deck of the *maheilah* for a break and breathed deeply of
the air after the antiseptic and sickroom odours below. Night
was falling and in the gathering dusk she could see how the
river, fringed by palms, ran through a marshland of water
and reeds. She felt some relief; they had a long way to go
but they were clear of Kut and moving.

Five minutes later they rounded a bend in the river and
she saw the tiny figures of men, beyond the palms and where
the marsh ended. She stared at them, wondering. Then there
was a prickle of flame and the crackle of rifle fire. She heard
the clang and drone as bullets struck the tugboat and rico-
cheted. A screech of outrage came from Winnie aboard the
Maid of Wallsend. Alison's heart sank. The Turks had got
ahead of them.

The tugboat turned around tightly, one paddle-wheel going
ahead, the other astern, and headed back up river, fleeing
from that fusillade. The Ark turned after it, dragging at the
end of the towing hawser. A few shots buzzed over Alison's
head, then the firing stopped as both vessels rounded the
bend again and were out of sight of the Turks. The paddle-
wheels stopped turning, the way came off the tugboat and
her anchor splashed down.

Tweddle popped up from below and asked wide-eyed,
'Wasn't that somebody firing?' Then, when Alison nodded,
'We'll have to go back to Kut.'

'No.' That was a gut reaction. She told him again, 'Wait.'

The Ark was drifting down with the last of her way to
nudge the rusty stern of the tugboat. One of the Arab crew
held it there with a grip on the hawser. Alison hitched up
her skirts and climbed aboard the tugboat. Winnie stood by
the wheelhouse, talking to Jimmy, who was rubbing his hands
on a lump of cotton waste. She looked round as Alison
arrived. 'This is a turn up.'

'What are you going to do?' Alison asked anxiously. 'Go back to Kut?'

'Not likely,' said Winnie, and Jimmy shook his head determinedly.

He went on, 'The Turks are around Kut and nobody will be leaving. We're going through here when it's dark. They fired rifles but not a gun so they probably don't have one. Tomorrow they will and there'll be no way through.'

Winnie asked of Alison, 'What do you want to do? We haven't the time to tow you back to Kut.'

Alison shook her head. 'We'll go on.'

She returned to the Ark and told Tweddle, 'We're going to slip past them when it's full dark.'

He nibbled at his lip. 'If they don't see us, they'll hear us. Can't we—?'

'If they can't see us they won't hit us,' Alison cut him off. She was tired and worried but sure she was choosing the right course. Tweddle would dither. She gave him something to do. 'Make sure they won't see us. Cover all the hatches so we don't show any light.' With the hatches shut the inside of the Ark would be airless and stifling but that could not be helped.

They moved again, dark and silent, when the night covered them. Alison went below and told her charges the facts and her intention. They accepted stoically that they might come under fire again. It was a minor matter compared to the pain of their wounds. She and the orderlies gave them aspirin to ease that pain as the *Maid of Wallsend* got under way again, towing the Ark astern of her.

She moved slowly ahead so there was hardly a bow wave or wake to mark her passing or provide a target for the Turks. She slipped round the bend again, keeping close to the bank away from them. Ten minutes passed before they heard her. Then there was a single shot followed by a volley, but no

bullet came near the tugboat or the Ark. Alison knelt by one
of the cots below and thought, *so far, so good*. But then there
came the shriek of a shell and a hammer blow against the
hull. She thought, *Oh God! They've brought up a gun!*

She made herself smile down at the man – just a boy,
really – in the cot. His mouth worked but he smiled back at
her and gripped her hand. She held it as the tugboat steamed
on, paddle-wheels threshing, while the gun on the shore
barked again and again. When tug and tow grounded on a
sandbank she held the smile, too, but turned her head so all
the men could see her. Then they grated over the obstruc-
tion and went on. The Turkish riflemen fired one last volley
then were silent.

Tweddle squeaked, 'We've done it!'

The men in their narrow cots forgot their pain for a
moment and cheered. One called, 'Three for Alison!' They
cheered her and she laughed, with huge relief rather than
triumph. She found her hand bloodless from the boy's grasp.
He smiled up at her and she kissed him. She thought it was
probably professionally unethical but they had survived
together. She could have kissed all of them.

Alison discharged her wounded into a hospital at Amara,
a hundred miles from Kut as the crow flies but twice that
following the snaking course of the Tigris. She had got
them out of the trap that Kut had become, that she and
Winnie had foreseen. After a long siege the starving gar-
rison had to surrender and were marched into captivity.
Few survived.

She bade farewell to the *Maid of Wallsend*, the skipper and
engineer. Jimmy patted her back and said gruffly, 'You're a
canny lass, Alison. One o' the best. Those lads were lucky
having you to look after them. They might ha' been left in
Kut to rot. I suppose there's a young feller waiting for you.
He's a lucky man.'

Alison denied it. 'No! There's no man.' She was sure of that but felt herself blush.

Winnie smiled knowingly, hugged her and said softly, 'Good luck, bonny lass.'

The hospital at Amara took Alison as well as her wounded and gave her a medical ward. Instead of surgical cases she was nursing men suffering from the fevers that were rife and some were dying. One of her new patients was a straw-haired young man: Private Cuthbert Price.

At first she could not believe it was him, though she recognised him on sight, this despite the passage of time, his haggard face and skeletal body. And there was his name printed on his chart. 'Cuthbert! Do you remember me?' She greeted him with pleasure as someone from home, a happier time.

He did, but showed no enthusiasm. 'Aye. Alison Bailey, isn't it?' His head rolled on the pillow, looking away. He offered no conversation, answered questions in monosyllables, if at all.

Nevertheless, Alison took him under her wing for old times' sake and tended him. She cared all the more when it became obvious that he was dying. She fought for his life but lost. He was dying not just from the fever but because he had nothing to live for. He lay and waited for the end.

Some of his comrades came to visit him and brought him small gifts of cigarettes. They were from Newcastle and called him 'Cuddy'. When Alison asked why, they said, 'He's a bit simple, and a cuddy is a donkey. And he's daft about horses. He volunteered for the cavalry but they put him in the infantry. It's good o' you to look after him like you do, miss.'

Alison said to him later, sitting at his bedside in a moment when she was free of duties, 'You're fond of horses, aren't you?' She hoped it would stir him to life.

It brought a smile to his face. 'Aye. A horse is a good friend.' And then, 'Like you. I don't deserve you.'

'I want you to get better.'

The fragile smile had gone now. 'You don't know—' He stopped and withdrew his hand from hers.

'What don't I know?'

His mouth worked. 'I was always thieving, right from school. The only honest work was with the horses. Your money – Francie's money that she kept in that old tea caddy – I saw her putting it away one day, and when she died I took nearly all of it. I didn't dare touch it before because I knew she would see some of it had gone. When she died I was sure you wouldn't know how much there should be, so I just left a few coppers.' He rubbed away tears with the back of his hand, a weak gesture. He whispered, 'I'm so ashamed.'

Alison tried to give him absolution: 'It doesn't matter now. I managed without it. Don't let it worry you.'

His hand sought hers again. 'Thank you.' It was a whisper. He died three days later, quietly in the night.

Richard came in a crowded troopship carrying reinforcements, steaming in past the oil installations on Abadan Island and into the port of Basra. He worked in the hospital there while Alison was in Amara, all through 1916 as the Expeditionary Force was built up. He went upriver for the final advance and the taking of Baghdad in March 1917. So did Alison. At that time they were only a half a mile apart but neither one knew of the other.

Alison was posted home in the autumn of that year. She travelled downriver from Amara aboard a river steamer, sitting in a deckchair under the awning. She saw the other steamer coming up river and watched as it came abreast, ready to wave as was the custom. Then with shock she saw that one of the figures leaning on the rail of the other steamer was a tall young captain in the Medical Corps. In the space of a heartbeat she was at the rail of her own craft and waving. She saw him wave, startled, and smile. Her heart turned over. He felt a flood of desire. Then it was over in seconds and the gap between them rapidly widening.

14

Sunderland, October 1917.

~~~~~~~~~~

'Alison!' Dolly Maguire squeaked the name. 'You're a sight for sore eyes. Come here, pet, and let me look at you. Moira! See who's here!' She ran around the counter of the sea-front Cookshop, threw her arms around Alison and hugged her. Then she held her at arm's length to eye her. 'You're looking a picture, brown as a berry.'

Alison had dropped her cases to hold Dolly and now laughed. She had just come from a Mesopotamian summer. 'Plenty of sunshine, too much, in fact. And plenty of cold and rain in the winter.'

'You're thinner,' said Dolly, but then added, 'It suits you; you're blooming. Your flat upstairs is ready for you.' She had written to Alison, telling her that Thelma had moved to Blyth with her husband, who had a new job in the shipyard there. Dolly had kept on her own rooms. 'I've given it an airing nearly every day.' Then she remembered her manners. 'Will you make us all a cup of tea, Moira love?'

'Aye,' said Moira, who had come through from the kitchen and smiled mechanically.

Alison sat down at a table and looked about her. The Cookshop was empty.

Dolly sighed and took a seat beside her. 'Nobody buying and we've practically nothing to sell. Butter, sugar, meat — everything's been short. I go to Cadwallader's and he just shakes his head. Mind, I think he has stuff hidden in the back that he could let us have, but he won't.'

Cadwalladder's was the wholesaler who had supplied them, but Alison suspected Harold Cadwalladder was nursing a grudge because she had bested him in an argument when she had first gone to him for supplies.

Dolly was going on, 'We had to shut down the other places because we weren't earning enough to cover the rents. We're only just keeping this one going. But I told you all that.' Dolly had written regularly, detailing how the Cookshops were faring. 'I'm sorry, lass, but I did the best I could.'

'Not your fault.' Alison squeezed her hand. 'It's just this war.' She had long since accepted that her little chain of restaurants had gone. Never mind; she would forge it again when this war was over – if ever. It had to end sometime, surely? She said nothing of this. Weren't they celebrating her return? And she was in a buoyant mood and wondered why? She asked casually, 'Are there any letters for me?'

Moira brought the tea, pot and cups rattling on a tray.

Dolly shook her head. 'Were you expecting one?'

'No,' said Alison. A better word would have been 'hoped'. She had written to Richard and posted the letter before she sailed from Basra. She had told him she was going home. *You might care to write to me. I would like to hear from you.* She had given him the address on the sea front. Now she reminded herself of the vagaries of the postal service in Mesopotamia; a letter from there might well take months to arrive. If he had written. She changed the subject quickly. 'I have two weeks' leave, then I have to report to a hospital in London. Sit down, Moira. We can all spare a few minutes.'

But Moira muttered, 'Got a lot to do.' She hurried away to hide back in the kitchen. The mention of letters as she brought in the tea had set the cups rattling.

'She doesn't seem too well,' said Alison. 'Her hands were shaking.'

'That's a new one,' Dolly shrugged. 'She's always got something wrong with her. She's still doing a day's work but that's only because she's afraid of the workhouse.'

Alison decided Dolly had little sympathy for Moira and could understand that. She also thought that Dolly had aged, but she would be sixty or close to it now and these war years had prematurely aged a lot of people.

Alison spent her leave in resting, interspersed with long walks along the shore where she and Richard had played as children. She found she remembered a lot more about those far off days than she would have thought. She also wandered down to the river by the Folly End, where Francie had taken her so long ago. Looking out over the Wear she could see the activity in the shipyards on both banks. This was the biggest shipbuilding town in the world and its yards were working flat out to replace the ships being sunk by the U-boats. Without the ships the country would starve and the war would be lost. Starvation was close now.

Alison recalled Simon saying, 'We'll never see women building ships.' They were helping to build them now because there weren't enough men to do the jobs. There were five hundred women working in the shipyards of the River Wear.

She could think of Simon without pain now, though still with sadness. She had given him a few brief hours of happiness and had no regret for what she had done.

She did not go near Bellhanger. Dolly had told her that it had been requisitioned for use as a hospital, as had so many big houses. Clara Skilton was still living there but Alison knew no one there now except the housekeeper and had no desire to see her. There was also the memory of the night she had held old Michael Tarrant in an attempt to warm him and save his life – and the charges that had been levelled against her. That had soiled the friendship and respect that had existed between her and that sadly treated old man.

Alison visited Cadwalladder's one morning, seeking supplies. Harold Cadwalladder was leaner now, cheeks sagging, and the watch chain hung with medals drooped lower across his paunch. Alison smiled and spoke him fair but he responded coldly and sold her only a meagre amount. He said curtly, 'We're all on short commons. It's this war.'

There were two young girls helping him in the shop and Alison would not beg. She asked about his son. 'How is Brian?'

His sagging face lengthened further. 'Just gone back after embarkation leave. He's off to France. His mother's worried sick.'

'He's a good lad,' said Alison. 'Tell him I was asking after him when you write.' And she came away.

Before she travelled south again she talked to Moira. 'You don't seem too well.'

The old woman now winced and muttered as she went about her work. She was quick to say, 'Nothing wrong wi' me; just a touch o' rheumatics.'

Alison doubted that and reassured her, 'I'm not going to put you in the workhouse.'

'I'm all right, I tell you,' Moira mumbled.

Alison had to be content with that. She caught her train and took up her duties in the London hospital. She had left her address with Dolly, and the injunction, 'Send on any letter for me.'

One was delivered a week after she left, but Moira found it first and threw it in the kitchen stove. Alison went back to the long huts full of desperately wounded men, cries of pain, discordant gramophones. She was left to eat her heart out over the long weeks and months of that winter.

'What are you going to do on your leave?' Richard was often asked that by colleagues on the troopship when he came home in early March 1918. He gave various answers, including 'Go home' and 'See some shows.' He did not mention the intention foremost in his mind. He had written several more letters to Alison in the past months and did not receive an answer to any of them – for the same reason. He had not given up, though telling himself he was a fool. He reasoned that the girl had made her wishes clear by her failure to reply. She had invited him to write out of courtesy – or because they had met a long way from home. Then she had found someone else. It happened, he knew. But while he had shrugged off Delia, he did not think it would be so easy with Alison.

He spent one night at home with Geoffrey Tarrant and his wife, Felicity, his guardians, both getting on in years now and delighted to see him. He told them, 'I want to visit someone but I'll be back in a day or two.'

When he had gone, Geoffrey said, 'He didn't say who he was going to see.'

'A girl, of course,' Felicity smiled. Then, more seriously, 'Not that Delia, I'm glad to say. I was relieved when I saw she'd married that brigadier – and sorry for him.'

Richard descended from the train in the evening as a woman porter squeaked, 'Monkwearmouth! Monkwearmouth!' He carried only an overnight bag and left that at the station. There was a cab waiting outside, the horse with head hanging. It was blanketed against the rain driven in on a cold wind from the sea. The ancient cabbie, caped and capped, dripping, carried him down to the sea front. He found Alison's Cookshop in darkness, pressed his face to the glass panel in the top of the door and peered in. A crack of dim light showed in the back of the building. The door was locked and he knocked, waited, knocked again. Finally he hammered on the door with his clenched fist.

The crack of light widened and spread to show him the

counter at the back of the café. An old woman came shuffling between the oilcloth-covered tables. She wore a dress of black bombazine, scowled out at Richard and shouted at him through the glass, 'What d'ye want at this time o' night? We're shut.'

'I'm looking for Miss Alison Bailey. I had a letter from her giving this address and wrote to her, but I want to see her.'

Dolly had gone home and Moira was alone. She guessed this tall young man was the writer of the letters she had destroyed. She thought of him as some lusting lover. 'She's gone. Went weeks ago. Didn't leave no address.' And then, still lying, 'Sorry.' But she was thinking, *serve the tart right*.

Richard stood in the rain, feeling it cold on his face. He had come on a fool's errand. He asked, with little hope, 'Do you know anyone who might tell me where she is?'

Moira shook her head and embroidered her falsehood. 'She said one or two things that sounded like she was off to see a feller.'

As he had suspected. He was not surprised. She was a very attractive girl and owed him nothing. That did not save him from the pain of loss.

He said, 'Thank you. Goodnight.' He turned and walked away.

Moira watched him go and felt a twinge of doubt for the first time. But she argued again, *serve her right*. She turned her back on him, returned to the kitchen and closed the door.

Richard walked back into Monkwearmouth. There was no reason for haste now. He reclaimed his bag at the station and then boarded a train to start on the long journey south. There was nothing to keep him there.

Alison had taken to seeking shelter in the café she had used before on her free half-days. She told herself it was

comfortable and convenient. It just happened to be where
she had seen Richard passing, long ago in 1915. She sat
at her usual table one day, in the window looking out, eyes
unconsciously searching. She thought that the café's owner
was lucky to have anything to sell, though it seemed to be
only tea and toast. Richard had not written. He had waved
when the boats passed so closely, and smiled – but had he
then forgotten her? She could not write again, throw herself at him. Or could she?

He was close. His leave was almost over and he had to return
to duty in France. He had left his kit in a hotel overnight and
intended to catch a train the following day. Now he was taking
a walk, aimlessly wandering, making the most of the last hours
of his leave. He tired of it after a while, the streets teeming
with the faces of strangers. He thought he would go to a show
that night. He had been heading towards where Alison sat but
now he turned to retrace his steps. He would find a taxi and
go to St George's hospital and look up old friends.

Alison had answered her own question. She could write
and she would. She would go back to the hostel and pen a
letter to him. It would not reach him in Mesopotamia for
weeks or months but she wanted to do it and had things to
say that she had held back before. She went to the counter
to pay and found herself waiting while a loud-voiced woman
argued over her bill.

Richard saw a cab and was about to hail it but hesitated.
He had left St George's to serve in the Medical Corps nearly
four years ago. Few, if any, of his friends would be left.
Doubtless all his contemporaries would also be serving. He
had had enough of disappointments. He would not go to add
to them. He turned yet again to follow his original course. After
a minute or two he recalled that it was just about here that
Alison had pursued him and they had another of their rows.

The vociferous woman finally conceded defeat and left

the café grumbling. Alison paid her own bill and hurried out into the street, her mind on the letter she would write. It would be a way of feeling close to him.

She appeared in front of him like the work of some genie. He said, doubting the evidence of his eyes, 'Alison?' Then, sure, 'Alison!'

'Richard!' Her daydream had come to life and in the shock of it she acted on instinct. She threw her arms about his neck, to be lifted off her feet, swung around and kissed. Then they were laughing and talking, both at once, oblivious to the staring faces of the river of people that eddied past them.

Esme, voluptuous in a silken day gown that clung to her figure, asked, 'Why are we going down to the coast? Can you tell me now? And why did you ask me to put on my glad rags?' They were seated in a first class carriage on a train out of Waterloo Station.

Oliver drew on his cigar. 'I'm going to do a deal with Jameson and I want you to soften him up.'

She raised her eyebrows. 'Again?'

He nodded. 'Again.' And, ironically, 'You aren't complaining?'

Esme smiled. 'He's – enjoyable.'

'He's also skipper of a ship that brings in sugar, tea, cheese and all manner of stuff I can sell. You did very well out of the last lot.'

'True,' she admitted.

'I didn't tell you before because I didn't want you gloating in advance,' said a jealous Oliver.

'I'll make it up to you,' Esme smiled.

Richard said, 'I wrote letters to you – several of them.' They were strolling, arm in arm.

'I never got them.' Alison heard him with relief – he had written!

'I went up to Sunderland, to your place on the cliff top. I spoke to an elderly lady there and she said you'd gone and left no address. She also suggested you might have a man already.'

'No!' Alison said vehemently. 'There's no one but you.' And now she knew there had never been anyone else, not even Simon, definitely not Julian. She recognised the 'elderly lady' in Richard's recounting of his visit to Sunderland and determined she would have words with Moira – some day.

Now he was intruding on her thoughts. 'I'll buy you a ring.'

She looked up at him, not expecting this, not sure what she expected. 'A ring? Are you proposing?'

'I am.' A moment's hesitation, then, 'I'm proposing an engagement. I don't want to marry in wartime.'

She knew he meant he did not want to leave her a widow. She also knew that she wanted whatever he did. 'I'll wed you or not, as you wish.'

He bought her a ring, a plain gold band and slid it on her finger in the shop, under the gaze of the blinking saleswoman. They took a cab back to her hostel. There she talked to the other girls and arranged for an exchange of duties, so she was free the following day. She rapidly packed a case. Back in the waiting cab with Richard, she held his hand as the trotting horse carried them to his hotel.

He registered at reception. 'My wife has been able to join me.' He eyed the clerk, daring him to question, while Alison rested her hand on the desk, the ring plainly visible.

'Thank you, sir. Good evening, madam.'

They ascended in the lift, a fresh-faced pageboy at the controls, and they held hands behind his back. The porter brought up Alison's case and Richard tipped him. Then they were alone at last.

Oliver found Esme reading a novel in the lounge of their Southampton hotel. He sat down in a chair beside hers and she asked, 'Well?'

He looked doleful. 'Jameson has been given changed sailing orders. He won't be putting in to Southampton any more. He's going up north instead.'

'I did my share,' Esme pointed out.

'I'm sure you did.' He was smirking now.

'So you're happy.'

Oliver said, 'I will be.' And when she raised her eyebrows he went on, 'You said you would make it up to me.'

He was always savage after these attacks of jealousy. Esme smiled, showing her teeth. She put the book aside. 'Shall we go up?'

They breakfasted late, the tall young captain and his wife, striking with her dark hair and huge dark eyes. Afterwards they made a handsome couple who turned heads as they strolled in Hyde Park. There was a bloom on her. Until he said, 'It's time for me to go.'

Alison felt fear clutch at her heart but she had known this moment would come, and smiled, 'Are you going from Victoria?'

'No, Waterloo.'

They claimed her suitcase and his kit and took a taxi cab. At the station he found a seat on the waiting train that was crowded with men in khaki. He stood with Alison by the open door and now they had nothing to say. Except, 'I shouldn't have brought you.'

'I wanted to come,' said Alison. She had known it would be painful but she wanted every moment of him that she could glean, to remember through the long days and nights of waiting. She stood on tiptoe to kiss him.

There was a break in the wall of khaki milling on the platform and Esme glanced that way and saw them. 'I don't believe it!'

'Don't believe what?' asked Oliver, at her side.

'The Bailey girl.' Esme pointed.

'Well, I'm damned! So it is.'

'I have a score to settle with that one,' said Esme. She started to make her way sinuously through the crowd and Oliver followed.

There was a shrilling of the guard's whistle, a slamming of doors as soldiers climbed into the carriages. Richard kissed Alison one last, lingering time, and boarded. He hung out of the window. 'I'll write.' He had her address at the hostel now.

'Yes, I—' Alison started, but did not finish.

Esme said stridently, 'I don't know this young man. Will you introduce me?'

Richard disliked her on sight and answered, 'I'm Richard Tarrant. What is it to you?'

Esme was put off for a moment then showed her teeth again in a smile of triumph. She swung on Alison. 'Now we know what you were up to with my husband, Michael, when I found you in his bed. You thought you'd inherit his fortune. So when you failed you decided to hook the man who did inherit – his nephew.'

The train was moving with a clanking of couplings and a spurt of steam. Alison saw Richard's shocked face and recovered enough to cry, 'That's not true!' She walked alongside the carriage. 'Richard, I—'

Esme went with her, screeching, 'It is true that I caught you in his bed! Isn't it? *Isn't it?*'

'Yes,' Alison admitted, shouting to be heard. 'But I was

trying to warm him.' She was bumping into people as she almost ran now to keep up with the train. Heads were turning but this time to stare at her and the shrieking woman in pursuit. She was being left behind. 'Richard!' She was blocked by a porter and his barrow, forced to stop. She called despairingly, one last time before he disappeared from sight, '*Richard!*' He was gone.

She stood with the tears on her face. She wept for her lover, to whom she had brought shame and doubtless heartache. She had laid a dreadful burden on him when he was to risk his life in the war. Alison stood looking out at the empty tracks where the train had gone. Finally she turned and walked back along the platform. There was no Esme, who had long since departed gleefully. Alison did not care. For a little while she had held the world in her hands but now she had lost it all.

15

London, March 1918.

Richard wrote the letter on the train from Waterloo, heartache and anger driving him. He posted it before his ship sailed for France. Alison received it the next morning, took it with shaking hands from the orderly who delivered it, and stuffed it in a pocket of her skirt. She was putting off the evil moment of reading that Richard was finished with her. Then she realised what she was doing, took a breath and ripped it open. Her heart was banging in her ears, her eyes would not focus for a moment. Then her vision cleared and his first words leapt at her off the page: 'I love you.'

He had more to say. He believed her, not Esme. If she had been in Michael Tarrant's bed then she must have had good reason. He did not want an explanation; he wanted her and he wanted her to write.

'Nurse!'

Alison dashed the tears from her eyes and hastened to answer the call. Not running; that was against the rules.

She wrote and so did he, sometimes a letter every day. This lasted for just two weeks. Then the matron of the hospital, a starchy disciplinarian but usually with a glint of humour in her eyes, sent for Alison. 'We're being asked to find volunteers to go to France – urgently.' There was no humour now. 'I believe it's very bad over there. I chose you because I thought you the most suitable with your experience.' Her gaze went to the strip of red braid sewn on Alison's sleeve, the 'efficiency stripe' awarded to nurses with a year of service in military hospitals and deemed highly competent.

Matron went on, 'Of course, you don't have to go. You can justifiably claim to have done your bit. It's up to you.'

Alison said, 'But we're needed. I mean, the volunteers.'

'Desperately.'

'I'll go.'

The crisis that had caused her to be called was an all-out German attack on the Allied lines.

Alison went that same day. Just twenty-four hours after her interview with the Matron she was in a hospital in France. She stood, ready for duty, in a long hut set among dozens of others. She saw how much she was needed.

A single nurse, a VAD, stood in the middle of the ward. Fluffy blonde hair showed under her cap and her baby blue eyes were wide and despairing. She might have been twenty but to Alison she looked like a child on the verge of tears. She was surrounded by cots holding forty grievously wounded men. The rags of uniforms cut from them littered the floor and their bodies were bound with bloodstained bandages. There was a smell of wet serge and disinfectant, sweat and the sickly sweet odour of gangrene, and fumes from the oil stoves.

'I'm Lottie Douglas,' said the girl, in response to Alison's question. 'We had a convoy come in. The girl who was on has gone off duty after a twelve-hour shift. There's six for X-ray and five D.I.L.' That was the 'Dangerously Ill List'.

Alison put an arm around her. 'I've come to help.'

They set to work.

It was a task that went on all through the summer and into the autumn. Two or three days a week they sent thirty or forty wounded back to England under orders to 'Clear the wards.' Then the next order would be 'Fall in!' That was to receive more wounded, the convoys of ambulances coming from the Front, and they would start the awful procedure

all over again. The never-ending changing of dressings,
making and dispensing tea, long nights spent sitting by a
smelly stove in the dimly lit ward or by the bed of a dying
man. Then laying out his body in the dawn.

The two girls always worked together if they could. They
both came from the same part of the world, Lottie from
Gateshead. She wore a gold ring but never mentioned her
husband. Alison did not enquire as it might cause pain; there
were enough young widows.

There came a day when Lottie fell into Alison's arms and
burst into tears. They had just come off duty, a day spent
trying to help men in pain and dying. Alison was worn out
but held the girl and tried to comfort her, thinking the con-
tinual strain had finally proved too much for her. Then Lottie
sobbed, 'My man – they brought him in. I did what I could
for him but he died in my arms. He used to get drunk and
knock me about. I took this job to get away from him and
I hadn't seen him for two years. Then at the last he didn't
know me. I wouldn't have wished this on him.'

A chill came over Alison. Suppose Richard was brought
in one day? That became another bad dream to come between
her and exhausted sleep. At the beginning she had hoped
she might meet Richard at some time, but it was a hope that
soon faded. Several times they tried to meet in Paris, only
for one or both to have their leave cancelled because of some
emergency.

Then one night she obeyed the order to 'Fall in!' She hastened to the ward and a voice called hoarsely, 'Alison? Is that
Alison Bailey?'

She was threading her way through the queue of stretchers
borne in from the ambulances by the orderlies. She spun on
her heel, thinking frantically, *Richard?*

It was not. This man was clearly not so tall. He was still
in khaki filthy with mud and blood, both arms and his head

cocooned in dirty bandages. His eyes peered out at her and
they were not Richard's. She went to him. 'Yes, I'm Alison.
Who—?'

'Brian Cadwalladder. You used to come in to us for your
stuff for your cafés.'

The son of Harold, the wholesaler. Alison smiled at him.
'Of course.'

'My dad wrote and said you'd been asking about me.'

'I did.' The stretchers were still coming in. 'I'll come back
and see you later.'

He said eagerly, 'Aye. Please.'

To Lottie and the other nurses she said, 'Brian
Cadwalladder is mine.'

Later she took charge of him, washed his body and rid
him of the lice, made his bed and fed him, saw to those
needs made difficult by the swathing bandages, dressed his
wounds, frightful as they were.

He told her, 'It was shrapnel, from a grenade. It came
over the parapet and I saw it but that's all I can remember.'

Alison fastened the last bandage. 'There you are, bonny
lad,' she said lightly, and smiled.

He was not fooled. 'I'll not be a bonny lad again.' They
both knew he would be scarred. But he was not tearful. 'Bit
of luck, really. My eyes are all right and I've got a blighty
one.' A 'blighty' wound meant he would be taken back to a
hospital in England, rather than treated in France and sent
back up to the line again.

Alison saw him off a few days later, the first stage of his
journey being on a hospital train, on one of the cots lining
the sides of the carriages. He held her hand in both of his
bandaged ones until it was time for her to leave. 'You've
been good to me, Alison. Bless you.' He waved, peering out
of the window, and she waved back until the train was out
of sight.

She went back to her duties and the war.

It seemed interminable, as if it would never end, as autumn edged in towards winter with rain turning the mud into pools of slime. But then the river of wounded steadily thinned to a trickle, almost ceased. The guns fell silent as the armistice was signed, bringing peace, and Alison was sent home.

Lottie said, 'Best of luck. My turn soon.'

'What will you do now it's over?' Alison asked.

'I don't know,' Lottie shrugged, 'but it won't be nursing, I'm sure of that.'

'I'll be stuck over here for a few weeks yet,' wrote Richard. 'But I will be with you as soon as I can.' He went on to say why, and a lot of other things that made Alison blush, but she saved the letter, as she had saved all his letters.

Clara Skilton celebrated the ending of the war along with the patients and staff of the hospital Bellhanger had become. There was singing, dancing and even some illicit alcohol, smuggled in by one of the orderlies. She entertained him that night but in the morning he was gone from her bed. Clara woke with a thick head and mouth and squinted blearily into a bleak future.

The final words of her companion of the night had been to crow jubilantly, 'They'll shut this place down now and we'll all go home.' Now Clara saw the consequences of this. The owner of Bellhanger, Richard Tarrant, would return. He might want a housekeeper but more likely he would bring a wife or find one soon. Clara would not be needed. And suppose he remembered, and noticed the absence of, some of the furniture 'Vincent Featherstone' had taken? She shuddered, foreseeing disaster.

There was only one person she could turn to. Clara sat down and wrote to him.

'Come out of there and put your glad rags on.' Oliver Crawshaw ripped the sheets from the bed and left Esme naked and squealing.

'What the hell!' she objected.

'We're going up north,' Oliver explained. He waved the letter, addressed to 'Vincent Featherstone', that he had just collected from the accommodation address. 'Now the war is over we'll have to find new ways to make a few quid; there won't be contracts for cheap and nasty hospital supplies. But I know of some furniture I left for a rainy day and I think it's time to cash in. We'll be in the money.'

Esme knew Oliver very well by now. She did not move save to stretch. She purred, 'First things first.'

They caught a later train and were settled in at the Palace Hotel in Sunderland in time for a drink before dinner.

Oliver left Esme seated in the residents' lounge and took a cab out to Bellhanger. His business there did not take long. At the back door he asked a soldier in shirtsleeves, a kitchen orderly, for Clara Skilton. She came out to him and he found a smile for her. 'I got your letter, but I see the army are still here. And what's going on in there?' He gestured to the stable block, where a light showed.

'They took most of the furniture out of the house and stored it in there, but it's a guardroom as well,' Clara answered, preoccupied with her worries. 'A sentry patrols all night.'

Oliver thought, *so that scuppers the idea of shifting the furniture.* He muttered an obscenity under his breath, then listened while Clara poured out her worries for her future. At the end he consoled her, 'I'll see you all right. I haven't let you down yet, have I? And I won't.' The time to dump her was not yet. 'I'll come and see you again in a week or two.' The army might well have gone by then.

He left her reassured and returned to the Palace in his

cab. He took a short cut through the public bar on his way
to the residents' lounge and Esme. It was full of men standing
drinking, many in their overcoats despite the big coal fire in
the grate. He only caught a glimpse of one bigger than most,
but he edged through the crowd until he could see – 'Hello,
Sharky!' He slapped the big man on the back.

He turned on Oliver with a scowl that changed to the
shark-toothed grin that was the origin of his nickname. 'I
thought you were still in London. Haven't seen you since
we did that furniture job up at Bellhanger, years ago, when
you were Vincent Featherstone.'

'Just up here for a visit,' Oliver grinned and ignored the
reference to his alias. This was a chance to acquire some
local knowledge. 'What will you have?' He fetched two pints
from the bar and they elbowed a space in a corner. He asked,
'So what are you doing now? Still driving a coal lorry?'

Sharky shook his head. 'I gave that up; too heavy and dirty.
Now I deliver grub from the docks to a depot in Durham.'
He winked. 'I get a bit for meself an' all. Sometimes a pound
o' butter, or a few rashers o' bacon. I carry all kinds.'

Oliver thought that was typical of the man, still indulging
in petty theft. He asked, 'Why don't you take the lot?' And
when Sharky stared he went on, 'The war's over but grub
is still short. People will pay for it and no questions asked.
But that won't last. Soon there'll be plenty of food shipped
in, so you need to do it now.'

Sharky said hungrily, 'Aye.' But then he objected, 'Where
would I store a lorry load? Me and the wife only have two
rooms.'

'Listen,' said Oliver. He talked and Sharky listened. Oliver
finished, 'Are you on?'

Sharky nodded eagerly. 'It sounds good to me.'

'I'll be round to see you.' Oliver made a note of Sharky's
address then left him to join Esme.

She greeted him. 'You're looking cock-a-hoop.'

He grinned. 'I am. I've just done some business. I'll have a drink and tell you about it, then we'll go in to dinner. Waiter!'

At that moment Pamela Baldwin was standing in the hall of her house, pulling on her gloves and telling Julian, 'We have to go out for dinner. We had practically not a crumb delivered today and Henri isn't able to cook.' She had engaged Henri Latour six months ago after dismissing the previous cook following a row. She was unaware that his real name was Joseph Higgins and that he was born and bred in Stepney. He had evaded being called up to the army by purchasing French papers, including a certificate of exemption from conscription into the army, from another French chef. The papers had belonged to the chef's deceased brother.

Now Henri was present in the hall in cap and apron, making his apologies with a gallic shrug and accent. 'I am sorry, but I cannot cook without the ingredients.' He was a handsome young man with oiled and waved hair and a thin pencil line moustache. When Pamela had interviewed him she was aware of the way he looked through the dress she wore and she felt a stirring of sexuality.

Julian thought that the previous cook had always managed to provide a meal he could enjoy. He also noticed that Pamela was already in a dinner dress, so this was no last minute decision. But the house was owned by his wife and its running was her business and he said nothing.

Pamela could feel Henri's eyes on her behind Julian's back and thrilled to it. She would have to do something about him.

In the Rolls Royce, with Julian at the wheel, he said, 'It's lucky the Palace and places like it are still able to find food to sell us, but we must exercise restraint, as the government says.' It was a request issued by the authorities to avoid allegations that the rich were not suffering from food shortages. A lot of the rich were suffering, but a few were not.

Pamela said curtly, 'Rubbish. I'm ready for my dinner.'

The head waiter led them to a table and Pamela scanned the menu. Julian opened his but first glanced around idly. A movement caught his eye: a couple had entered and the man was staring at Julian, was now smiling. They followed the head waiter but as they came abreast of Julian and Esme, the man paused. He chuckled, 'There's a surprise! Imagine meeting you.'

Julian looked up at Oliver as if mesmerised. Here was the man who had blackmailed him and given him away. He could only be there for one reason, to squeeze more money out of Julian. And betray him again to Pamela? It was four years since Pamela had confronted him in the London hotel but he still shuddered at the memory.

She was staring now, curious. 'Are you going to introduce me, Julian?'

He lurched to his feet but Oliver jumped in. 'Allow me. I'm Oliver Crawshaw and this is my wife, Esme. Mr Baldwin and I met in London. Business. We shared in a deal I put together and made a few pounds.'

Pamela asked, 'What kind of business are you in, Mr Crawshaw?'

'I turn my hand to all sorts of things. At the moment I'm into shipping, but I look out for any opportunity.' He smiled at Julian and Pamela. 'I mustn't keep you from your dinner.' He followed Esme and the waiter as they went on to a table.

Pamela snapped the menu shut. 'I'll have the soup and the beef. You never mentioned any business deal to me.'

'I'll have the same,' Julian told the waiter. He was not hungry, felt sick. 'It wasn't important. Just a few pounds, as he said.' He had also said he was on the lookout for any opportunity. Oh God!

'I've known you get into some funny business in London.' Pamela's hard eyes bored into him. 'There was that trollop who ran the cafés – Alison Bailey.'

Julian thought, *I can't go on like this*. He could see he faced another humiliation. What would Crawshaw tell Pamela? He had to get out, and there was a way . . .

Esme said, 'That man has a hunted look.'

'Does he?' Oliver smiled.

'Yes. Do you have business with him now?'

'No.' His smile was that of a bad little boy pulling the wings off butterflies. 'Not now.' He found it amusing to see Julian stew in his own juice.

Julian only picked at his food, without appetite. It was all he could do to carry on a conversation with his wife. She noticed and snapped, 'You're quiet. Cat got your tongue? And you've hardly eaten a bite. Are you "exercising restraint"?'

He mumbled something about a hard day at the yard but she was no longer listening. Instead she ate voraciously and thought of Henri.

Julian drove her home. He had no desire for her but neither did she want him. They slept in their separate rooms, but he lay awake making his plans.

He acted the next day, calling his typist into his office and ordering her, 'Shut the door.' She obeyed, watching him with worshipping eyes. Valerie Bagwell was dark and seductive under the prim skirt and high-necked blouse she wore for working in the office. Julian knew just how seductive. She had come from somewhere vaguely 'down south' and had worked at Baldwin's yard for some six months now. For most of that time he had lusted after her and she had yielded to him, passionately.

Now he said, 'I'm ready to take you away from all this. Can you be ready tomorrow?' Now he had decided, he was in a fever to go without delay.

Valerie rounded the desk to kiss him and breathe, 'Yes. And the bureau?'

He thought it was his scheme to run away but in fact she had suggested she could be more available if . . . It was also her suggestion to start up a secretarial bureau. He would put up the money, be the chairman and manager while she supplied the knowledge and experience. It appealed to him, to be freed from the noise and dirt of the shipyard. And he foresaw a constant procession of young girls seeking employment.

Now he nodded agreement. 'I'll go to the bank today.'

Valerie stroked him. 'You don't want a cheque or a transfer. Your wife might trace you through that.' She had worked in a bank and knew the procedures, had been dismissed but was clever enough to evade prosecution.

The thought appalled him. 'I'll take cash.'

'That's a good idea.' She kissed him again and his hands became busy on her body. Then there came a knock at the door and she slipped into a chair, notebook on knee and pencil poised.

Julian croaked, 'Come in!'

He visited his bank that afternoon and told the manager what he wanted. 'I need the money for a private business venture.' The following morning he drew a thousand pounds in big white five pound notes. His shipyard labourers were living on less than three pounds per week. On the train thundering south, Valerie asked, 'Have you got the money?' They were alone in the compartment so he let her see the thick wad of white notes buttoned away in his inside jacket pocket. She kissed him. 'I can't believe it's really happening, just you and me, forever.'

'It really is,' he assured her. He felt an enormous surge of relief and release. Every turn of the wheels took him further away from Pamela and what he saw as the prison sentence she represented.

When they disembarked at Kings Cross they booked in at a nearby hotel for the night. They were both in a celebratory mood and took a cab to a restaurant for dinner. Valerie was kittenish and wanted champagne so Julian ordered a bottle but drank all of it himself. Valerie found it too dry and instead sipped at a glass of sweet white wine. They returned to their hotel and celebrated again in the privacy of their room, but Julian carefully hid his wallet under his pillow as they undressed by the light of the fire glowing brightly in the hearth. Then she came to him, their shadows dancing on the wall.

Julian woke with a ray of pale sunlight shafting through a crack in the curtains. The fire was cold and dead. He had a headache and a dry mouth and concluded the champagne had not been very good. He groaned and turned over then realised he was alone in the bed. Valerie was not in the room. Her suitcase had gone. With a dreadful suspicion he threw aside his pillow. His wallet was not there. He found it lying on the floor by the crack in the curtains. Valerie had opened it in the light seeping through from the street lamps and taken the thick wad of notes. She had left him the few pound notes in there. If she had done it out of kindness he was not impressed.

What could he do? Call the police? They would ask why he was carrying so much money. What could he tell them? They would want confirmation from his bank. Would they contact Pamela? Would they find Valerie? He doubted it.

He could not go back, that was certain. He shuddered at the thought of returning to Pamela. Whatever position he sought in the shipyards, he would need references. He would have to seek some menial employment where a reference was not wanted.

He dressed and paid his bill, ignoring the censorious look from the clerk, who had obviously noted the absence of Julian's 'wife' and concluded he had smuggled in some street-walker, who had slipped out once her work was done. Which, in a way, was true.

He left the hotel carrying his case and saw an office on the other side of the street with the sign 'Secretarial Bureau'. He thought miserably that he might find work there, prob-ably as a clerk. He crossed to it, picking his way through the droppings left by the numerous horses pulling carts and cabs. Next to the bureau was 'The Cosy Café', with bright chintz curtains and oilcloth-covered tables. There were a dozen or so customers, workmen or women cleaners, drinking mugs of tea and eating toast. Putting off the moment of entering the bureau, he entered and sat down at a table.

A woman in her thirties stood languidly by a till behind the counter while a girl of twelve or so skipped among the tables taking orders and serving. Three small boys popped in and out through a curtain behind the counter, bearing orders. Now a man of fifty or sixty emerged, a white apron tied round his waist and a few strands of grey hair parted in an oiled quiff. He carried a mug in one hand, a plate of toast in the other. He called out, 'Now then, Millie! Serve this order! Busy day today!'

'Righto, Dad!' The twelve-year-old dashed over to him and bustled off with plate and mug.

George Grindly, for it was he, thought that Millie was a right good little worker. She reminded him of that lass as worked for him years ago. What was her name? Alison.

He also thought the toff in the good suit looked as mis-erable as sin. He did not know that they shared a common experience: flight. Dolly Maguire had been right when she predicted that Una would have him running around, but George was sublimely happy with her and the love and children she had given him.

'Damn him! Damn him to hell!' Pamela Baldwin was not happy. When she heard from the shipyard that Julian had not gone to work, learned from the bank that he had drawn a thousand pounds, she finally accepted that he had run away. She raged through her big house, hurling his photograph against the wall and throwing his clothes at the feet of the startled gardener. 'Burn them!' Then she dressed carefully and went out to tea, driving herself in the Rolls.

This was a gathering of ladies who were kindred spirits and met to gossip and complain about the food shortages. In the course of conversation she announced casually, 'Julian has left me.' And as they stared and murmured in astonishment, she shrugged and lied, 'Not surprising. I told him I was sacking him as manager of the yard. He had become useless. I suspect drink was at the bottom of it all.'

The murmurs were now sympathetic. She thought that they had better be.

Maudie Hamilton, overweight and tightly corseted, sighed, 'Still, the yard is going well.' Shipbuilding was booming. 'I wish the same could be said of my investments. Some of them are looking uncertain.' That was said with the comfortable certainty that she would be all right anyway. She went on, 'There's that café on the sea front: Alison's Cookshop. It's a property of mine but it doesn't seem to do much business these days. I wonder how long I will go on receiving my rent. The lease runs out soon.' Then, 'Is something wrong, dear?' She blinked nervously at the glaring Pamela.

Who was wondering if Maudie was slyly reminding her of Julian's escapade with that Alison Bailey. Then Pamela remembered that no one knew of that. She gave a brittle smile. 'Nothing, dear.'

But she was thinking . . .

She drove back to her big house and in the hall told the maid, 'Tell Henri I want to see him. I'll be in my room.' And when he came to her, in his whites but cap in hand, she ordered, 'Lock the door.' He obeyed and he was looking at her in that way. She said, 'I'm going to buy a restaurant.' She knew Maudie would sell like a shot. 'I want you to run it.' He nodded and smiled, licked his lips. She went on huskily, 'We'll dine at the Palace tonight but first I must change. You can help.' She turned her back to him and he began to fumble with the hooks.

Alison returned to Sunderland on a day in early December. The rain fell coldly as she stepped off the tram on the sea front and collected her luggage from its place by the driver.

'Have ye been far?' he asked as he handed the two suit-cases down to her.

'Aye,' she replied as she took them. 'France.'

'You've picked a cauld day for it. But better than ower there, though.'

'That's true,' she laughed.

'What were you doing out there?'

'Nursing.'

'Are you finished now?'

'Aye.' Finished with nursing, with bloody death and pain and burials.

So she believed.

'Alison! Bonny lass!' Dolly was delighted to see her but looking tired. Alison recalled thinking a year ago, when she had returned from Mesopotamia, that Dolly had aged. It was more evident now. This last year had taken its toll. There were more lines in her face, a weariness slowing her movements. And now she gave voice to her worries. 'It's not a cheerful welcome I have for you, pet. My Sheila has lost her man.' That was her daughter, living in Glasgow and married to a merchant seaman.

'Oh, no, Dolly!' Alison put an arm around her.

Dolly went on, 'She sent me a telegram. I got it last night and never had a wink of sleep. His ship was torpedoed and sunk off Ireland. He'd gone all through the war without a scratch and then to be killed at the finish. And her with three little bairns. She wants me to move in with her and look after them so she can get a job.' She stopped and swallowed and the tears came now. 'I'll have to go. Her and them bairns are all I have in the world.' Her only son was killed early in the war and her aged mother died of grief soon afterwards, another casualty. 'But I feel so badly about leaving you when you've just come home.'

Alison held her, felt the sobs racking Dolly's body, and it had a boniness now. She recalled holding Francie so long ago. She steered the old woman to an oilcloth-covered table and sat her in a chair. 'We'll have a cup of tea. Is Moira in the kitchen?'

Dolly sniffed, 'She's in the hospital in Roker Avenue, has been for the last week. I wrote to you but the letter must have passed you.'

'I'll make a pot,' said Alison, heading for the kitchen and thinking, *Dear God! What next?*

Her mind was busy as she made the tea. It did not take her long to decide the right thing to do. She took the tea out on a tray, sat down at the table with Dolly and said, 'You must go, of course, and as soon as you can be ready. I'll miss you but I'll manage. I've learned a bit about that these last few years.'

Dolly dabbed at her eyes with a handkerchief and found a tremulous smile. 'It's good of you to take it like that. I've

got to sell most of my few bits o' furniture and see about
sending on one or two I want to keep. Can I finish tonight?
Or do you need me to work my notice? I won't want any
more money. I have some savings.'

'You can finish now,' said Alison, 'and I'll pay you what's
owing. You've worked hard for me, before the war and all
through it, and I appreciate it. So I'm going to give you an
annuity.' And as Dolly stared uncomprehending, 'That's a
pension. It'll only be for a few shillings a week but it will
help.' Alison would buy it with the hundred-pound legacy
left to her by Michael Tarrant and saved for a 'rainy day'.
She had planned a use for it now but would have to cope
without it.

'Bless you,' said Dolly. Then she added sadly, 'There's
more bad news.'

Alison tried to keep her smile in place while she thought,
What now?

Dolly went on, 'A chap came in to look round the place.
He looked and sounded like a foreigner to me. He said he
was going to take it over. I wouldn't let him in the kitchen
and I chased him as soon as I could, but he said the lease
was up, I'd be getting a letter and he would be back. There
was a letter came for you this morning. I'll fetch it.'

From Richard? 'I'll go,' said Alison.

'It's on the dresser.'

Alison found it, a stiff white envelope, her name and
address typed on it. So not from Richard. She ripped it open
and read. The freehold of the premises had changed hands.
Her lease would run out shortly and the new lease would
have an increased rent. The figure made her blink. It was
impossible, ridiculous. Then she read the signature of her
new landlord and all became clear. It was written with a
flourish – 'P. Baldwin.' Julian Baldwin's wife was taking her
revenge by putting Alison out of business. Belatedly, because

the opportunity had only just come? No matter; she was going to do it. Or so she doubtless thought.

Alison felt a cold rage. She slid the letter back into its envelope and went out to Dolly. 'Nothing to worry about.' Nothing for Dolly to worry about, anyway. 'Now you finish up here and get away.'

Dolly obeyed, but not without more tears and thanks. Alison turned over the sign on the inside of the door to read 'Closed'. The sea front was deserted, no sign of any customer. She carried her suitcases upstairs to her flat. She thought: *not mine for long*. And: *one thing at a time*.

Down to the kitchen again, where she made herself a light meal of cheese on toast; there was little else. Then she set out to walk to the hospital in Roker Avenue. She arrived during visiting hours, asked the nurse on duty for Moira Grindly and was told gravely, 'Down at the end of the ward. The sick note is out for her.' That meant she was allowed visitors outside the usual hours. It also meant that Moira was seriously ill.

Alison found her lying with the sheet drawn up to her chin and clutched with bony fingers. Her wasted body was thin under the covers, her face drawn in pain. Her eyes were closed but she was not sleeping, her head turning restlessly. She was a shadow of the woman she had been. Alison was shocked at the sight of her; she had seen that look before.

'Hello, Moira,' she said softly.

The eyes opened and Moira said, 'Alison?'

'Aye. How are you?' Alison asked out of courtesy; it was obvious how Moira was.

'Bad.' Moira put it in a word. She whispered, 'Can I have a drink?' She watched as Alison filled a glass from a jug of water on the small bedside cabinet, lifted her head and held the glass to her lips so she could drink. When she had done she whispered, 'Ta. I see you have a ring on your finger.'

Alison smiled, 'I'm engaged to a soldier in the Medical Corps.' That was said without thinking, a happy response to a question she was happy to answer. She saw the reaction, the shamed turning of the head away, and knew she did not need to ask about the letters from Richard that had never reached her. She had come home with the intention of taking Moira to task, about the letters and her turning away of Richard when he had come in search of Alison. That was impossible now, of course, and no longer necessary.

She asked, 'Can I fetch anything in for you?'

Moira's head turned and she blinked. 'Are you coming in again?'

'I'll be in tomorrow. So what would you like?'

'Nothing. But come. Please.'

Alison left the hospital and set out for the town, walking down Church Street and crossing the river by the ferry, paying her halfpenny fare. The Wear was busy, thronged with shipping now safe from the U-boat threat. The yards stretching along both sides of the river were filled with the clangour of men building more ships. Alison drank it all in, the salt wind off the sea, the smell of coal smoke from the yards and the houses ranked in terraces behind them, the screaming of the swooping gulls, the sirens of ships and hooting of snub-nosed tugboats. She was home.

She climbed the hill of High Street East and went on to Cadwalladder's, the wholesaler's tucked away behind the station. Harold Cadwalladder was behind the counter in the store, double chin only skin now, hanging over his stiffly starched collar, watch chain with its medals looped loosely over his reduced paunch. Shortage of food and worry about his son had done that. He nodded at Alison but kept on dealing with a customer. 'That's all I can give you. I'm sorry, but there it is.'

The man he addressed grumbled, 'What you've sold me will hardly see the week out.'

'It'll have to do.' Harold's bass voice was implacable. 'Now the war's over we should get a bit more stuff in, but it hasn't happened yet.'

The customer muttered under his breath and stalked out.

Harold turned to Alison and she prepared to give battle, remembering how he had turned a stone face to her back in 1917.

He said, 'I see you're back, then.'

'I am and there are a few things I need.' Alison took out the pencilled list she had made out.

Harold rumbled, 'Our Brian said he'd seen you in France.'

Disarmed, Alison smiled at the memory. 'It was good to meet somebody from home. How is he?'

'Getting better. He's in a hospital down south but they're going to move him up here soon. His mother and me, we went down to see him. He said you were up to your neck in wounded but you kept an eye to him.'

'I did what I could.'

'Aye. He's grateful and so are we.' He reached out and took the list, glanced at it and nodded. 'I'll see to that for you.'

'Thank you,' said Alison meekly, and came away.

She walked back in the dusk, this time crossing by the bridge. She cut through by Dundas Street and paused when she came to the first of her Alison's Cookshops. Pressing her face to the glass, she saw the furniture was still there. Dolly, in her letters, had said it was, together with the stove and oven. The place had been closed down because it was losing money, only as a 'temporary' measure. But no rent had been paid since it shut two years ago.

Alison walked on back to her flat, lost in thought.

She crossed the river by ferry again the following morning

and saw Ezra Arkenstall, the solicitor, in his offices in High Street East. His pointed beard was greying now but the eyes behind his wire-rimmed spectacles were still shrewd and he remembered her. 'Miss Bailey!' He gestured her to a chair. 'Please sit down. And what can I do for you?'

'I want to start up my café in Dundas Street again. I think you know the one.'

He pursed his lips, then said cautiously, 'I do, but I can see difficulties. The lease has run out and no rent has been paid for some time. A Mrs Maguire returned the keys.'

'She was acting for me in my absence. I was a nurse, serving in Mesopotamia.'

'Good Lord!' said Arkenstall. 'I would like to assist you but I will need to contact the owner of the property. When you first took it on it belonged to Michael Tarrant, but on his death it passed to his nephew, Richard. He will have to be consulted and I do not know his present whereabouts.'

'I do,' said Alison. As he stared she delved into her bag and produced Richard's latest letter. She reached across the polished desk to lay it on the blotter and pointed at the address. 'There you are. Captain Tarrant and I are engaged to be married.' They were already as man and wife, in fact, but she did not embarrass Arkenstall with this information.

As it was he said again, 'Good Lord!' Then, recovering, 'I offer my congratulations to you both. I will write to Captain Tarrant at once. Meanwhile . . .'

Alison came away with the keys to the Cookshop and the promise of a lease just as soon as the solicitor received Richard's formal agreement. She spent the following days scrubbing and cleaning the property, windows, stove and oven. She paid a man owning a horse and cart to transfer from the sea-front restaurant the furniture, crockery and other items she needed. They laboured together to load the cart. As Alison emerged carrying a box full of cutlery she found Pamela Baldwin, with a smartly dressed man at her side, standing just across the road and watching. Pamela's huge silver Rolls Royce squatted against the kerb.

Pamela smiled unpleasantly and gloated. 'I see you are moving out.'

Alison was about to make an angry reply but then her helper asked, 'D'ye want these casseroles, miss?'

'Aye, put them on the cart.' Then Alison turned back to Pamela to smile at her. 'That's right. I've no further use for the place. Like we sometimes find we have no more use for a man or a husband. I'm sure you know what I mean.'

Pamela saw the reference to Julian and glared. She suffered the frustration of not being able to find an answer. But then the man with her asked, his voice accented, 'Can I get in now?' He was dapper in a sharply pressed suit, a silk handkerchief flopping from his breast pocket and another tucked into his sleeve. He wore patent leather, elastic-sided boots.

Pamela smiled at him. 'Soon, Henri.'

Alison judged him to be the 'foreigner' that Dolly had turned away. She smiled at him. 'I think you are a restaurateur.'

'*Oui*.' He gave a little bow.

'I suppose you have plans for a restaurant here?' Alison put what was half a question, half statement.

'Of course, but a place with *ton*, of class, you understand. With everything of the finest.'

'I wish you *bonne chance*.' That almost exhausted Alison's knowledge of French but she had learned all she needed to know, said all she had to say. Pamela gave her a suspicious glare but Alison only smiled. She knew such a restaurant would not make a profit but Pamela would find that out. She had acted out of spite so serve her right.

Alison finished loading the cart and climbed up to sit by

its driver. She left Henri making plans with Pamela. She returned to the Cookshop in Dundas Street and set to work unloading the cart. At the end of the day she was ready to open up. Her last act before turning off the gas lamp was to write to Lottie Douglas in France.

She still had to sleep one night on a bed laid on the floor of her new Cookshop. She reflected ere she slept that she had come full circle. She had started out sleeping on the floor here twelve years ago.

Her first day of opening was quietly successful in that she had a steady run of customers. This was in large part due to her having let it be known at the nearby tramway depot that she would be open. In the evening she closed in time for her to visit Moira Grindly, who said little but held her hand and thanked her. 'It's good o' you to come.'

'I'll see you tomorrow.'

Alison walked home and heated a hotpot she had cooked earlier. She was about to sit down to it when there came a knocking at the street door. She wound her way through the tables, wondering who it might be at that time. Outside was blackness and rain driven against the windows. She opened the door and Doreen Grant, the mother she had not seen for twenty years, said, 'Hello, Alison.'

16

Monkwearmouth in Sunderland, December 1918.

'It is Alison – isn't it?' Now Doreen peered uncertainly at her daughter.

'It is.'

'I wasn't sure for a moment, but as soon as you opened the door I thought I could see your father in you.'

Alison was having her own moment of uncertainty. Doreen Grant – if that was her name now – was a wreck of the young woman she vaguely remembered. Even in the half-light of the doorway, Alison could see the black hair was now a dirty grey, the slender, curvaceous body was thick and shapeless and her face lined and blotchy. She wore a three-quarter length coat with a collar of mangy fur. The coat and the skirt beneath had been shortened to show more of the veined legs shod with cracked button boots.

Doreen said, in a querulous whine, 'It's colder than charity out here. Are you going to ask me in?'

'Aye.' Alison stood back to let her pass, 'Come in.' She did not use the word 'mother'. It did not come easily to the tongue. She followed Doreen back to the kitchen where her mother pulled a chair up to the stove and held out her hands to warm them. Alison saw they were chapped, the nails black-rimmed. Now, in the light, she looked a very old woman, though Alison thought that she would only be in her early fifties.

Doreen raised her head and sniffed. 'Something smells good. You've been cooking. I could eat a horse.'

The hotpot was only big enough for one – Alison was suffering from the shortages – but she said, 'I'll cook some more potatoes. They won't take long.' She started to peel them while her mother looked about her. She was aware that Doreen had a musty smell about her. She asked, 'How did you find me?' She did not ask 'why', thinking uneasily that she would find out.

Doreen grumbled, 'I've been back in the town for nearly a week and looking for you. I started at Bellhanger but there was only some housekeeper there. I didn't know her and she didn't want to know me, so I told her to go to hell. I asked all over after that, then today I was outside a pub ower the watter.' That was on the other side of the river. 'This feller came out and I got talking to him.' Her face darkened. 'He was bloody rude, started to walk away, but then I asked him about you. He gave me another funny look but he said he worked on the trams. He'd heard you were opening up a café and gave me directions.'

Alison guessed why the man had been 'bloody rude', being accosted by this old woman. Her mother had not changed. 'What happened to Mr Tobin?' Cecil Tobin had gone off with Doreen when she had left Alison with her grandmother, Francie.

'God knows, I don't,' Doreen said absently, uninterested, and stared into the flames of the stove. 'He just up and went, years and years ago.'

Alison thought, *and after that another man – and another*.

She cooked the potatoes and served them up with the hotpot, sharing the meal with her mother. Doreen ate hungrily, wiped her mouth on the back of her hand and looked about the kitchen. 'Have you got a drink in the house?'

'No, but I'm going to make a pot of tea.'

'Lend me a bob and I'll run out and fetch something from the Beehive.' That was a nearby public house. And, wheedling, 'We have to celebrate.'

Alison was not sure about that, but gave her the shilling and she hurried out. Her daughter washed up and sat down by the stove. She was trying to come to terms with this new twist in her fortunes. For years she had thought her mother would, then might, come back to her. The hope had finally faded. Now it had happened and she felt nothing but unease, and guilt because of that. She asked herself, as she had on many occasions when she was uncertain how to act, what would Francie say? But this time she did not have an answer.

Doreen returned with a quarter bottle of gin. Alison found a glass but politely refused to join her in 'celebrating' with neat gin. 'I've had a cup of tea.' Doreen did not press her and steadily emptied the bottle herself. She did not bring any change from the shilling.

Alison gave up her bed to Doreen and made up another on the kitchen floor for herself. As she lay there, in the darkness save for the dim glow from the stove, she could hear the drunken snoring of her mother.

That was the pattern of their joint lives for the next few days. Doreen would rise late and sit by the stove while Alison ran the café. After supper in the evening she would repeat her request for 'a bob', then go out to the Beehive. She realised that Alison would not be drinking so she would sit in the 'Bottle and Jug' at the pub, keeping company with the old women sipping their stout. She would return in a mellow mood, say how glad she was to have found her only daughter again, then doze by the fire until Alison pushed her upstairs to bed. There was never any change from the shilling.

All this while Alison was visiting Moira in the hospital in Roker Avenue every day. The nurses came to know her and where she came from. Then one afternoon a porter came bearing a message for Alison, that Moira had taken a turn for the worse and was asking for her. She closed the café, tidied up while waiting for the last customer, then hurried off to the hospital. She told Doreen, sitting by the stove, 'I don't know how long I'll be. Help yourself to a bite if I'm not back.'

She was with Moira all through the last hours, holding her hand and talking softly while she was conscious, sitting patiently when she lapsed into sleep. The nurses brought her cups of tea. One said quietly, 'You've done this before, haven't you?'

Alison nodded.

Moira was not conscious when the end came. Alison stood up stiffly and sought out the nurse on duty to tell her, 'She's gone.'

'It was kind of you to visit and stay with her. She wasn't a relative?'

'No.

'A good friend, then.'

Alison thought of Richard's letters to her, that Moira had destroyed, and the way she had turned him away with lies when he had come seeking Alison. 'She used to work for me. It was a duty.'

She walked home through the empty streets and arrived just on midnight. She felt in her bag for her key then found the door was unlocked. Alison hesitated. Who might be in there waiting for her? Surely Doreen would have locked the door. She saw the light was on in the kitchen, entered cautiously and threaded through the tables towards it. The kitchen door was ajar and she peered around it. Doreen lay back in an armchair, her mouth open and snoring, her muddily booted feet propped up on another chair.

Alison was weary to the bone, worn out physically and mentally by her vigil. Her anger with this parent of hers had been building for days and now burst out. She swept Doreen's feet off the chair and shook her. 'Wake up!' She smelt the rum then, looked round and saw the empty half-bottle lying on its side and empty on the table. 'Where did you get the money for that?'

Doreen was still barely awake, mouth loose, eyes blinking owlishly. Alison went out to the café on a sudden suspicion and pulled open the drawer in the counter that she used as a till. It had held a number of coppers and some silver. The coppers seemed to be there but the silver coins were few.

'You stole it from me!' Alison charged, outraged and incredulous. Could her own mother have done this to her?

Doreen whined, 'I only borrowed it. I—'

'Borrowed? How will you pay it back?' Alison shook her head. 'No! This is the last straw.'

'Don't turn me out,' Doreen pleaded. 'I've nobody but you, nowhere to go.' She was frightened, crying, maudlin. She groped for Alison's hand. 'I don't know what happened to your father. I should have stuck by him but I thought when he found out the truth he would blame me.'

Truth? Alison gripped the hand and demanded. 'What truth? Tell me!'

Doreen sobbed. 'That Sean Rafferty, he said I was nothing but a whore and your father hit him and he died. But it was true. Sean knew me before I met Matt, knew what I'd been up to. I couldn't face your father and tell him that. I said nothing to him but I told you he was a jailbird and you should forget about him. I'm sorry.' Then she pleaded again, 'Don't put me on the street.'

Alison had never intended to turn her out; Doreen had mistakenly read that into her angry outburst. Now she said, 'I won't, but you'll have to change your ways.'

Doreen responded eagerly. 'I'll help about the place, work in the café.'

'All right.' Alison was still trying to take in what she had learned. So many years she had believed her father to be a murderer she must forget. He had killed, it was true, but it had been a tragic accident. Her picture of him had been painted by Doreen. Francie had never known him.

She said, 'I'll make some supper then I must go to bed.' In the morning she would have to make the arrangements for Moira's funeral.

They ate supper, Doreen picking at the food in a subdued mood, and retired. Before Alison slept she thought that she would have to find her father. But how?

Doreen was downstairs and helping with breakfast soon after she heard Alison moving below. Her daughter noted this change of routine but did not comment. Nor did she when Doreen offered, 'I'll wash up so you can get on.' Later, drying dishes as Alison prepared to go out, Doreen ventured, 'Can I have some new clothes for working in here, please?'

Alison agreed. 'You'll need two brown skirts and some blouses and aprons. Try Blacketts; I think they are having a sale now.' She dipped into her purse again. It was looking thin; her savings were running low. She wanted to open the Cookshop as soon as she could today, to catch some trade and earn a living. She set out with Doreen determined to do this.

In the town they went their separate ways, arranging to meet back at the Cookshop.

Alison returned first at mid-morning, opened the café for business and had all she could handle. Noon came and went in a blur of work and it was two in the afternoon when trade slackened off and she thought she could make herself a cup of tea. But Doreen had not come home. Alison bit her lip. It seemed she had mistakenly trusted her mother again.

She made the tea and was sipping at it as she sat behind the counter, when one of the tram drivers from the depot came in. She stood up, ready to serve him, but he was followed by a policeman. The driver said gravely, 'It's about your mother.'

Alison saw something terrible in that look and sat down again as her legs gave way under her. 'My mother?'

'Aye. I've seen her two or three times when I've been in here, so I was able to identify her. The pollis here asked me to come and tell you.'

Alison said dully, stunned, 'You mean she's dead?'

'I'm afraid so,' said the policeman, grey-haired without the helmet now cradled in one arm, too old to be in the army. 'There were numerous witnesses to the accident . . .' He explained how Doreen had tried to jump from a tram before it stopped but stumbled and fell under the wheels of a lorry.

Alison kept going, moving in a nightmare, identifying the body, attending the inquest held at the Albion Hotel. The coroner said apologetically, 'The deceased had been drinking and this may have been a contributing factor.' His verdict was 'accidental death'. Alison listened but found a crumb of comfort in the fact that Doreen had with her two brown skirts, blouses and aprons, all brand new. She had weakened but was coming home, was trying to change.

Alison arranged and attended two funerals, of Moira and Doreen, inside a week. She inserted a notice in the *Sunderland Daily Echo* of the funeral of: 'Doreen Grant, née Bailey, of Alison's Cookshop in Dundas Street. Mourned by daughter Alison.' She did the same for Moira.

No one came to either interment in the frosted ground. Alison, dry-eyed, was the only mourner. She sat by the stove alone at night and told herself she would not give way to grief. What was done, was done. Now she would look forward.

The next morning brought a new day and a letter from Richard. He hoped to be home – with her – soon. He told her of his plans for their future and they delighted her. That evening brought another welcome surprise: Lottie Douglas, fluffily blonde and blue-eyed, walked in carrying a suitcase then dropped it to fall into Alison's arms. Laughing and wiping away a tear, she declared, 'I've finished with France and nursing and come to take on that job you offered me.'

Alison gave up her bed yet again, this time for Lottie. She brushed aside the girl's protests and joked, 'I'm used to it. I might change the name to "Alison's Boarding House" if I take in any more guests.'

They talked far into the night and the next morning saw Lottie working in the Cookshop, serving while Alison cooked. She was popular with the young men now starting to come back from the war, demobilised. Alison suspected she might not have her assistant for long, but now she fitted in well.

After a week Lottie came into the kitchen where Alison was cooking and giggled, 'We have a new boy friend, but he's a bit older than the others.'

'What do you mean – "we"?' Alison laughed. 'You are the one with the admirers.' Though she knew she had her share, only put off by the ring on her finger.

Lottie said, 'But he's asking for you.' And when Alison stared, 'He said to me, "Are you Alison?" I told him you were in here.'

'Excuse me.' The voice came from the doorway leading to the café. They turned and saw its owner standing there. He was a man in his fifties with greying hair, not tall but broad and powerful. He said uncertainly, 'Did you put this in the paper?' He held it out, a much crumpled copy of the *Echo*. She could see her notice of the funeral of her mother ringed in pencil. He went on, 'Are you Alison?'

'I am.' She knew who he was. She had not forgotten her determination to seek him out, had thought about ways only that very morning. Now she could not remember the man she had not seen since she was a child of four or five but she was sure he was –

'I'm Matthew Grant,' he said. 'I think I'm your father.' He glanced at Lottie then back to Alison. 'I don't want to embarrass you. Can we talk somewhere, just the two of us?'

Lottie said hastily, 'I'll go.'

'No. I'm not ashamed of anything I've done.' Alison reached out to take Matt's hand. 'I'm not ashamed of you, either.'

Lottie was circling around Matt to the door. 'I'll look after the customers and give you a chance to talk.' Then she was gone.

Alison felt her knees like jelly, sat down on a chair and pulled Matt down onto another beside her. 'I was going to look for you, but all these years I didn't try because I'd been brought up to forget about you. Then my mother came back and admitted she'd blackened your character to save herself from blame. She said she couldn't tell you the truth.' She stopped there, realising she might have said too much.

But Matt said, 'It's all right. I know the truth, what she was afraid to tell me.' He smiled ruefully. 'I looked for you when they let me out. That was September 1915.'

'I was in Mesopotamia,' Alison said, squeezing his hand.

'So there was no chance of me finding you.' He shook his head. 'I was looking for Alison Grant, anyway. I never thought that you might have – or your mother might have – changed your name to her maiden name. I went back to sea, to Argentina first, then on a ship running back and forth to America. In between voyages I stayed in a seamen's mission or boarding house, all in Liverpool. But a week back I signed on in a collier carryng coal from here to London. I was going down to the river to join her when I bought this paper.'

He flourished the *Echo*. 'But we sailed and I didn't open it until I came off watch, when we were out at sea. I saw the notice of the funeral, thought you would be the Alison, my Alison, but I had to wait until the ship docked here again.

We got in late last night. Then this morning I stood around for an hour before I had the courage to come in.' He was silent then and Alison felt his fingers tighten on hers. She was too full to speak but he said, 'I still can't believe I've found you.'

'Nor me,' choked out his daughter.

Then Lottie entered apologetically. 'I have an order for two teas and cheese on toast twice.'

'I'll get it,' said Alison.

'I'll bear a hand,' added her father. And when she glanced at him, surprised, he went on, 'I can. I'm a pretty good cook, can manage tea and toast, anyway. I worked as a cook for the last ten years of – of my time.'

Alison noted the slight hesitation but did not remark on it. Instead she laughed and dabbed at her eyes with her handkerchief. 'I'll do the toast and you make the teas.'

In fact all three busied themselves and as they worked Alison remembered, 'You said you were staying in the seamen's mission or a boarding house.'

'I stayed aboard last night but, aye, I'll be looking for a place later.'

'No, you won't. You'll stay here.'

He paused in pouring the tea. 'Are you sure? Will you have room?'

'I want you here and you can have my bed. I'll sleep down here in the kitchen. I've done it often enough before.'

'You won't do it again for me.' Matt was firm about that, but he grinned. 'I have my own bed I'll bring with me, my "donkey's breakfast".' That was his seaman's straw-filled mattress.

They laughed, but after lunch he went off to his ship and brought back his big seabag holding all his belongings besides his mattress. Then on Alison's order he set forth again, this time to buy a bed. It was delivered next day so he only slept one night in the kitchen. Thereafter he slept upstairs. The three rooms up there had been used for service, as Alison had planned in the early days of opening the Cookshop. Now she was using them as bedrooms by the simple expedient of stacking the spare tables and chairs in one corner. As she had told Lottie, 'It's a bit like camping out but we've done that before. If it has a bed then it's a bedroom.' She thought, *And we'll need the furniture when we open another place.*

Now she and her father would go walking, arm in arm, down by the river. They did that one day when Alison closed the Cookshop early because they had run out of supplies, had nothing to serve. They talked, learning about each other and the lost years. At the Folly End they paused and she told him, 'Francie, my gannie, used to bring me down here to watch the ships steaming up and down the river.'

Matt asked, 'Was she good to you?'

'And good for me,' Alison said definitely. 'She brought me up and anything good in me is due to her. She's always been with me. Whenever I didn't listen to her, I regretted it.' She remembered the disastrous affair with Julian Baldwin.

'I should have been with you!' The cry was wrung out of Matt.

Alison was quick to ease his pain. 'It wasn't your fault! It was just bad luck and you are here and we're happy now! We have to look forward. I made mistakes.' And she told him about Richard and how they had fought, until the day they looked at each other and everything changed.

'He sounds a good man,' said Matt. 'I'm looking forward to seeing him.' Then he grinned. 'He'll have to ask me if he wants to walk out with you.'

'I expect you'll see him soon,' Alison laughed happily. 'I hear the army will be closing down the hospital at Bellhanger very soon. Richard wants me to look it over as soon as they have gone, to see what condition it's in. He's planning on living there and starting up in general practice. I'll be meeting the housekeeper again, Mrs Skilton.' She was not looking forward to that.

Clara Skilton was not looking forward with any pleasure. She did not like the sound of the proposal just made to her but could not see how to avoid it. The housekeeper sat in her room at Bellhanger, staring nervously at her visitors. The years had not dealt kindly with her. The once-generous bosom had spread and sagged, her face become lined and jowly. She had once been able to excite Oliver Crawshaw, albeit he had then had an ulterior motive, to gain access to the house and steal its furniture. She could not excite him now, could see this in his false smile. Clara could not help but see the contrast between her and Esme, sitting by him now. Her well kept figure was expensively gowned and she exuded a hard-faced sexuality, despite her age.

Oliver asked, 'When do the last of the soldiers go?'

'Tomorrow.' Clara added, 'There are only two orderlies and a corporal left. Why do you want—?'

He cut in, 'So there'll only be you here? What about the owner?'

Clara thought she saw a way not to become involved in his plot, and said quickly, 'He's coming back here to live. I had a letter from his agents.'

'Did it say when?' And as Clara hesitated he guessed she was hiding something. 'Let me see this letter.' He held out his hand. Clara stood up and took it down from behind the picture of George V on the mantelpiece. Oliver scanned the sheet quickly, then lifted his cold eyes to give her a glance that chilled her. 'It says he *may* be here at Christmas. You wanted me to think he'd be back in a couple of days or so. You thought that might put me off.' He was silent for some

seconds, eyes boring into her. Then he said only, 'Don't try
to lie to me again. We'll bring the stuff in one night this
week. By Christmas we'll have sold it on and gone. It'll be
hard luck on anyone who tries to stop me.' He paused again,
watching her, saw her eyes fall before his, her hands shaking
where they lay in her lap. He saw she understood the threat
and he nodded, satisfied.

His tone became silky, his smile wide. 'You wrote to me
for help and that's what I'll give you. We'll make a mint out
of this and you'll have a share that will keep you in comfort
for a year or two.' He rose to go, but warned, 'We'll be back.
Keep your mouth shut.'

Clara nodded dumbly and saw them out of the house. She
shut the door behind them and leaned her back against it,
her eyes closed. She was frightened, knew she was dealing
with a dangerous man. He had promised her a lot of money
and that meant risk – of prison. She had lost sleep on many
a night, fearing repercussions from the theft of the furniture
years ago. Suppose the police found out about this latest
theft planned by Oliver? Suppose, as a result, they discov-
ered the earlier crime as well?

She could see herself in a cell, and moaned, 'Oh, God
help me! What am I going to do?'

~~~

'Oh, no!' Alison's cry was anguished, torn from her. 'Why?'

Matt put his arm around her where she stood at the table in the kitchen of the café. She was rolling out pastry for pies and flushed from the heat of the stove. He said gently, 'Because I can't stay here living off you all the time. So I walked over to the shipping office this morning and signed on again. It's the same ship but the dockyard's finished the work on her. We're sailing tomorrow night.'

'But you've only just come home,' Alison wailed.

'I've been here a week and I'll be back in another two weeks or so.' He hugged her. 'I'll keep on coming home, you can be sure of that, but I'm a sailorman so I'm bound to go away for spells.'

Alison saw there was no moving him, sighed and accepted.

Pamela and Henri lay side by side on her big bed, slack and exhausted after their lovemaking. She stared up at the ceiling, thinking lazily, and stretched. She drawled, 'When do you expect to open that restaurant? It's cost a fortune to do it up and we need to recover some of the money.'

He yawned and stretched in his turn, reached out a hand to fondle her body. 'When I can get something to serve. The official issue of food is just about enough to make a plateful of sandwiches. We need meat, butter, eggs – I could go on all day.'

'We need some of them for this house. We're having to eat out most nights. I'm paying you to cook and I'm getting nothing.'

'Nothing?' He leaned over her where she lay spread-eagled.

She was aroused again and pulled him down onto her.

The lorry came after midnight. The glow from its acetyl-ene headlamps washed over the window of Clara's room at the back of the house. She saw the light flit across the ceiling, through a gap at the top of the curtains where they did not meet. She tensed involuntarily, was already awake, had been sleeping badly. She guessed who it would be; the last of the soldiers had gone and she had the house to her-self.

Clara crawled miserably out of bed, knowing she would have to open to him. She pulled on a dressing-gown and lit an oil lamp. By its light she wended through the stone-floored passages and the kitchen and opened the back door.

'You took your bloody time,' Oliver snapped at her and pushed into the passage. 'I thought you might have changed your mind, but you wouldn't do that, would you?' He gripped her by the throat, forcing her head back.

Clara choked out, 'No!' She could see beyond him the looming figure of Sharky Spraggin with his shark's tooth grin. A woman was with them but this was no Esme. She was burly, hard-faced, thick-lipped. Behind them was the lorry, reversed up to the door. It was a three-ton Dennis flatbed, its canvas canopy closed and lashed with rope. Headlights extinguished now, it blended into the darkness in the shadow of the house.

Oliver's smile was thin. 'That's right. You don't want to lose what's left of your looks.' He jerked his head at the others. 'This is Sharky Spraggin and his wife, Bessie. She's going to give us a hand.' He released Clara, but only to order, 'We'll be needing a drink or two when we finish. Get on with that.'

Clara rubbed her throat where his fingers had left weals and said huskily, 'I've nothing but a bottle of stout. Will that do?'

'*Stout!* No! Hell's flames! Just make us some tea, and you can leave us that light. Nobody will see us around the back of the house.' He took the lamp from her and turned back to Spraggin. 'Let's start carrying the stuff in.'

They unlashed the canopy and drew it aside. Clara saw the inside of the lorry was crammed full with crates, bulging sacks and casks she recognised as holding butter. Then Oliver saw her staring and barked, 'What the hell are you gawping at?'

Clara scurried away.

The two men and the woman worked quickly at the unloading, Bessie as strong as any navvy. There was reason for haste. As Sharky said, 'They'll be expecting me at the depot and when I don't turn up, they'll start looking for me.' They stacked the cargo in rooms and passages. The furniture had been put into store in the stables when the Army took over the house as a hospital, but inside their beds were still *in situ*, their narrow iron and wire frames propped up against the walls.

The work completed, they sat in Clara's kitchen and drank the mugs of tea she had brewed. Now she sat by the stove, twisting her fingers nervously in the cord of her dressing-gown. Oliver said with satisfaction, 'I'll shift this lot in no time. There are people out there with money to spend and starving. They'll snap it up.' And he would make a lot of money, but he did not say that.

Sharky drained his mug, banged it down on the table and

stood up. 'I'll be off. Let's have what we agreed.' He held out his hand.

'Of course,' Oliver pulled a wad of pound notes from his pocket and passed it over.

Sharky counted the notes with thick fingers, then he nodded, 'Ta.' He handed the wad to his wife, who had been watching with greedy eyes and licking her lips. She stuffed it in the cavern between her breasts and buttoned her dirty blouse over it.

Oliver said, 'You can give me a lift for part of the way back.' Then he grinned at Clara. 'Don't go helping yourself. I'll see you right for money, but if you let anybody in here—' He did not finish but she took in the threat and swallowed. Oliver said, 'I'll be back.'

He followed Sharky and Bessie out to the Dennis and they all climbed into the cab and drove away. Clara watched from the back door of the house until the glow of the headlamps faded and died. Then she locked the door and returned to her bed, to lie awake until the dawn.

Sharky set Oliver down on the outskirts of the town, from whence he walked to the Palace Hotel, where he was staying with Esme. The night porter let him in, Oliver explaining, 'I'm suffering from insomnia so I took a long walk.' He smiled and slipped a shilling tip into the man's hand. 'Sorry to be a nuisance.'

'That's all right, sir. No trouble at all.'

'I should sleep now.' But when he entered the room he shared with Esme he woke her and was not ready for slumber.

At first she protested sleepily, 'What? Now? It's the middle of the night.' But she yielded. 'All right, come on, then.'

Later she asked, 'So it went well?'

'It did.' He lay on his back, head on hands, grinning up at her where she hung over him. 'All we need now are customers and we should find them without any trouble.' He closed his eyes, then opened them again. 'What are you doing?'

'What do you think?'

Sharky drove out on the road to Durham and his depot, until Bessie grumbled, 'How much further? Remember I've got to walk back to the town. It'll take me all bloody night at this rate.'

'Stop whingeing!' Sharky snapped at her. 'We have to do the job right. I marked a place just along here.' They came to a turning off that was little more than a cart track. He turned into this and switched off engine and lights. He and Bessie opened the canopy again, pulled it aside and climbed into the empty back of the Dennis. He laid down and Bessie tied him with some rope they had brought from the cab. She sat back on her heels and asked, 'If you're all right I'll go home.'

'Aye, you be off. Somebody will come along and find me before too long.' Then he grumbled, 'It's going to be bloody cold, though.'

He was right; it was a winter's night. When the sixty-year-old farmer trudged along the track at first light that morning he found Sharky blue and shuddering with chattering teeth. The farmer bawled for his labourer, an ancient like himself. Together they untied him and walked him between them to the farmhouse. There they sat him by the fire and the farmer's wife heated some broth and spooned it into him.

The local policeman was summoned by the farmer. He was also too old for the army and arrived pedalling sedately on his bicycle. Sharky, now warm and fed, gave a dramatic account of how he had been robbed of his cargo. 'This feller waved me down. When I stopped he said his missus had slipped and fallen into the ditch and could I help him to pull her out. I got down and went to the ditch. There was no wife, but four big lads waiting for me. I had no chance wi' them. They tied me up, drove my Dennis up a track and took my load.'

The policeman took it all down in his notebook, licked the point of his pencil and asked, 'Can you describe any of them?'

'Just the one that stopped me. He was the smallest, about five foot six, sharp faced. The others had scarves or summat over their faces.'

The constable climbed onto his bicycle and set off to start the investigation. Sharky returned to his lorry, reported to his depot in Durham and retold his story. Then he drove back to Sunderland, repeated the tale yet again to his supervisor in the docks, and finally walked back to the two rooms he shared with his wife.

Bessie was sitting before the fire, toasting bread on a fork held out to the glowing coals. The grate, oven and fire irons all needed cleaning. She asked anxiously, 'What happened?'

'It all went like we planned.' He said it with the satisfaction of a job well done, sat down and started to take off his boots. 'And you needn't sit there. Make me some breakfast.'

'Aren't you the man who claimed to have business dealings with my late husband?' On Tuesday evening Pamela stopped at Oliver's table in the restaurant of the Palace Hotel. Henri hovered at her shoulder. Her tone was harsh and her eye hard. She went on curtly, 'Julian Baldwin. Do you remember?'

'I do.' Oliver rose from his seat. He had noted that 'late', and answered gravely, 'I'm sorry to hear—'

'I'm not sorry,' snapped Pamela. 'The cur ran away with some girl half his age and I'm delighted. He only had his job because of me. I expect he will starve and serve him right.' She started to move on but paused to add, 'Mind you, we're all close to starving. I'm sure there's plenty of food but the government has it locked away and won't let us buy it. Then they keep on about exercising restraint when we go out to a place like this.'

Oliver noted that, too, and offered, 'Please, why don't you join us?' And he lowered his voice to urge, 'I think I can help you with your problem of supply. I have sources . . .' He winked and suggested, 'We can have dinner and then go to somewhere more quiet to talk in private.'

Pamela had taken in his hint and looked at him hungrily. 'Thank you. We will. This is Henri, my chef, who also manages my restaurant.' She indicated him with a wave of her hand. He gave a little bow.

Oliver returned it while Esme smiled and thought, *I'll wager the restaurant is not all he manages – Gigolo.* She had experience of the type.

They all sat down, kindred souls, and after dinner they struck a bargain.

Alison and Matt walked through the gaslit streets, she with her shawl about her shoulders, her hands in a muff against the cold. He carried his big seabag slung on his shoulder. It held all his kit, including his 'donkey's breakfast'. They crossed the bridge then descended to the level of the river. Matt's ship lay by the quay and they wound to it through dark valleys between stacks of timber and piles of coal, glinting black in the gaslight.

They stopped at the foot of the gangway and Matt set down his seabag and stretched his wide shoulders. 'I'll leave you here.' Then anxiously, 'Will you be able to walk back by yourself?'

Alison laughed. 'I'm not afraid of the dark.' Not after Mesopotamia and the shelling in Flanders. She looked up at the night sky, sprinkled with stars. 'It's fine. I may walk up to Bellhanger, to look it over for Richard, as he asked me.

I'll have to go again in daylight, of course, but I'll be able to see how the army have left the inside.'

'I'm looking forward to meeting Richard,' Matt smiled. 'Hopefully when I get back from this voyage.'

'Hopefully,' Alison agreed and reached up to touch his face. 'I'm going to miss you. Take care and come back soon.'

'I will.' He put his arms around her and hugged her. She kissed his cheek and he said, 'Hey! No tears.' He held her out at arm's length. Alison dabbed at her eyes with a corner of the shawl and smiled up at him. He heaved up his seabag onto his shoulder again. 'That's better. Now, off you go.' He turned her around with his free hand then gave her a gentle shove to send her on her way. 'Goodbye, bonny lass.'

'Goodbye, Dad.' She looked back once then was gone into the dark canyons between the stacks of timber.

Matt sighed and blinked, close to tears himself now. He whispered her final words: 'Goodbye, Dad.' He shook his head and climbed the gangway, found a bunk in the seamen's quarters in the fo'c'sle and lay down. He stared up at the rust-speckled deckhead above him and whispered again, 'Dad.'

Alison walked home, still regretting the departure of her father but consoling herself that he would not be away for long. And she had found him again after all the years of separation.

She was passing the Palace Hotel, on her way to cross the bridge into Monkwearmouth, when movement flickered in the corner of her eye. She glanced in the direction of the hotel and just glimpsed the man. He was strolling past a window and his head was turned to look out, or so it seemed. She saw him for only a second but that was enough. She recognised that big-bodied, apelike figure, the silky moustache, the cold-eyed smile. This was the man who had tried to take her by force, that she had seen on the hospital roof, who had murdered Percy Digby.

Instinctively she stepped back and lifted a hand before her face as if to ward off a blow. Then she realised that he, looking out into the darkness from the light, could not see her. She still took another two backward paces but then turned away from him and hurried on. The sighting had shaken her, like waking from a bad dream out of her past. What was he doing there? No good, she was sure of that. And what could she do? Nothing. Past experience had shown that. She had gone to the police over the murder of Percy Digby but Oliver had evaded arrest.

She grew calmer as she crossed the bridge with the trams rattling by, clanging and grinding. She told herself to calm down, that Oliver might be gone as soon as he had appeared, that he could not know of her existence.

She – almost – did not mention the experience when she arrived home.

Lottie sat by the stove and smiled, 'Matt did go, then?'

Alison nodded. 'Didn't you think he would?'

'I wouldn't have been surprised if he'd changed his mind. He's awfully fond of you.'

'I'm fond of him.' Alison hesitated, then admitted, 'On my way home I saw an evil man. He did not see me but it frigtened me for a while.'

'Frightened you?' Lottie had always leaned on Alison's courage, was shaken by this admission.

Now Alison shrugged. 'Just for a while, but I'm all right now. You see, I saw him kill a man.'

She told how Oliver had thrown his victim from the hospital roof to his death – and got away.

Lottie listened to the end then said indignantly, 'So he's still walking about scot free! That's disgraceful!'

Alison smiled wryly, 'It's the law.' She changed the subject, glancing up at the clock on the mantelpiece. 'I've time to walk up to Bellhanger, just to look at the inside. The rest will have to wait for another day. I've a feeling there'll be a lot of work to do to the place.'

Lottie said doubtfully, 'Will it be worth it?' Then hesitatingly, not wanting to hurt this dear friend's feelings, 'I've only seen it once and it looked a bit – grim.'

'I know what you mean,' Alison laughed, 'but it could be a happy house.'

Lottie said uneasily, 'D'you think you should go? What about that murderer?' And reluctantly, 'Would you like me to go with you?'

'No!' Alison was firm. 'I can't stay in forever because of someone who's probably forgotten I exist.'

She resolutely put Oliver out of her mind and set out, walking briskly, thinking of Richard and Bellhanger. He had been there when they first met, though he had not known she was living at Bellhanger. It had been a part of their childhood, their lives. It had been Michael's house, a place of sadness because he had given his heart to a woman who had wrecked his life. It had been a haven for Alison, a home and a place of love with her 'gannie', Francie. Now it would be a house which Richard would share with her in happiness.

She was coming to it now and it towered tall and black against the night sky, hanging over her. The windows reflected what light there was from the stars, as if coldly watching her. But there was no light inside.

She passed the steps lifting up to the front door, never thought of using it, the habit of her childhood too ingrained. Instead she walked round to the back door. There was no light but she could see the huge silver motor car. It looked to be the Rolls Royce belonging to Pamela Baldwin. She thought there might well be others like it owned by ship-builders or shipowners, but Pamela's was the only one she knew.

It gave her pause. She wondered why it was there? What could Pamela want at Bellhanger? Or – could it be a car borrowed from a brother officer by Richard? That caused a leap of the heart, but then she remembered he was still in France, and if he had come home she was sure he would have come first to her. So, not Richard. There was a way to find out, and to carry out her task. She reached out her hand to the bell pull and yanked at it, as her mother had done so long ago, while she had waited, apprehensive.

She shivered now.

The bell jangled in the kitchen and startled them into silence, froze them like statues. They were all there, Pamela and Henri, Oliver and Esme. They sat round the table, drinking the tea Clara had made for them, by the light of two oil lamps. She stood by the stove, her hands to her mouth now, shocked by the bell's tolling. They stared at the board high on the wall where the bells were mounted on springs. The one that still vibrated was lettered in faded gold paint: *Rear Door*.

Oliver was first to stir, glared at Clara and demanded, 'Who's that?'

'I don't know,' she whispered.

'Have you talked to anybody, had any visitors?'

'No.' She shook her head. 'No.'

'Answer it. I'll come with you. Take one o' the lamps.' And to the rest, 'Put out the other. Keep still and quiet.'

Henri said nervously, 'What if it's the police?' He wanted no truck with them, peering at his false papers and asking questions.

'The police would come to the front,' Oliver told him. He looked round at their faces, yellow in the lamplight. His own was malevolent. 'Nobody runs, nobody talks. I'm not being taken. They've been shooting deserters in France and they jailed a shopkeeper for overcharging a few pennies for margarine. What would they give me for taking this lot?' He gestured at the stacked crates and sacks. 'Remember.'

They all took in his threat, knew he would kill to save himself, and it chilled and silenced them. He nodded and shoved Clara towards the door. '*Move!*' She led the way from the darkened kitchen, her mouth working, and he followed her.

They traversed the passages, came to the rear door and Oliver stood with his back pressed against the wall. 'Watch what you say. Give nothing away,' he hissed. 'I'll be here.'

They heard the bell jangle distantly, the unknown caller on the other side of the door becoming impatient.

'Go on, open it,' Oliver urged.

Clara obeyed, turned the key in the lock and dragged back the bolts. She pulled the door towards her, so Oliver was hidden behind it, and fearfully looked out. Despite Oliver's reassurance she still expected to see a policeman. She felt a surge of relief when the oil lamp she held showed her the beshawled figure of Alison. She croaked, dry mouthed, 'Hello, Miss Bailey.'

'Good evening, Mrs Skilton.' Alison thought the woman seemed distraught, pallid and nervous. 'Is anything wrong?'

'No!' She was quick to deny it. 'Nothing! No!'

Alison was suspicious; there was something amiss here, but she did not press the matter. 'Is that Mrs Baldwin's motor car?' She indicated it with a nod of her head.

Clara stared blankly, 'I don't know nowt about it.'

Alison was sure she was lying, but that was all the more reason to find out what was going on. 'Mr Tarrant asked me to look over the house, to see how the army have left it. So, if you please . . .' She stepped forward, not prepared to accept a refusal.

Clara yielded perforce, shuffled back but held on to the door with one hand, offered the lamp with the other. 'You take the light and go on. I'll fasten the door and follow you up to the kitchen. We can get another lamp there.'

Alison complied and started on her way through the passages, a well remembered route. The door closed behind her with a snicking of shot bolts, grate of turning key. Then she heard Clara shuffling behind her. That shuffling hid any sound made by the soft-footed Oliver as he brought up the tail.

Alison paused when they came to the sacks standing against the wall. 'What are these?'

'It's just stuff the army left, I suppose.' Clara shrugged, 'They're nowt to do wi' me.'

The army had gone but left these sacks – and Clara had not looked at the contents? Alison felt that breath of suspicion again, that there was something amiss, but she said nothing and moved on.

They came to the kitchen door. It was closed and Alison paused again, conscious of Clara's rapid breathing just behind her. She shoved at the door, opened it wide and stepped inside, then held up the lamp. Its pool of light spilt over Pamela Baldwin and her chef, Henri. Alison moved it slightly and now it took in Esme Tarrant. They sat around the kitchen table and blinked owlishly at the light.

Alison set down the lamp among them and demanded, 'May I ask why you are all here?' Then she realised. The table held a plate with a wedge of cheese, a dish of butter. She looked further, taking up the lamp again, circling the kitchen. Stacked around it were crates, and sacks like those she had seen earlier, but some of these were open, showing they held flour, or cheeses like great wheels. There were sides of bacon and casks of butter.

She whirled to return to the table and put down her lamp

there, rested her hands on the board to lean towards the three who sat there, and she cried, 'There's food here to feed dozens of people for weeks! These are rations for hungry folks, starving children, and they've been robbed!' She stared her disgust at the three at the table.

'Light that other lamp,' said Oliver, and stepped into the room.

18

Monkwearmouth in Sunderland, Tuesday 17th December 1918.

◆～◆

Matthew Grant stepped over the coaming and out of the fo'c'sle onto the deck. He was one among a dozen sailors who had turned out at the call of 'All hands' to take the ship to sea, but now he hesitated for long seconds. He was thinking of Alison, this daughter of his that he had finally found after a parting of more than twenty years. He had thought of nothing else since he had left her on the quay and now a truth forced itself on his attention. His mind was made up.

He hurried aft and found the mate, in blue jacket and brass buttons, just below the bridge. 'Mr Thompson!'

'Aye?' The mate turned and saw who had called him. 'Hello, Matt.'

Matthew did not waste time, could not because the ship would soon sail. 'I'm going ashore. I mean, to stay ashore.'

'Bloody hell!' swore the mate irascibly. And he pointed out, 'You signed on for the round voyage. What do you think we're doing aboard this tub, pleasure trips round the flaming harbour?'

This was no more than Matt expected and he apologised. 'I know, but I can't go. I've found my daughter that I've been seeking for years. She was five years old when I lost her and now she's a grown woman. I can't leave her again. I thought I could, that I ought to go to sea again, but I can't face another parting. I'm going back to her and I'll find a job ashore.'

Thompson had sailed with Matt before and more than once. He knew Matt's worth as a sailor and a man, respected him. And he had a daughter of his own who was soon to be married. He shoved out his hand to grip that of Matt and shook it. 'I'll tell the skipper. He'll moan like hell at sailing a man short but he'll be all right. You fetch your kit and go ashore before they take away the gangway.'

Matt ran back to the fo'c'sle and crammed his 'donkey's breakfast' into his seabag. Five minutes later he stood on the quay, panting and waving up at his erstwhile shipmates on the deck above him as a crane removed the gangway. Then he turned and started to walk, seabag on his shoulder, back to the town, Monkwearmouth and Alison's Cookshop. He stepped out, light of heart.

Clara lit the second lamp, scraping a match into flame that wavered unsteadily with her shuddering body. Its light underlit Oliver's face making black holes in which his eyes glittered. His voice was harsh. 'Hello, Miss Bailey.'

Pamela spat out, 'Harlot!'

Esme followed, 'Bitch!'

'Ssh!' Oliver held up a hand for silence, his glare fixed on Alison. 'You asked what we were doing here. It's a private party and you were not invited. You'll have gathered you aren't popular with some of us, but I'm glad to see you.' And, as the others stared at him, questioning, 'Miss Bailey and I have unfinished business.'

Esme demanded, thinking she knew and jealous, 'What kind of business?'

Alison also thought she knew, and thought, *never*. She sought a way of escape.

He proved them both wrong. 'She knows too much. She could send us all down. We have to shut her mouth.'

That frightened them. They stared at him, transfixed.

He still stood in the doorway that opened on the passage going to the back door. Alison saw that was no way out for her, but ... Her gaze shifted to the other door, that which led to the main house. Oliver saw that shift, foresaw what she intended and started towards her, but Clara stood in his way. He hurled her aside as he leapt to seize Alison but that moment's delay had given her a chance. She skipped past the table, yanked the door open and was through and running.

Behind her came Oliver's voice, raging, 'After her!'

She ran light-footed through the passages and rooms. The furniture that had been sheeted like ghosts was gone, but she flitted like a phantom on flying feet. Instead there were the army beds propped up against the walls and looking in the gloom like the doors of cells. She reached the front of the house, fetched up against the front door but found it locked and no key to be seen.

She sobbed, panting and breast heaving, and raced back to the stairs. Oliver was pounding up from the back of the house, trying to cut her off, but she beat him to the stairs, albeit by only a stride and a half. She whipped the shawl from her shoulders and flung it at his head. It wrapped around his face, blinding him and she flew up the stairs, gaining on him again as he fought out of the hampering wool.

At the top were more passages, more rooms. She swerved in and out of stacked army beds, hearing him pounding at her heels, racing for her life. She leapt, three at a time, down the back stairs she had climbed so often with a loaded tray, through the long room where as a child she had seen the naked woman standing pale in the moonlight. Alison was running an obstacle course that was a kaleidoscope of memories.

Now into the dining-room, where as a girl she had stood at the door and watched Richard dining with his uncle, 'Mad

Michael' Tarrant. Through that door, round the long table – had the army used this as the officers' mess? Through the other door and doubling back. All this way and never an open window to set her free, but now she was heading back to the kitchen. She had been slamming doors behind her, each one delaying Oliver slightly, building up her lead. The next turning would bring her to the green baize door and the kitchen. She would force her way through there, was certain Clara would not resist, that the other two would not stand against a determined attack. Then she swung around a corner – and into the arms of Henri.

He had failed to keep up with the chase. A stranger to the house, he had lost his way in its twists and turns. He had only just found himself near the kitchen and was about to return there. He was as surprised as Alison by their collision, but all he had to do was wrap his arms about her and this he did.

He bawled excitedly, 'I've caught her!' He nearly lost her again as she jammed an elbow into his midriff. He gasped with pain but he held on. She stamped on his foot and that made him howl but it did not break his hold. She kicked out in a flurry of legs and lace and wrung moans of agony out of him. Then Oliver came up with them, seized Alison's wrists and forced them up her back. The green baize door was opened by Esme and she held it wide. Oliver ran Alison through into the kitchen, threw her face down on the floor and knelt on top of her, his weight crushing her. He was breathing heavily, his face shining with sweat. He panted, 'Got you, my beauty. Now you're going to pay.'

He looked for Clara and saw her standing by the stove, her hands twisting in her apron. He ordered, 'Bring me some rope.'

'Rope?' She repeated dully, in shock.

'Aye! Rope! Something strong, not bloody string.'

She scurried to a cupboard, delved in it and emerged with an old clothes line. He used it to lash Alison's wrists and ankles, drawing the knots tight so that she sobbed with the pain of it.

Pamela sneered, 'Serve you right.'

Oliver looked up at her, 'I'm taking her in your car.'

She did not like the idea and demanded, 'Why?'

'Because it's the only one we've got, you damn fool!' he snarled at her.

She turned red with anger but said nothing, cowed by his glare.

He stood up and turned on Henri, who was sitting on a chair and nursing his bruises. 'You can give me a hand to carry her down.'

Alison twisted her neck to peer up at Henri and warn him, 'Whatever he does, you will be an accessory.'

Oliver grabbed a drying cloth from the table and used it to gag her. To Henri he said, 'Take no notice of her. She won't give us any more trouble.' He glowered around at them all, looking for signs of wavering. They did not meet his gaze but did not defy him, either. 'Clara!' And when she started nervously, 'You come and fetch a lamp, open the door. The rest of you wait here till I come back.'

He stooped, turned Alison onto her back and lifted her by her shoulders while Henri took her long legs with their button boots. The two men carried her easily, Clara leading the way with one of the lamps. She unlocked the back door and set it wide, stood aside to hold it open and to let the men pass with their burden. As she held up the lamp she caught a glimpse of the girl's eyes above the cruel gag, saw the tears in them. They seemed to mirror her own fear. Then Oliver opened the rear door of the Rolls and he and Henri dragged their bundle inside.

Oliver slammed the door and told Henri, in a hushed tone

now they were outside the house, though there was no one to hear them. 'You go back and wait with the rest. I'll manage on my own from here.'

Henri hesitated, then asked, 'Where are you taking her? What are you going to do to her?'

'To a place down on the river, called the Folly End.' Then Oliver added, 'Never mind what I'm going to do. I'll arrange matters so there's no backlash. Tell that to the others. It'll stop them worrying.'

Henri was still uneasy but backed away. Oliver slid into the driving seat of the Rolls and drove off around the front of the house. Clara stood at the back door with the lamp. She had not heard the muttered conversation. As Henri entered she passed him the lamp and said, 'You go on. I'll see to the door. I'll be along in a minute.'

He took the light and walked on, heard the door close behind him and the key turn in the lock. His thoughts were not pleasant. He remembered Alison's warning of being an accessory to – what? He had an awful fear it might be murder.

Matthew Grant knocked on the door of Alison's Cookshop and it was opened by a surprised Lottie Douglas. 'Matt! I was just thinking that you would be out at sea by now. Didn't the ship sail?'

'She did but I didn't.' Matt edged through the doorway with his cumbersome seabag and dumped it in a corner. 'I changed my mind. I'm staying with Alison, as she wants me to, and finding a shore job.'

'That's marvellous!' Lottie clapped her hands delightedly. 'She'll be so pleased.'

'Aye,' he grinned. He looked around the kitchen. 'Where is she?'

'She said she was going up to Bellhanger.' Lottie glanced

at the clock on the mantelpiece. 'I thought she would be back by now.'

Matt frowned. 'It's a bit late for her to be out.' Then he grinned sheepishly. 'I sound like an old-fashioned father already, though when I remember what she told me about her time in Mesopotamia and France, it seems she can look after herself.' But now he saw Lottie was not smiling. 'Are you worried for some reason?'

'When she came back from seeing you off, she said she had just seen an evil man on her way home.'

There was a clatter of hooves outside. Looking out through the door to the café they could see the cab stopped outside and the nodding head of the horse. A tall figure showed through the glass of the door and a fist beat a *rat-a-tat*. Lottie hastened to open it. The tall, wide-shouldered young man was in khaki service dress, with a gleaming Sam Browne belt and, on the cuff of the jacket, the three stars of a captain. Lottie did not need to ask and said with certainty, 'You're Richard Tarrant.'

'Yes. Is Alison here?' His smile was wide. 'I won't be demobilised until January but they've given me leave over Christmas and the New Year.' He saw they were not smiling and his grin slipped away. 'Is something wrong?'

'Aye,' said Matt. 'There might be.'

'Are you Alison's father?' asked Richard.

'I am.'

'She wrote me about you. But what's wrong?'

Matt and Lottie related how Alison had gone to Bellhanger, and had seen 'an evil man'.

Lottie added, 'She said she didn't think he'd seen her, but suppose he did?'

That was enough for Richard. 'I'll find her.' He turned back to the waiting cab.

Matt said, 'I'll come with you.'

They jumped up into the cab and Richard shouted to the driver, 'Bellhanger House!'

'Where?' asked the baffled cabbie.

'Straight ahead and I'll direct you! Fast as you can and I'll double your fare!'

The cabman understood that. He shook the reins, shouted at the horse and it broke into a gallop. The cab careered down the road and Lottie watched it go, anxiously.

They came to Bellhanger with the horse in a lather as it halted before the dark pile. Richard was first out of the cab and took the steps up to the front door in one bound. He yanked on the bell pull, hammered on the door and shouted, 'Open up!'

A bell jangled again in the kitchen. The three sitting round the table started as one, their nerves overstretched. They heard the distant banging – of a fist? And they stared up at the board that told them which bell had rung. Esme licked dry lips. 'That's someone at the front door.'

Henri jerked to his feet as if plucked on a string. 'I don't want to be caught here with this lot.' He gestured at the sacks and crates filled with food, then snatched up one of the two lamps from the table.

Pamela shrieked, 'Where are you going?'

'I'm getting out of this.' He made for the door leading to the back of the house and the two women were quick to follow. For a moment they all three crowded in the entrance, then Henri elbowed his way through and led the way down the passage. They came to the back door and found it locked. Henri lifted the lamp high, looking for the key and saw that the bolts were drawn but the key was not in the lock.

Esme squawked raucously, 'Don't just stand there! Open it and let us out!'

He swallowed and his voice shook in time with the lamp. 'I can't. It's locked on the outside.'

They stared at each other, yellow-faced and sweating in the lamplight. They were caught like rats in a trap.

Richard set his shoulder to the door and it burst inward. The hall gaped dark before him and Matt. He said, 'We need a light.' He went back to the cab where his canvas valise still rested on the seat. It was mud-stained and worn but had been with him through four years of war. He dug into a side pocket and took out an electric torch, a 'flashlight', another veteran piece of kit. He shone its beam into the hall, showing the stairs lifting up to the next floor, the passage running on to the back of the house.

He called over his shoulder as he ran, 'Ground floor first!'

'Coming!' Matt was at his heels.

They raced down the passage, crashed through the green baize door and so came to the kitchen. They halted, panting, looking about them in the light of the single oil lamp standing on the table. They saw the scraps of food on the table, the sacks and crates, the sides of bacon. Richard breathed, 'What the hell has been going on here?' But: 'Where's Alison?' And he bellowed, '*Alison!*'

There was no answer and he crossed the floor with long strides and plunged into the passage beyond. He called back to Matt behind him, 'There's a light down here!' So they came on the three, huddled wide-eyed and blinking as the beam of Richard's torch flitted over their faces. They found no comfort in his glare when he demanded, 'I'm looking for Alison Bailey. Where is she?'

Oliver stopped the Rolls on the deserted quayside that was the Folly End. He looked out across the river to the ships lying out in the stream. They twinkled with riding lights but here was only darkness. He left the engine of the car running and hauled Alison out of the car. He dragged her by the shoulders to where the stone steps, slimy with weed, ran down into the black water of the river. The tide was beginning to flow, lapping at the steps. He dragged her down them until she lay along the bottom exposed tread on the edge of the water. She guessed what was in store for her.

Oliver did not leave her in doubt. He sat on the steps just above her and mopped his sweating face with a handkerchief. Then he dug a hand into the pocket of his jacket and pulled out a clasp knife. He thumbed out the blade, long and wicked, and she thought for a second that he was going to end it brutally then and there. She closed her eyes and steeled herself for the blow, but there was worse to come. He explained, 'The tide is coming in; it will be over your head in a few minutes. Once it's finished I'll cut off the lashings and take them away. When they find you it will look like an accident or suicide.'

Oliver smiled down at her and she closed her eyes.

A ripple rolled in against the step on which she lay and water splashed up onto her face, as if in warning of what was to come. The stone beneath her was wet and cold, the very air of a winter night was chill against her skin. She could feel the tears that squeezed out between her tight-closed lids. In her pain and fear and despite them, she still found sorrow for Richard because they had wasted so much time when they could have been together.

She thought she heard the distant clangour of iron-shod wheels on cobbles, but then she felt Oliver's hands on her cringing body.

Henri cracked. There was no Gallic accent now; he spoke the cockney of Stepney. 'I only came here on account of her!' He indicated Pamela Baldwin with a jerk of his head.

'I just – got involved. He said to give him a hand to carry her down here to the car.'

Richard broke in, 'Who said? And where—'

'Oliver Crawshaw. He was taking her to some place called the Folly End, down on the river.' He added, voice breaking, 'God help me, I think he means to do away with her.'

Matt said, 'I know the Folly End. Alison took me there when we were out for a walk.' He and Richard raced back the way they had come. They jumped down the front door steps and the driver of the cab greeted them with, 'Here! What about my fare?'

'You'll get it!' Richard boosted Matt into the cab with a hand thrust in his back, then pulled himself up beside the cabbie. 'The Folly End! And it's a matter of life and death!'

The driver looked at him, read sincerity in his face and reached for his whip. But now came an open touring motor car carrying four policemen. One was an ageing sergeant but the other three were Special Constables, recruited from young men not conscripted into the Army because of having reserved occupations. The car stopped in front of the cab with a screech of brakes.

The sergeant sitting beside the driver stood up. He eyed Richard, and Matt with his head out of the window of the cab. He bawled, 'Where d'ye think you're going?' Then he recognised Richard's uniform and rank and became doubtful. He turned to ask a woman, sandwiched between the pair of burly policemen in the rear of the car, 'Mrs Skilton! Are these two of 'em?'

Clara, who had decided to save herself and turn King's Evidence, shook her head, 'I've never seen them before.'

Richard ordered the cabbie, 'Drive round!' And when the driver hesitated, 'Drive on or I'll throw you off!'

The car was already moving out of the way, the sergeant waving them on. Richard shouted to him, 'You'll find three of the people you want inside! There's another on the Folly End.' Then the cabbie was whipping up his horse and swinging the cab around the car. With a hammering of hooves they charged down the road into Monkwearmouth.

Richard and Matt shared a single fear: were they too late?

Water splashed over Alison again; the step on which she lay was now awash. She blinked it from her eyes and pulled up her knees to foil Oliver's fumbling. He cursed her but paused, the din of wheels bouncing on the cobbles now joined by the clash of hooves. It became louder, came closer with every second, intruded on his thoughts. He raised his head but his hands still groped. Alison kicked out desperately, both feet together perforce, tied at the ankles with the rope. She caught his forehead a stunning blow that rocked him. His hands went up to it so he did not see Richard launch himself from the seat of the cab in a flying leap.

Alison saw him suddenly appear, swooping down on Oliver with a face hard with rage. In a camera blink of memory she remembered another Tarrant, his uncle 'Mad Michael', who challenged and beat two louts who mocked him.

Oliver first knew of Richard's arrival when his shoulders were gripped by strong hands. Despite his ape-like bulk and the strength that had made him feared, he was thrown across the steps.

Richard hauled Alison out of the water and up the steps, but he kept a watchful eye on Oliver. He now recovered and lashed out with the knife but Richard evaded the blow. He seized the wrist of the hand brandishing the blade, smashed it down on the stone step and the knife fell between them. Richard scooped it up and Oliver turned and ran.

Matt was descending the steps. He tried to stop Oliver but slipped on the slimy green weed that covered them and crashed down. Oliver scrambled past him and up to the quay. He ran to the Rolls where its engine ticked softly, and slid in behind the wheel. Matt pursued, ran up to the driver's door and grabbed the handle. But then the car pulled away in reverse; Oliver was turning it to drive away up the slope from the river, intent on escape. Matt was dragged along until he let go and sprawled on the cobbles.

Richard had used Oliver's knife to cut away the bonds that held Alison. Now he carried her up the steps. Oliver squinted through the blood trickling down from the blow on his forehead inflicted by Alison. He saw them come out onto the quay, did not know who the man was but there was the girl who could see him jailed. He rammed his foot down on the accelerator and drove at them.

Matt rolled away desperately out of the path of the car, its wheels missing him by bare inches. The cab driver was fighting to control his horse. The poor beast had taken fright at the wild manoeuvring of the Rolls. Now it reared, charged forward and dragged the cab across in front of the car. Oliver spun the wheel to avoid a collision, succeeded and shot past the cab – then ran off the edge of the quay. The Rolls somersaulted as it plunged bonnet first into the river, settling on its roof. The wheels went on spinning until they just showed above the black surface. Oliver was trapped underneath.

Richard set Alison on her feet but she clung to him, not trusting her legs, shaky from being bound and from her escape from an awful death. Matt came limping to join them, wrapping his arms about them. The cabbie had calmed his horse, though it stood trembling, and there was a moment of blessed near silence. Then the police car came down the hill, bouncing on the cobbles. The sergeant still sat by the driver but he had picked up reinforcements on the way. Two constables sat in the rear seats and two more rode standing on the running boards either side and clinging to the hull of the car.

The sergeant was out of the car as soon as it stopped and addressed Richard. 'Now then, sir, what's going on here?'

'There's a car upside down ten yards out from the quay with a man inside it.' Richard pointed.

'Good God!' Then the sergeant bawled orders. Two of his men, strong swimmers, stripped down to their drawers and swam the few yards out to the car. They ducked below the surface and pulled Oliver from the car but it was all for nothing. Richard pronounced him dead. 'His neck was broken when the car fell on top of him.'

The sergeant sighed. 'I've left the others up at the house, handcuffed together and with a man to keep an eye on them. And I've sent two more constables to arrest another man and his wife, who had something to do with this business.' He was talking of Sharky Spraggin and his wife, Bessie; Clara had told of their part in the theft of the supplies.

He took out his notebook. 'Now I have to take down some details.' He poised his pencil and looked at the pale-faced girl in the arms of the young captain. 'Who are you, miss, please?'

She leaned against her lover, her father close by, and smiled at them. She was Alison of the 'Cookshop' restaurants, soon to be the wife of Dr Richard Tarrant of Bellhanger, and no longer a jailbird's daughter.

IRENE CARR

Fancy Women

'You fancy woman! Adulterer! Harlot! Murderer! You'll find no forgiveness here! Trollop! You come here flaunting your finery, all bought with the wages of sin!'

The harsh urban life of 1900s Sunderland is no place for beautiful, innocent Laura whose determined spirit brings nothing but trouble. In love with wealthy Ralph but rejected by his family and threatened by her cruel stepfather, she flees to London. But here she finds only heartache and treachery.

Amidst the brutality of World War I she is forced to think twice about everything she holds dear, and when the bloodshed finally ceases she faces another struggle – with her past. The fancy woman must return to the scornful streets of her birthplace; unbeknown to her, it may offer love, in the last place she'd ever imagine looking.

HODDER

IRENE CARR

Rachel

Orphaned at a young age, Rachel is left penniless and alone in the streets. However, her mother has left her a valuable legacy: her jewellery and the support of Rachel's desire to educate herself and become a governess. When she lands a post with a good family she believes her struggle is over. Until she is blamed for a crime she hasn't committed.

In spite of her indomitable spirit, Rachel is soon destitute. Then she learns that her eccentric uncle has left her his house in Sunderland. But it comes at a heavy price: she can only inherit if she marries her childhood friend Martin. She believes Martin a philanderer and she has vowed he will never break her heart . . .

HODDER

IRENE CARR

Liza

Unjustly sacked as a lady's maid to an English family in Germany, Liza returns to 1907 Britain penniless, without a job or any hope of a reference. Aboard the SS *Florence Grey* she meets spoilt, rich Cecily Spencer who, keen to elope to London, persuades Liza to switch identities for a month.

In order to support her family, Liza trades her rags for riches and moves in with Cecily's guardian, William where she encounters life in the Sunderland mansion from the other side of the servants' quarters.

But when she falls in love, she is torn apart by conflicting loyalties. Will she lose everything if the man she loves finds out who she really is?

HODDER